THE WIDOW'S WAGER

CLAIRE DELACROIX

The Widow's Wager
The Ladies' Essential Guide to the Art of Seduction #3
By Claire Delacroix

THE WIDOW'S WAGER

PROLOGUE

London, England - March 5, 1817

On this particular Wednesday afternoon, Brisbane's Emporium was remarkably crowded. Catherine Bettencourt, Baroness Trevelaine and daughter of one partner of Carruthers & Carruthers' Publishers and Booksellers, appreciated the bustle even as she made her way to the back counter. Business was brisk, perhaps because ladies felt the need for the cheering activity of shopping for oneself, perhaps because many were returning to town from their country estates and yearned for diversions. Either way, Catherine knew that the proprietress, Sophia de Roye, had to be pleased by the influx of clients.

She saw Mrs. de Roye at the back counter, her tall figure distinctive even at a distance. To Catherine's relief, Eurydice Montgomery, Countess Rockmorton, was chatting with Mrs. de Roye. Catherine would not have to wait upon Eurydice, a most reassuring detail for she had many errands to fulfill on this day. She smiled when she heard Eurydice make a jest and Mrs. de Roye laugh—Sophia had once been Eurydice's tutor and the pair were still close.

Brisbane's Emporium was a popular destination for ladies with a taste for fine fabrics. Their selection of silks was unrivaled and the vast array of ribbons and bonnet trimmings available in their haberdashery meant that even a lady with the most modest of budgets could find a delightful item to acquire. The previous autumn, the large shop had been divided into smaller rooms, in the style of the exchanges, and it was clear that the clients had embraced the transformation. A central corridor mimicked an arcade, with windows for the various departments on either side, their goods artfully displayed. Near the entry from the street were the silk shop on the left and the millinery on the right, followed by fans and hosiery on the left and haberdashery on the right—adjacent to the millinery, for convenience. Against the back wall was a display of jewelry, a space that appeared to be leased to a goldsmith, and a perfumery. In the middle of the rear wall, Mrs. de Roye reigned, organizing deliveries, orders, and gifts. Catherine knew that lady's husband, Lucien de Roye, managed the books and ensured that payments were collected. On this day, Catherine had no doubt that the tea shop next door was also busy.

Even though she was married to Rhys and a baroness now, Catherine would forever be the daughter of a man who had earned his way in trade and thus, an active shop always made her smile.

Mrs. de Roye nodded a greeting to her and the countess turned to greet Catherine with characteristic enthusiasm. "Mrs. de Roye has arranged for us to have a private room to view the silks," Eurydice said, winking rather broadly. "I know you prefer to be discrete about your opinions."

It was an excuse and Catherine knew it. In truth, the pair had met to discuss the future of the collection of intimate advice that both had used to advantage. They had need of privacy not only to ensure their plans remained secret, but also that no one realized they were meeting (and conspiring) with the notorious courtesan, Miss Esmeralda Ballantyne.

"Irene will show you the way," Mrs. de Roye said, gesturing to a young woman beside her.

In that moment, a collective gasp echoed through the crowd of shoppers. Like everyone else, Catherine turned to look.

Miss Esmeralda Ballantyne had entered the establishment. She wore a striking dress of striped silk in mint green with black accents. Droplets of rain glistened like diamonds on the shoulders of her deep green coat. Her hat was graced with no less than three ostrich plumes, her dark hair was elegantly arranged, and she wore a magnificent choker of pearls of so many strands that it covered her neck completely.

But it was her presence alone that excited such a reaction.

Her reputation had clearly preceded her.

Miss Ballantyne surveyed the store and its occupants with a small smile, then strolled toward the perfume counter. The shoppers parted before her like the Red Sea, more than one lady whispering behind her hand to her companion. If they were scandalized, Miss Ballantyne was only amused.

"Goodness," Catherine said, because she felt she should say something that sounded as if she was shocked.

"We must go immediately to the private room," Eurydice whispered, as if she did not wish to encounter Miss Ballantyne. Irene quickly led them away and Catherine glanced back to see Miss Ballantyne surveying the wares.

"I would not scent the entire store," she said in the dulcet tones famed throughout England for their seductive allure. "But I must smell them all. I have need of a specific scent, you understand, to tempt a most discerning gentleman." Then she smiled and the clerk, as Catherine might have anticipated, was incapable of doing anything other than ensuring Miss Ballantyne's satisfaction.

The door to the private chamber was secured behind Catherine and Eurydice, the table piled with striped silks of enthusiastic hues which neither had any intention of buying, and the two friends watched each other as they listened for approaching footsteps. Catherine smiled at the sound of Miss Ballantyne's voice drawing near. Eurydice smiled when there was activity in the adjacent room. That door was audibly closed, then Esmeralda herself opened the adjoining door between the two viewing rooms.

"We must be hasty," she said, bustling into the room with the silks, her voice low. "I welcome your plan to publish the book for the education of other ladies. Indeed, it was my hope all along."

"I still must make a compelling argument to my father and uncle," Catherine said. "I fear they will not be readily convinced to publish such a guide."

Eurydice made a dismissive sound but Esmeralda was studying Catherine. "It must have endorsements," she said. She indicated one of the bottles of perfume surrendered to her and Catherine read that it was evidently a favorite of a crown princess in Europe.

She nodded understanding. "But how?"

"Who is the greater question," Esmeralda said. "I have no suitable references, but you must know more dissatisfied wives."

Eurydice and Catherine exchanged glances. "None that would lend their names to such an endorsement, even if impressed," Eurydice said.

"Perhaps an advertisement?" Catherine suggested, dubious of its success.

Esmeralda chuckled. "There is a notion. Leave the references to me." She raised a finger. "Upon the matter of the book itself, I intend to add some chapters."

"Oh! *Details*," Eurydice said with enthusiasm.

"I am not certain there is a need," Catherine objected.

The courtesan's famously green eyes gleamed. "How else would you have known that dear Rhys was not telling you all of the truth, if not for details?"

"But that reference was a medical volume."

"Where else will women discover the truth?" Esmeralda demanded, seeming to take umbrage. "It is imperative that we include *all* the information they desire and require. The entire point is that women should be informed about matters of intimacy. That is the reason they will want the book. This is why it will *sell*."

Catherine frowned, knowing her father was conservative. "I cannot guarantee that it will be published in that case."

"And there is the injustice of this world laid bare," Esmeralda said. She pulled a small volume from her purse. Catherine was surprised that it was a bound copy of *Childe Harold*, a book she thought unlikely to lend much to the courtesan's argument. "Look at that," she challenged, handing the book to Catherine with an imperious air.

There was little to be done except open it as bidden.

But it was not the poem of Lord Byron inside the covers of the book. A different book had been crudely sewn into the hard case binding, a book much smaller and printed on inferior paper. It looked disreputable even before Catherine read the title: *Harris's List of Covent Garden Ladies*.

"This is the reference available to men," the courtesan said. "It was published from 1757 to 1795, a highly popular volume and one far more explicit than I would ever be. My descriptions would be poetic and tasteful."

Eurydice, meanwhile, had seized the book from Catherine. "It includes names and addresses!" she whispered, clearly both scandalized and fascinated. She changed her tone to read aloud. *"She has a wonderful art in raising up those of her* male friends *who are inclined to* droop *while in her enchanting company."'*

Catherine felt her eyes widen. "Oh!"

Esmeralda merely smiled, reminding her of a contented cat.

Eurydice read on. *"'She never wishes a gentleman to* come *a second time unless he proves himself to be a man of honour at the* first *visit;* five pounds five shillings *is the present this lady expects for the distribution of her private concerns."'* She looked up, her amazement clear.

"It's a guide to courtesans," Catherine guessed softly.

"With prices," Eurydice added.

"With *details*." Esmeralda reached over and turned the pages for the book, tapping one with a fingertip.

Eurydice obediently read. *"'She is celebrated for bush-fighting with a birchen rod, which she wields with dexterity to the uncommon gratification of many gentlemen who have occasion for this operation to rouse the Venus lurking in their veins."'*

"Birchen rods?" Catherine echoed.

"You see what an education can be found in such volumes." The courtesan reached out and turned the pages again.

Eurydice read with even greater enthusiasm. *"'She is perfectly mistress of all her actions and can proceed regularly from the dart of the tongue, and the soft tickle of her hand, to the ecstatic squeeze of her thighs; the enchanting twine of her legs; the elaborate suction of her lower lips and the melting flood of delight with which she constantly bedews the mossy root of the tree of life and washes the testimonies of manhood...'"* Eurydice fell silent in apparent astonishment.

"Goodness," Catherine said again, feeling flustered.

Eurydice smiled wickedly. "The ecstatic squeeze of her thighs," she repeated, then raised her brows.

Catherine had to avert her gaze for her cheeks were burning.

"We are at a disadvantage," Esmeralda insisted. "There must be additions to our text before publication to right the balance." She offered a sheaf of pages to Catherine. "Here are my current suggestions. Take that book also, to show your father that such details are not unprecedented." She smiled again. "I suspect he knows as much, but he may insist otherwise to his daughter."

Catherine could not imagine how she would even show the volume to him. Birchen rods! She busied herself in packing it all into a satchel she had brought in the expectation of new chapters from Esmeralda. It felt particularly heavy now.

"I want to read it all," Eurydice said, perhaps predictably. "Both the other book and your additions."

"I am certain you do," Esmeralda purred.

"Let me talk to my father first," Catherine said. "I will return the book to Miss Ballantyne afterward."

"Then I will lend it to you," Esmeralda promised Eurydice in a whisper. "Ask Sebastian about anything you do not understand. I recall that he was rather adventurous."

"Oh! The fiend!" Eurydice did not look as appalled as she sounded.

In fact, she looked to be anticipating the discussion with her husband.

Countess and courtesan smiled at each other, then Esmeralda retreated to the other room, closing the door behind herself. Immediately, the scent of various perfumes crept beneath the door, a combination of musk and floral scents that was sufficient to make Catherine blink.

"The jasmine with vanilla," Esmeralda informed the clerk who had apparently returned to that chamber. "It will suit admirably."

"I cannot persuade the baroness to indulge in the crimson stripe," Eurydice told Irene when she appeared. "Though I favor this silk of two hues of blue."

Catherine could not even think of making an acquisition. It was upon her to win her father's favor for this change in the scope of this project, and wondered how best it might be done.

Birchen rods. Did she dare to ask Rhys about that?

DAMIEN DEVRIES, the Duke of Haynesdale, waited impatiently in his carriage outside the house of Miss Esmeralda Ballantyne. He had not seen the lady since she had set him on the trail of Jacques Desjardins, the jewel thief who had been deported and banned from Britain for a year. He knew he had done his duty but he was restless with the implications of his choice. His agitation grew with every passing moment that he and the magistrate—in his own carriage—awaited the return of Miss Ballantyne.

But there was naught for it. A criminal had to pay the price of his or her crimes. That was the law.

His leg ached, though, as if his old wound would protest the very idea of having any part in the persecution of Miss Ballantyne, a woman whose wit and humor had surprised Damien on more than one occasion, a woman who had given him the clue to apprehend the real thief.

Who had then implicated her.

If she had been attempting to rid herself of an accomplice, the scheme had not been planned well.

Damien suspected that Miss Ballantyne always planned well.

If that was true, then the search of her home would reveal nothing at all, and all would end well. Even that assurance did little to reassure Damien and he rubbed his aching thigh as he sat impatiently, waiting.

It was late afternoon when a hackney cab stopped in front of the magistrate's carriage and the rain had finally stopped. Miss Ballantyne alighted from the cab, attired in green and black. She looked both delightfully feminine, to Damien's view, and in dire need of the protection of a man like himself.

Save that he had been the one to bring the authorities to her door.

He descended from his own carriage as she halted before the magistrate. Something flickered in her glorious eyes, something that might have been trepidation, but it was gone before Damien could be certain of it. The magistrate explained the need to search her home and Damien knew he did not imagine that she paled slightly.

But she stood a little taller when she replied. "Of course. Your Grace, it is an unexpected pleasure to see you again. Shall I assume that you are involved with this expedition?"

He bowed, feeling like a lowly cur. "You may indeed, Miss Ballantyne. It was the evidence I gathered from Jacques Desjardins that brought the magistrate to your door."

She definitely paled at that, but did not falter. "I see. Perhaps you would care for a cup of tea while this investigation is pursued. I find myself in rather great need of one." She did not wait for his reply but led the way to her door, which was swept open by the older butler Damien recalled. That man hid his uncertainty well but not completely, but was as efficient as previously.

The magistrate and his men headed into the house with purpose.

By the time Miss Ballantyne had shed her gloves and jacket, proceeding into the front room, the butler appeared with a laden tray of tea. Damien smelled the fresh scones and his stomach responded with enthusiasm. He saw that Miss Ballantyne's hand shook slightly as she offered him the cup of tea.

"You appear to be distressed, Miss Ballantyne," Damien dared to say.

She flicked a glance his way, which he might have called poisonous if it had lasted longer than a heartbeat. As it was, he wondered whether he had imagined it, for it was banished so quickly. "You anticipated that I would welcome the arrival of a magistrate to search my home?"

"Perhaps you experience distress, as a result of guilt."

The look she granted him at that was searing in its ferocity. "I fear only that my life has been stolen by a lie," she said, biting off the words with vigor. "And worse, one that I should have anticipated."

Damien was startled by the vigor of her claim. In that moment, he had absolutely no doubt of her innocence, but it was too late for such a realization.

The magistrate was at the door, a necklace of rubies carved in the shape of berries in his hand. "I must insist that you accompany me, Miss Ballantyne," he said.

She looked at the gems and inhaled deeply. Damien was certain he heard her swear under her breath with an earthiness that made him blink. Then she stood and beckoned to her butler for her coat. "Of course," she said, leaving the room and her house without a backward glance.

Damien put down his tea, convinced to his very marrow that he had erred in bringing the law to her home.

One way or the other, he had to set this matter to rights. His honor demanded no less.

IN THE END, Catherine had no opportunity to present her argument to her father, at least not with the book. She returned to Carruthers & Carruthers specifically to speak with him, only to find that the shop was as deluged with clients as Brisbane's had been. Her younger sister, Patricia, was nigh overwhelmed, to the point that the youngest of the three sisters, Prudence, had joined Patricia behind the desk. Both were slender and blond like Catherine, and both adored books as much as Catherine did. Patricia, content that she would remain unwed now that she had reached twenty-one years of age, had a tendency to sound knowing. The family jest remained that Prudence was *not*. The youngest sister was eighteen and flitted from one fascination to another with dizzying speed. As Catherine had helped in the shop for years before her marriage, she took a place behind the great circular counter, as well.

By the time the crowd had thinned and it became clear that her father was in no mood for a discussion, Catherine was more than ready to return home to Rhys and dinner. She could not find Esmeralda's book, however. She had removed it from her satchel while approaching the shop, steeling her confidence to address her father, then placed both satchel and book beneath the counter on the back side. Now, only her satchel was there.

"Whatever happened to the book?" she demanded of Patience.

"Which book?" Patience asked, sparing a meaningful glance at the full bookshelves surrounding them.

"There was a copy of, um, *Childe Harold* on my satchel."

"That was packed with Lady Beckham's order," Prudence contributed, even as she strode past them with an armload of books to return to the shelves. "She had requested it, so she said, but it was not in her order."

Catherine felt herself pale. Lady Beckham was a great patroness of the shop but also an opinionated dowager of conservative views. She had a rakehell of a son and a much younger daughter whose sweetness Catherine did not wish to be responsible for despoiling.

As if the gods meant to mock her, Prudence pivoted to smile at her, pushing up her glasses as she did so. "She said it was for Amelia."

Catherine gripped the counter. "But that was my book."

Prudence laughed. "That cannot be. You have never liked Byron's poems. It just ended up on your satchel instead of in the order. Fear not—I set all to rights."

"You set all awry," Catherine said, knowing she sounded stern. "The book must be retrieved at once."

"What difference?" Patricia asked. "We have several copies of *Childe Harold* in circulation and one is much like the other."

"This one is different," Catherine insisted.

"Because it was yours?" Patricia asked archly. "Take another, Catherine, and cease to make such a fuss."

"That book must be retrieved with all haste," Catherine said, seeing her return to Trevelaine House delayed.

"If you insist upon it," Patricia said with forbearance. "I will send word to Lady Beckham, explain the confusion and request the return of the book."

"No, someone must go there and see the book exchanged immediately."

"Do you have love notes in the margin?" Prudence asked with delight. "Shall I tell Papa that you now write in books like a wretched heathen?" She did a reasonable mimicry of their father, who called all those who abused books 'wretched heathens'. Prudence frowned. "Why does he say that? There is nothing particularly Christian about taking care of one's books. Why, I've heard that…"

"The book," Catherine said with force, interrupting her sister. "It must be retrieved immediately." She eyed Prudence. "You put it in the wrong package so you should see the matter repaired."

"There is nothing of import that cannot wait until the morning," Prudence said with a confidence Catherine did not share. "Oh, do not scowl! Amelia is unlikely to race to read that volume tonight. I wager it might even be returned unread. I will send word in the morning, and all will be well."

"You should return home to your lord husband," Patience advised. "You would not wish for dinner to be delayed at Trevelaine House on your account."

Catherine looked between the two of them, then at her father's stern countenance as he chastised a new worker beside the printing presses. It had been a long day, and somehow she would ensure the book was collected in the morning.

BUT IT BECAME clear the following day that Esmeralda's volume, hidden within the case of Lord Byron's book, would not be retrieved soon. Lady Beckham, her son and daughter, had left England for sunny Italy and their return was not anticipated for three months.

There was far worse news than that, however. By midday, Catherine learned that Miss Esmeralda Ballantyne had been imprisoned for the theft of a ruby necklace, one with gems carved in the shape of fruit.

Everything had gone awry and Catherine had no notion of where to begin to repair the situation.

CHAPTER 1

London, England - March 12, 1817

Mrs. Eliza North was vexed.

She had told one lie in all her life and that single falsehood had returned to haunt her with vigor, precisely as she had been warned by her childhood governess. In fact, the untruth plagued Eliza in such inconvenient fashion that Mrs. Whittemore might well have ensured as much from beyond the grave, simply to prove herself right.

It was most annoying.

It had been precisely ten years since Nicholas Emerson—the love of Eliza's life and closest friend of her older brother Damien—had bought a commission and left for Europe without a single word of farewell. It had been almost ten years—one day less, in fact—since she had accepted the persistent suit of Reverend Frederick North, a decision wrought of despair. It had also been ten-years-less-a-day since Eliza had lied to her father and insisted that she loved Frederick beyond all men, in order that her father would permit her to wed a country parson some twenty years older than herself.

It had seemed to be a solid choice at the time, when

15

she had wanted nothing other than to be far beyond any place Captain Nicholas Emerson might ever show his handsome visage.

But now the war was over and Frederick was dead. Eliza had heard from Damien that Nicholas had returned finally to London, but it would have been vulgar to admit her comparative lack of feelings for Frederick at this point. She had been fond of him, to be sure, and his had been a comforting presence, but love? No. It was Nicholas who had always held Eliza's heart captive, Nicholas who had gone abroad with that token firmly in his possession, Nicholas who was utterly unaware of its burden and apparently oblivious to Eliza herself.

And now that Frederick was gone, Eliza's lie stood barrier between herself and her desire.

Eliza did not doubt that Mrs. Whittemore was laughing at her, wherever that good lady had discovered her place in the hereafter to be.

Alone in the pale yellow breakfast room of Damien's London house, Eliza did not find that her own disposition matched the sunny hue of the room.

She had come to London with high hopes, but thus far, there had not been a single opportunity to speak to Nicholas since his arrival in town the week before. In fact, her brother had shown a shocking return to the dissolute behavior of his youth in the past week, perhaps due to Nicholas' influence. It seemed to Eliza that the two men were determined to visit every establishment of dubious repute in London. No decent woman could follow the pair on such a course and she had little opportunity to speak with even her brother, given that he was either out with Nicholas or sound asleep when home.

Why were men so obsessed with pleasure, even at the risk of their own welfare? These two had survived a war, though certainly Damien had sustained an injury to his leg that would never heal. Even so, she could not understand why they were so determined to drown their sorrows. They were home, alive, and more fortunate than most.

She knew that voicing any objection would only make her sound like the prim widow of a parson, but Eliza was concerned by their indulgences. Their mother, also in residence, remained blithely disinterested in her son's habits or disposition. There was nothing of import in the dowager's world beyond the cultivation of roses. It was a marvel that she had come to town at all, and Eliza could only assume that a quest for a clipping from a rare breed of rose was behind her mother's choice.

Eliza read her brother's newspaper while she lingered over her tea, a habit of which Damien was aware but disapproved. The dowager duchess did not know that Eliza read the newspaper and would have disapproved much more vehemently if she had. There was little chance of that lady discovering the truth, though, since she never left her rooms before noon. Eliza could not imagine why anyone would be concerned: the political news was sufficiently dull that it could not be unseemly for her to read about it.

She was just about to put the paper aside when her gaze fell upon an advertisement.

Ladies! Does your husband prefer his mistress's bed to yours? Is your betrothed to be found with actresses and widows? The Ladies' Essential Guide to the Arts of Seduction can teach you the skills your governess, your mother and your sisters never shared. Be assured that all enquiries after this volume are treated with the greatest discretion.

Eliza could well imagine that it would be intriguing to know secrets such as these. Why, a woman with such skills would never be overlooked by a man whom she held in affection.

Eliza's own amorous experiences with her late husband had been less than idyllic and certainly not particularly informative. Not only had Frederick been a man of the cloth but he had possessed a moral adversity to pleasure: their couplings had been few and of short duration. Rendering the marital debt had felt to Eliza like a chore Frederick was obliged to perform, and thus it had become one to her.

They had met abed so infrequently that it was no surprise they had never had children. Though Eliza had always wanted a family, she had come to doubt that Frederick shared her ambition. If she wed again, she desired it all: love, a family and a secure future.

At this juncture, it seemed likely that she would never marry again.

Intrigued, Eliza read the advertisement again. It was only logical that there might be more to the deed than she knew. It also made sense that those who knew the secrets found pleasure in it. Why else did people so often indulge? Eliza did not doubt that the ladies who frequented the same establishments that her brother and his friend had taken to patronizing would know all such details.

She wanted to know them herself.

Oddly, there was no address in the advertisement.

How peculiar.

Eliza did like a good puzzle. She supposed the advertisement could be a hoax or a jest, but hoped it was genuine. She read the short paragraph again. It appeared that it was a book she sought. She wagered the volume did not appear in any library, so it must be the author she had to find. Sadly, there were no hints as to that person's identity.

Eliza had to assume that the author was a woman.

What kind of woman would know of such matters? While the author could be any woman of a certain age with knowledge of intimacy, this last detail—that she had written them down to share with others—hinted at an uncommon measure of audacity.

Could the author be a courtesan? Eliza felt a little thrill at even the daring possibility of conferring with one. She had never spoken to one of the Cyprians who flitted through society, though she had seen them at a distance in her debut year and knew something of them. Frederick had been scathing about their immorality—Jezebel appeared regularly in his sermons, almost inevitably after they made a rare visit to London —but Eliza had never been so convinced of their evil. It seemed to her that the transaction took two parties, one male and one female, and it was unclear to her which bore the greater blame for any resulting sinfulness. Courtesans were reputed to be educated and clever, which would make one precisely the kind of woman capable of writing not only a book but this particular reference.

Did she dare to ask her brother for a list of potential candidates?

The dowager's bell rang, summoning Hastings upstairs. The girl was always prompt in responding and sure enough, Eliza heard her brisk footsteps in the upstairs corridor. The front bell sounded and Higgins moved crisply to respond. Doubtless some other soul intended to leave a card. The silver salver was thick with them each morning since their arrival in town, evidence aplenty that the Duke of Haynesdale's eligibility was tempting to many an ambitious mama, and this despite his injured leg and his rediscovered tendency to be a wastrel. Doubtless, some even declared his limp and cane to be dashing, though Eliza guessed her brother's fortune was the true lure.

While Higgins dealt with the caller, Eliza studied the newspaper from front to back once again, but found no further references to this mysterious *Essential Guide*.

If her brother did know more—he knew everything, it often seemed—he might not share his knowledge with Eliza. She was fairly certain he would disapprove of her question.

There was altogether too much disapproval at the current time, her own notwithstanding.

"Of course, he is at home," declared a man firmly in that moment, interrupting Eliza's thoughts. Her heart leapt at the familiar deep tones. "I carried him here myself not four hours ago. His Grace may not be awake, but he is most assuredly at home. Fetch him, if you please, Higgins. I will not tolerate his excuses after my assistance to him just hours ago."

Nicholas!

"But, sir, I must insist," Higgins protested, to no avail. Eliza often thought the man should have despaired long ago at the herculean task of securing protocol in Damien's house. Such established habits had disappeared completely with her father's demise.

The dining room door swung open before she could feel more sympathy for Damien's loyal butler.

Caught, Eliza hastened to arrange Damien's newspaper as if it had been untouched. She spilled tea into her saucer in her haste, then froze when a man laughed. She looked up and was snared with a single glance.

Captain Nicholas Emerson was leaning in the doorway.

Eliza's heart stopped, and then it raced. He was as tall and handsome as he had always been, but worse, the effect of his presence upon her was as potent as ever. Her mouth went dry and she could not summon a coherent word to her lips. She had always become a stammering idiot in this man's presence and hated that absence only made her reaction worse.

Nicholas' tawny hair was a bit longer than she recalled and it appeared to have more curl as a result. His necktie was loosened and there was stubble upon his chin. The combination gave him a rakish air that made her heart flutter. Indeed, there was a daredevil glint in his eyes, making him seem less honorable than she knew him to be. He was also more tanned than she remembered, and it seemed that his shoulders had become more broad. His eyes were as blue as ever, but there were shadows lurking in their depths when she looked, and a grim edge to his familiar smile.

Indeed, there was a good bit different about Nicholas when she studied him more closely. He seemed larger and more dangerous than he once had been, less predictable and perhaps more volatile. He had been wounded, she knew that from Damien, but she could not discern where he had been hurt. He appeared to be as vital as ever and if anything, his presence made Eliza tingle with greater vigor.

She doubted that Nicholas regarded lovemaking as a chore to be completed at regular intervals.

She would have wagered that those intervals would be far more frequent than Frederick had decreed they should be.

A part of her wanted desperately to know for certain—regardless of the price.

"Mrs. Eliza North," Nicholas chided. "Surely you, a paragon of the feminine gender, are not reading a newspaper like a bluestocking?" As ever, he teased her and prompted her smile, treating her like a second sister.

"Whyever not, Captain Emerson?" Eliza managed to say, even if her voice was not as even as she would have liked it to be. "I was curious this morning and in need of its distraction."

Nicholas' smile broadened an increment, prompting Eliza's heart to leap. She had always thought him strikingly attractive but had his smile always been so wicked? "Curious? I should not have expected curiosity to be numbered among your many attributes."

"Oh?" Eliza silently chided herself for such a feeble attempt at conversation.

"Practical, sensible, clear-thinking, reliable—these are the traits I associate with Mrs. Eliza North and surely no others are more appropriate for a parson's wife. But curiosity? No, no, that is the stuff of temptresses like Pandora and Eve."

Eliza straightened, finding the litany of her qualities less satisfying than she might have done. "You have been absent for ten years, Captain Emerson. People change." She sounded prim, precisely as she did not want to sound, but the words were out and the damage was done.

Her companion sobered immediately. "Indeed, they do," he said and inclined his head politely. "I was sorry to hear of your loss," he said softly, his gaze searching hers for a heart-stopping moment before he crossed the room to the sideboard.

Eliza thanked him for his kindness, then grit her teeth. All she had wanted was a moment to speak with him, and in less time than that, she had managed to secure his conviction that she was a sensible woman in mourning. She would rather have been a temptress, though she had no idea how to embark upon such an endeavor.

If only that ad had contained an address...

"My lady?" Higgins hovered in the doorway, exuding disfavor as only he could do. Higgins was not easily surprised, not in this household, but his eyes fair fell out of his head as he watched Nicholas help himself to Damien's brandy.

Eliza protested. "A brandy for breakfast? Captain Emerson, you are intemperate!"

His eyes widened slightly as he turned to regard her, but the merry twinkle she expected to find in his eye was not there. Instead, he seemed predatory, a man who should not be challenged over his choice of indulgence.

"It is true," he admitted, then added another increment to the glass. "And me, custodian of my sister Helena's chastity. Appalling, is it not? Someone should do something about my lack of wholesome attributes. Someone sensible and responsible." He cast her a glance, then turned and raised a brow. He looked positively diabolical and something deep within Eliza began to hum. "Perhaps someone, Mrs. North, like you." Then he saluted her with his glass and took a long sip, his gaze unswerving.

His was a dare, Eliza did not doubt it, and she began to rise to her feet to accept it.

Then Nicholas smiled a small knowing smile that made Eliza reconsider. He gestured to the decanter. "Would you care for one? You might become intemperate with me, Mrs. North. We could be two drunken wastrels by the time Haynesdale makes his appearance, and all this before the stroke of noon."

"No, thank you." Eliza sat down hard and shook her head. "Although I am not certain that I should be thanking you for your offer to share Damien's brandy."

Nicholas chuckled darkly. "Probably not." He sipped the brandy again as he took a seat at the other end of the table. He had already consumed half of what he had poured. Even with the expanse of mahogany between them, Eliza could feel the heat of his gaze upon her. He had carried the scent of wind and sunshine and horseflesh into the dining room with him, and she yearned suddenly to ride alongside him and hear his laughter.

Although Nicholas did not look as if he laughed often these days.

"You smile," he fairly purred.

"I was recalling the morning you took the horses from the stables at Haynesdale and we rode out together."

Nicholas laughed. "The squire's son and the duke's daughter, and unescorted!" His eyes widened in mock horror. "I could not sit down for a week after that thrashing." He pretended to wince as he moved in his chair. "Perhaps there is much to be said for good behaviour."

"Tell me your father did not do as much," Eliza protested.

"It is the same with horses," he said readily. "The right lesson delivered at the right moment is never forgotten."

"But what was the lesson?"

"The most obvious one. Though your brother and I were friends, our situations would never be comparable, and I should never be so fool as to forget it." Their gazes locked for a potent moment and Eliza averted hers first.

"You could not have known then that he would inherit the dukedom."

"Even if he had not, the disparity would have remained great." Nicholas did not appear to resent this, but presented it as a known fact.

It was on Eliza's lips to ask if their adventure had been worth it, but she had no chance to do as much.

"My lady?" Higgins fairly squeaked.

"Perhaps you might see if His Grace is home, Higgins, as Captain Emerson seems inclined to wait upon him."

"Very good, my lady." The butler did not let his gaze stray from their visitor and Eliza could fairly taste his distrust. "Shall I send Phipps for another pot of tea, my lady?"

"An excellent idea. Thank you, Higgins."

Higgins spared Nicholas one last grim glance then departed, pointedly leaving the dining room door open behind him. There were maids in the hall, tending the fire in the foyer and cleaning the floor, so Eliza knew their conversation was being observed. She might be a widow, but she still had a reputation to protect. She appreciated Higgins' thoughtfulness, though she thought his worries misplaced.

Nicholas was no more interested in seducing her than in, well, kissing his young sister. Eliza felt a surge of dissatisfaction and wished heartily that she could become the kind of woman with whom men liked to dally.

Eliza North: temptress.

No, she would have to use her maiden name, if anyone was to believe the appellation.

Eliza DeVries: temptress.

She liked the sound of that. That lady would have read the volume advertised in this morning's newspaper and done so unflinchingly.

A temptress might have composed such a work.

Perhaps it was time Eliza was less demure and predictable.

Nicholas watched her as he drank, his expression enigmatic. "You smile again," he fairly purred.

Eliza chose to provoke him a little. "I was considering the merit of becoming a temptress. The choice must have its advantages."

He laughed in surprise, leaning back in his chair. His eyes gleamed as he watched her. "I should think you would need a tutor, Mrs. North, given the respectability of your nature."

"You may be right, Captain Emerson," she replied mildly, feeling that she had found her footing. "Have you a candidate to recommend?"

"I already offered to lead you astray."

Eliza held his gaze. "And what would you do, Captain Emerson, if I agreed?"

"I believe I should fall off my chair in shock, and then I would realize that you were teasing me." He gestured to the open door with his brandy. "Is that a comment upon my reputation or your own?"

"I could not begin to speculate upon your reputation, Captain Emerson."

Nicholas laughed shortly. "Well put, Mrs. North. We both know that you are above reproach in all circles." There was no malice in his words but they still stung. He tilted his head to regard her, his gaze sharpening again. "Are you always so alarmingly composed in the morning?"

"I fail to see anything alarming about the fact that I slept well." Eliza smiled. "I shall endeavor to sleep poorly, if you believe it more fitting."

Nicholas snorted and sipped his brandy. Eliza waited until he was mid-sip, then spoke with the intent of surprising him.

"Or you could drink less, fornicate less and sleep more yourself," she suggested.

His reaction was highly satisfactory. Nicholas choked on his drink, then regarded her over the rim of his glass. His eyes were so very blue that she could not look away. "I believe you startled me on purpose, Mrs. North."

"Do you?" She strove for a tone of innocence but was not entirely certain of her success.

"How delightfully wicked of you." He leaned an

elbow on the table, a smile curving his lips. Eliza's heart fluttered. "But how can you be certain of my sins?"

"Brandy at breakfast," she said, indicating the emptied glass. "And you noted a lack of sleep yourself."

"But the subject of fornication, Mrs. North, has not yet been broached." He was watching her closely and could not have missed the flush of color that suffused her cheeks. Eliza had to drop her gaze to her tea and she heard him chuckle to be proven right about her reservations. "But such mischievous commentary, Mrs. North, compels me to wonder whether it is true what they say."

"Surely you give no credence to gossip, Captain."

"None, unless it is supported by observation."

"And what is said and implied?"

"That the talent of those with DeVries blood for finding trouble is unrivaled—save among the daughters of the house. Is it true, Mrs. North, that the DeVries ladies are spared the wild tendencies of the sons of the line? There was a time when Haynesdale seemed incapable of consuming his fill of pleasure. Perhaps he returns to indulgence to savor your measure as well." His brows rose. "Or perhaps the daughters are just as wild, but hide the truth rather better."

Eliza swallowed, so keenly aware of his intent gaze that she flushed. "I wager you would like to know the truth, Captain."

"I would, indeed, Mrs. North."

"Suffice it to say that I should think life would be rather dull without pleasure."

"And does a good night's sleep count as pleasure?"

"It can."

He laughed shortly. "You have always shown the most unnatural inclination to be sensible, Mrs. North. You will not fool me about your character."

"It is only good sense to recognize that a sound sleep is restorative."

"I shall take your word upon that matter." Nicholas toasted her with his glass. "For I do not intend to discover the truth of it myself anytime soon."

Eliza and Nicholas fell silent as Phipps brought a hot pot of tea. There was only the slight clatter of cups in saucers in the dining room as the maid set down the tray and the weight of Nicholas' burning gaze upon Eliza. She offered a cup to Nicholas, which he declined.

Upon the maid's departure, Nicholas spoke softly. "I am sorry. I truly am a beast."

"You are not so bad as that."

"You are being polite, as always you are."

"No. I am not."

"Not being polite now, or not always polite?"

"Both."

"Nonsense." Nicholas regarded her, a disconcerting warmth glimmering in his eyes. "I am certain you are the most sensible, polite and honest woman I have ever known. All the greater a riddle that you, of all women, should have wed for the impetuous fancy of love."

Eliza caught her breath and fixed her attention upon her tea. "I fail to see the riddle in that."

"Because love is not logical. Certainly no one could have predicted that the Reverend Frederick North, so many years your senior, would have captured your heart so securely."

Eliza tried not to fidget beneath his bright gaze. She could not tell Nicholas the truth in this moment, not when he applauded her practicality and counted her outside the company of temptresses. "Love must be beyond explanation, then."

"You inspire me, Mrs. North. How many other women wed against their best financial interests, simply for love alone?" Nicholas lifted his glass and the crystal sparkled as it caught the morning sunlight. "It must be devastating to lose the love of one's life."

"Yes, it is." Eliza agreed quietly, though she was not speaking of Frederick. "Is that why you come to London? To seek a bride?"

Nicholas shook his head and put down his glass firmly. "No. I am charged with finding a suitable match for my sister Helena. My aunt is most resolute that she must be settled before the end of the season."

"Your aunt," Eliza said. "Lady Dalhousie?"

"The very one," Nicholas agreed readily. "Though I am Helena's guardian since the demise of our parents, my aunt was sufficiently good to take my sister into her care when I bought my commission."

Eliza remained silent, doubting there was anything good about the gesture. Lady Dalhousie, as she recalled, was most concerned with wealth and stature. Nicholas' father had left little save his debts and Southpoint, a small holding adjacent to Haynesdale. The sale of it to their father and the duchy had been barely sufficient for Nicholas to buy his commission after discharging his father's gambling debts. Lady Dalhousie would have spent the past decade grooming his much younger sister for a good marriage. The girl had always been uncommonly pretty and a rich match would ensure the aunt's comfort in her old age.

Nicholas continued. "Helena had her debut season last year and undoubtedly enjoyed herself enormously, but made no match." He considered his words for a moment. "You must remember her?"

"Of course. I recall her being quite high-spirited, though she was only a girl when last I saw her. Exceedingly pretty, as well."

Nicholas nodded agreement and his expression turned rueful. "The years have changed little. She favors her mother."

"Your father's second bride?"

"And a woman consumed with the pursuit of pleasure at any price. Helena is precisely like her, if perhaps a little more reckless. Indeed, there could be no woman less like you. It will be either a marriage or a scandal for Helena and, were I a gambling man, I would wager on the latter."

Eliza recalled his aversion to games of chance, a legacy of his father's choices. She kept her tone light. "Then perhaps you should mend your own ways, to better provide an example for her."

"I rather thought I should find a more suitable chaperone instead." Nicholas leaned forward, his eyes darkening to that arresting shade of blue. "I know that you, for example, could be relied upon to steer Helena upon a sensible and prudent course."

"She is not my sister, Captain."

"But sadly, she is mine, and I am the last who might offer such guidance."

"You might endeavor to change, sir."

"I might recognize a futile task when I hear of it." Nicholas smiled at her so warmly that Eliza's heart skipped a beat.

Could she chaperone Helena? Instinctively, she doubted the wisdom of undertaking the task—though she was tempted by the possibility of more time with Nicholas. "Surely your aunt has employed tutors and chaperones?"

"Indeed, and at great expense. Helena dances beautifully, and speaks both French and German. It is decorum that eludes her and I fear my aunt's example is not one she finds compelling."

"No?"

"No." He visibly fought a smile and Eliza was glad when he lost. "Helena has informed me that when she is as ancient as Aunt Fanny, then she will be sedate but not before."

"Ah."

"It is my own conviction that Helena has need of the counsel of a lady closer to her own age."

"Did you come here this morning to see Damien or me?"

"You, of course." That Nicholas' voice lowered to a tone of intimacy that made her reservations melt away. "Will you do it, Eliza? Will you aid in my quest, for Helena's sake?"

It did not hurt that he called her by her Christian name, as he had many years before. It certainly did not injure his cause that he appealed to her with such sincerity. It seemed to Eliza that the room had become uncommonly warm.

She met his gaze steadily. She would do what he asked, but not for Helena's sake. Although she would have been happier to have Nicholas see her as more than useful, chaperoning Helena might give her own objective a greater chance of success.

Indeed, it could not injure her cause.

"Of course," she said. "For Helena's sake," she amended, fearing she had agreed too readily.

"Yes," he murmured softly. "For Helena's sake." Their gazes held for a long moment, then he looked away so abruptly that Eliza wondered whether she had imagined the flicker of heat in his gaze.

"And that will grant you the opportunity to seek a match of your own," she said, then immediately felt she had been too forthright.

Nicholas shrugged. "I have no intentions of wedding."

Eliza was surprised. "Surely now that the war is over?"

He shook his head. "I cannot afford a wife, Mrs.

North. You might applaud me for being so prudent as to put practical considerations in their rightful place."

"You might wed an heiress and secure your future."

Nicholas laughed easily. "I think that an unlikely scenario."

"Why? You are a man of fine features, though you hide your gallantry…"

He leaned closer, his intensity making her words die on her tongue. "I will not wed simply for the sake of comfort, much less for the sake of conformity. Thus, I have no plans to wed at all."

"But then you will be alone!"

"I have my sister, just as you have your brother." His eyes narrowed in assessment. "Surely *you* cannot mean to wed again after losing such a great love."

Eliza was flustered. "Who can say?"

He sipped his brandy. "Ah yes, who can say when the heart shall be captured anew?"

"You need not mock me."

"On the contrary, Mrs. North, I admire you. How many have the confidence to follow the urging of their own hearts?" He clearly did not expect a reply, for he rose to his feet to refill his glass again. "Indeed, wedding for love seems such a feckless thing to do, that it might be precisely the kind of amusement I should like. Perhaps I should follow your example, and wed only if my heart demands it. It is wildly improbable that I should succeed in finding such an affection, of course, but I rather prefer long odds."

"So do I," Eliza said without meaning to do so. She spoke so resolutely that Nicholas glanced up, impaling her with his bright gaze.

"Oh, I do not believe that," he teased. "Such frivolity, Mrs. North, seems quite out of character for you."

"If you like long odds, you should have accepted

Galveston," Damien remarked from the doorway and the pair turned as one to regard him.

How long had he been listening?

As dark as Nicholas was golden, Damien had once looked far more wicked and disreputable. It was more than his coloring. His manner was imperious and often audacious. Eliza had to admit even as his sister that he was devastatingly handsome. The limp that was his souvenir from the war only seemed to make him more dashing. His manners were impeccable, his manner often inscrutable, and Eliza always felt that Damien had many secrets that would never come to light. Or would the right woman unfurl them? She hoped she lived to see that day.

On this morning, Damien was also unshaven but his stubble was a dark shadow on his chin and far more noticeable than Nicholas'. They were a matched pair of this day, each appearing to be as much of a rakehell as the other. Damien was leaning more heavily on his cane, she noted with concern. He visibly noted Nicholas' choice of beverage and poured himself one of the same, then turned to Eliza. "Galveston has five thousand a year, which would keep you well enough, although the odds of him making you happy were long indeed."

Eliza could not help but grimace, a response that made both men chuckle.

"Would it have to be ten thousand a year to abide him?" Damien teased, his eyes dancing with familiar devilry. "You took Frederick for two."

"Two?" Nicholas echoed in mock astonishment. "This then is the price of love?"

"In your circumstance, you can scarce afford such affection," Damien noted.

"Damien! You should not speak thus!" Eliza said, realizing too late that her words only proved Nicholas' assessment of her nature.

"What is the point of an old friendship if we cannot be forthright with each other?" Damien demanded.

"Hear, hear," Nicholas agreed. The pair toasted each other cheerfully and drank.

"I could not abide Galveston for a fortune, and you know it," Eliza said with heat. Damien laughed but Nicholas watched Eliza with disconcerting intensity. She felt her color rise again.

"How intriguing, that the sensible Mrs. North can ignore practical considerations when it comes to marriage," he noted.

"Galveston is an inoffensive man, but scarce one who might kindle the admiration of a lady," Damien supplied, musing into his glass.

"A practical man, then?" Nicholas asked.

"Very. Undoubtedly unconvinced of the merit of love, or perhaps even affection."

"Alas," Nicholas said.

Eliza knew that both were teasing her and enjoying it. The simple truth was that Mr. Galveston was far too similar to her late husband. He was a sensible, prudent man, not given to flamboyance or lavish gestures. Unlike Frederick, he was just a few years older than Eliza, which meant a marriage to him would likely be of long duration.

She could not have borne it.

"Additionally, he has the misfortune of being possessed of fleshy lips," Damien said and Nicholas snorted. "I suspect kissing him would be rather like kissing a fish."

"Damien!"

"Well? Was it?" Her brother had the look of the devil about him, as always he did when he teased her.

"I never kissed him."

"I thought he kissed your hand."

Eliza flicked a lethal glare at her brother, which produced no good effect.

Indeed, he grinned at her.

Nicholas sat back in his chair, folding his arms across his chest. "How alarming that a woman would decide upon a man's merit, or even the fate of his suit, on the basis of how he kissed her hand."

"Perhaps you should see yourself assessed," Damien suggested to Eliza's dismay.

"Perhaps I should." Nicholas unfolded himself from his chair with easy grace, eyes glinting with purpose.

"The pair of you are unfit company for a lady," Eliza began to protest. She rose to her feet, intent upon leaving them to each other's supposed wit.

But Nicholas was already crossing the room to her and she could not flee from him. He claimed her hand with admirable grace, arching his brow as he lifted her fingers to his lips.

Of course, Eliza wore no glove. She was at breakfast. The prospect of his mouth against even her fingers was sufficient to make her heart leap for the heavens. She found no words upon her tongue. She stared at him, savoring the warmth of his hand upon hers and the strength of his grip. Nicholas watched her avidly as he bent lower. A lock of his hair fell over his brow, tempting her to push it back from his brow. She inhaled sharply at the first touch of his lips against her flesh and felt a tingle launch from that point of contact. His lips were firm and dry, brushing across her hand with an intensity equal to the heat of his gaze. He was gentle but there was a deliberation about his gesture that spoke of strength held in restraint, of a power that could be unleashed with her slightest gesture.

Of passion that could be loosed, on her command.

This man would take all night to seduce the woman he desired.

All night.

Perhaps she should ask him for lessons and forget the wretched book. Eliza felt slightly faint at the notion and did not doubt that her eyes widened. Her knees weakened in a most delicious way and she knew she swayed a little. As Nicholas ended his kiss, his gaze swept over her with a hunger that left her yearning.

A sound night's sleep held markedly less appeal than it had possessed just moments before.

"Well?" he asked, the question no more than an exhalation.

Eliza swallowed. "I doubt any woman would refuse you on that gesture alone."

Nicholas' eyes gleamed. "I am most gratified to know as much, Mrs. North."

Eliza pulled her fingertips from his hand, fearing that he was mocking her. "There might, indeed, be merit in the prospect of being led astray by a man such as yourself. Perhaps I erred in declining your earlier generous offer."

"You intend to corrupt my sister?" Damien asked.

"I offered, but she declined."

"Of course. There is one woman in the world immune to your charm, to be sure." The duke indicated to Nicholas' glass. "I suppose you would like another."

Nicholas turned to his friend, giving every sign of forgetting Eliza completely. She should recall that he shared Damien's ability to charm without meaning anything by it. "Indeed. I was about to conclude that your hospitality had become rather mean."

"We are simply unaccustomed to guests with manners such as yours, given your long absence from our company."

Nicholas snorted. "You mean that you have lacked

companions prepared to carry you home after your revels. I am certain, Haynesdale, that you have gained some weight in my absence."

"Perhaps you possess only a fraction of the strength of your youth," Damien retorted.

"Perhaps I shall leave the two of you to your nonsense," Eliza interjected and the pair bowed to her politely. It was clear they wished her to leave.

Undoubtedly, they had plans to make for this night's debauchery.

"Perhaps you might accept my aunt's invitation to tea today," Nicholas said when Eliza reached the door. "She has a schedule for Helena that she wished to share, if you could be persuaded to undertake this favor."

"You spoke to her of it already." Eliza had the unwelcome sense that she had been granted a responsibility that Nicholas did not desire, simply so that he could enjoy himself instead.

There was nothing worse than being considered useful, in her view.

He winced. "There was a decision pending. I sensed as much last evening so I offered your assistance, if it could be won." He saluted her with his glass. "My aunt was most gratified by the suggestion."

Eliza wondered at this. Lady Dalhousie once had been a rival of her mother's, but that had been decades before, in their debut season.

Surely such an old feud had been put to rest?

Perhaps not.

Eliza thanked Nicholas for his trust and agreed to visit his aunt, then left the room. She heard their voices when she reached the hall, just before she pulled the door closed behind her, and paused to listen.

"She seems quieter," Nicholas commented as glasses clinked.

"It has only been nine months since Frederick died,"

Damien said, his tone more somber than it had been. "I expect it takes rather longer than that to recover from the loss of a great love."

"I expect so," Nicholas agreed.

Eliza grimaced in her frustration. The situation was entirely her own fault, but there had to be a way for her to repair what she had done. There had to be a way for her to become a temptation to Nicholas Emerson.

The Ladies' Essential Guide to the Art of Seduction was the solution to her woes, Eliza knew it.

She merely had to locate that volume or its author. Somehow.

She would ask at Brisbane's Emporium before visiting Lady Dalhousie. The proprietress Sophia de Roye, once Sophia Brisbane, knew everyone and everything. Eliza had relied upon Mrs. de Roye's knowledge in the past.

Indeed, she felt a sudden and most desperate need for a new pair of gloves.

CHAPTER 2

Captain Nicholas Emerson was beginning to suspect that the more matters changed, the more essentials remained the same.

Miss Eliza DeVries had always been able to enflame his soul, though she was as beyond reach as the sun itself. He had become certain since buying his commission and leaving England's shores that this effect had been a result of his youth. Other women possessed only a passing allure—he had noted time and again how ladies could only fascinate him for a short while. They became predictable, if not worse; they began to pale in comparison to his memory of Eliza, and invariably, his interest faded.

Eliza, he had assured himself, remained an icon of female desirability because he had not spent sufficient time in her company in recent years. On the one hand, he welcomed that the end of the war would provide the opportunity to return home and diminish her power over him; in another, he had dreaded the loss of yet another reliable lodestar. He had dallied on the Continent, delaying the inevitable in a failed effort to concoct a plan for his own future. On this morning,

Nicholas had entered the breakfast room of his best friend, confident of results.

Only to be astonished by the vigor of his response to Eliza's welcoming smile.

Despite the passing of time, her influence had not diminished a whit. Nicholas had recognized the magnitude of his error with a single glimpse. Eliza was every measure as alluring as she had always been, perhaps more so than he recalled. She had always been pretty, but not conventionally beautiful. It was the glint of intellect in her eyes and the impish curve of her smile that enticed him. He admired that she could surprise him and often did. But now there was a confidence about her, as well as a sense that not all of her thoughts were readily declared. She had become mysterious and intriguing, a riddle he yearned to unfurl, and that was perilous to his hopes, indeed.

The girl had become a woman, he supposed, though Eliza was only twenty-eight years of age to his own thirty-five. He felt immediately that they were on a more equal footing than when she had been a maiden—though that made no sense given that he possessed little more than his own name. Nicholas was as smitten as ever, and in even less of a position to act upon his interest.

If that revelation had not been cause for a drink, he did not know what was.

The first brandy had gone down easily, perhaps too easily, but then he was still feeling the influence of the night before. Alcohol might not be good for a man's wits or his future prospects, but it was ideal for ensuring a dreamless sleep.

After he had picked his heart off the floor and emptied that first glass of brandy, the notion had come to him. His aunt had been complaining ever since his return about Helena's antics, almost demanding that he take charge of his younger sister. He had been sure to tarnish his own reputation sufficiently in the past sennight to persuade Aunt Fanny to reconsider the wisdom of that notion before it became a command.

It had been an impulsive whim to suggest that Eliza chaperone his sister, a suggestion made before Nicholas considered the repercussions.

He had never expected her to respond favorably, but Eliza had been agreeable. Perhaps his suggestion fit with her own expectations. He could readily imagine that a woman who had until recently been the wife of a parson was accustomed to providing useful service to others. To return to the duke's abode and become idle might be abhorrent to her.

He could think of no other reason for her ready agreement.

The challenge would be to win his aunt's approval. There was some matter between his aunt and Haynesdale's mother of long-standing enmity, and Nicholas did not wish Eliza to arrive for tea before he had eliminated any objections.

If indeed, it could be done.

"The shame of it is that there were no children," Haynesdale said quietly and Nicholas realized that his friend had been watching him.

And he had been staring at the door, where Mrs. North had vanished, like a lost hound.

"I had assumed there was no desire for any," he said, when in truth he had not considered the matter at all. "After all, they were wed the better part of a decade."

"Precisely," his friend agreed. "And Eliza always wished for a family, the larger the better." Those words only added to Nicholas' conviction of the unsuitability of his interest. He feigned interest in his glass lest Haynesdale guess the truth. "It must have been Frederick who declined."

"Perhaps it was a decision made of frugality," Nicholas suggested.

"He had a good living. Not a rich one, but they could have supported a family." Haynesdale shook his head. "Perhaps there was another issue."

Nicholas was keenly aware of one possible reason. Had his friend guessed the truth of his own situation? Nicholas risked a glance to find the duke apparently lost in thought.

"Frederick was very concerned with the spiritual and physical health of his parishioners," Haynesdale continued. "Eliza often noted the extent of his charity in giving food or comfort. She said he would go to anyone who summoned him, regardless of the hour, and laughed that he often gave away their own dinner to those in greater need. She worried about his health, especially near the end." He nodded. "Perhaps he did not have the fortitude to care for a family, as well."

His concern, to Nicholas' relief, was solely for his sister.

"But that is over and done. Eliza is young enough that if she weds again, she can have those children." Haynesdale looked up and smiled, even as his words were like a knife to Nicholas' heart. "And have you satisfied your need for indulgence?"

"I have only begun to drown my sorrows," Nicholas replied lightly. "Have you already lost your enthusiasm for such revels?"

"I have other matters requiring both my attention and a clear head," his friend growled, then spared him a piercing look. "You must have a scheme for your future."

"I have few prospects now that wages have been halved."

Haynesdale shook his head. "There is no cause to be grim. You are home. You are hale. You are decorated.

You have a commission. Take a wife, Emerson. See yourself settled instead of drinking yourself to an early grave."

"*You* recommend marriage to me?" Nicholas was incredulous. "Perhaps I have missed my opportunity to meet your new wife, the duchess who keeps you so contented."

"There is no such woman and you know it well." Haynesdale was gruff, though, which meant some female *had* snared his gaze.

Perhaps he had no intention of wedding the lady in question. That would be characteristic of the man Nicholas knew.

"Then who are you to commend the office to me?"

Haynesdale raised his hands. "I thought only to surrender a little advice. A wife might see you settled. A marriage might give you purpose."

"A wife might see me miserable," Nicholas countered. "Or I might ensure the same to her." He shook his head with resolve. "You waste your breath, Haynesdale. I will never wed."

"And you will accept no gifts. Truly, you have become vexing company, Emerson." There was a glimmer of humor in Haynesdale's dark eyes despite his manner. "It is a shame you have such an aversion to gambling, for I never met a man more fortunate at the tables. You might win yourself a fortune, though your dislike of such pastimes was well-earned."

Nicholas froze in the act of taking a sip of brandy, struck by the notion.

His friend nodded, unaware that he had granted inspiration. "Your father's lesson was a harsh one. I have always respected your resolve not to follow his path."

Nicholas had been compelled to sell the family manor to pay his father's gambling debts after that man's demise, and had vowed then to never to turn the tables himself. He knew the fever of being compelled to return to the game despite one's mounting losses and feared to succumb to it as his father had.

If he was sober, though, he invariably won.

"What if I could play for one night only?" Nicholas mused.

Haynesdale straightened, a gleam of interest in his eyes. "Then you must play at Brooks's, where the stakes are higher."

"I am not a member."

The duke smiled. "There is your luck showing itself, for you are in the company of one. I will see you admitted."

For the first time in months, Nicholas saw hope in his future. "And if I succumb to the fever on that one night, there can be little lost," he said softly, then raised his glass. "I thank you, Haynesdale, for the suggestion."

"However inadvertently it was made. Shall we make it tomorrow?" Haynesdale asked. "Thursdays are said to be busy nights. I will escort you there myself."

"Excellent." Indeed, Nicholas felt a measure of excitement. Could he do it? If the benefit was his entire future, he had to try.

"What would you do with such gains?" Haynesdale asked.

Nicholas had no need to ponder the question. "Breed horses. Of course."

"Of course. You have a fine stud in Sterling, to be sure." Haynesdale drained his glass and set it aside, turning to consider the sideboard and the offerings upon it. He rose with an effort and leaned heavily on his cane as he filled a plate. "There was a time when I thought it inevitable that you and Eliza should meet at the altar," he said with apparent idleness, and Nicholas was glad that his friend's back was turned. "You always teased her so."

Nicholas' heart clenched that he had been discovered, but he kept his tone light. "Because she always came back for more. Most maidens would have wept in dismay but Eliza always retaliated in kind. I admired her spirit, no more than that."

"Truly?" Haynesdale glanced over his shoulder.

"The daughter of a duke and the son of an impoverished country squire?" Nicholas scoffed. "I should never have imagined such a match probable." He had no intention of confiding his most intimate secret in anyone, but he would entrust Haynesdale with it if necessary.

Preferably not on this day.

"My father would have agreed with you, to be sure." Haynesdale's plate was filled with eggs and ham, potatoes and grilled tomatoes when he settled before it with contentment. "You were slow to return home after the end of the war," he said finally, as if changing the subject.

Nicholas was aware again of the differences in their circumstances. Haynesdale had been spared any lack of direction at the end of the war by his unexpected inheritance. "I seized the chance to take a Grand Tour of a sort."

The duke consumed his meal with more enthusiasm that Nicholas would have been able to summon for food on this morning or any other morning of late. "I had wondered whether your heart had been engaged. I thought you might return home with a bride."

Nicholas seized upon the excuse. "It seems that many ladies are practical in these times."

"Ah." Haynesdale cleared his throat before he continued in a brisk tone. The subject of matrimony appeared mercifully to have been abandoned. "Thank you for the suggestion that Eliza chaperone your sister. It will be a suitable activity for her and an interest like this should help to revive her enthusiasm for life." He nodded at Nicholas with satisfaction. "And Miss Emerson might not be the sole one to find a suitor this season. It is an admirable solution and I thank you for it."

"You are welcome, of course," Nicholas said, though his throat was tight. If he had foreseen the possibility that he might be providing the means for Eliza to encounter an appropriate suitor, he might not have made his suggestion in the first place.

"There is a ball at Almack's tonight. Rather than continue our revels, I plan to attend."

Nicholas laughed aloud in surprise. "You, at Almack's? You will need every able man in London to defend you from ambitious matchmakers."

Haynesdale smiled. "Perhaps just one would suffice. Join me? You might ensure that Eliza and Helena find a footing with each other."

As much as he knew it was folly to give himself the opportunity to see Eliza courted by other men, Nicholas could only agree. If she greeted such attentions with enthusiasm, that might banish his own interest.

Either way, he would not be a fool who yearned for what he could never possess.

~

Eliza had to wait for the opportunity to talk to Mrs. de Roye as that lady was occupied with other shoppers. She looked at gloves with indifference, for she did not actually need another pair, then at various ribbons in the haberdashery. She was beginning to despair that she would not be able to delay longer, when the proprietress presented herself.

"I do apologize, Mrs. North. This month has been

uncommonly busy so far." Mrs. de Roye smiled. "How may I be of assistance?"

"I have need of a pair of ivory gloves," Eliza said. "And cannot decide between kid and velvet."

"Surely that will depend upon when and where you mean to wear them."

"I suppose kid is more practical."

"We have a very fine kid suitable for the most formal of occasions." Mrs. de Roye placed such a pair on the counter. They were wondrously soft and the leather so thin that it might tear while they were pulled on. Eliza had no doubt that they were expensive for they were as soft as butter.

"Perhaps the velvet," she said, as if indecisive.

A pair of velvet gloves was presented for her perusal. "We also have some long satin gloves for evenings, and short leather gloves that are more sturdy than kid. Irene would be happy to show you all of the options that you can better decide…"

"But I wished particularly to consult with you."

Mrs. de Roye hesitated in the act of summoning a clerk. "Indeed?"

"Indeed. This is most awkward." Eliza lowered her voice. "I wondered whether you might have read the newspaper this morning."

Mrs. de Roye shook her head in confusion. "Is there a reason for your query?"

"There was an advertisement for ladies this morning." Eliza dropped her voice yet lower. "One recommending a book."

"Did it have a title?"

"*The Ladies' Essential Guide to the Art of—*" Eliza looked left and right, then leaned across the counter to whisper the last word. "*Seduction.*" It seemed to hang in the air, a sibilant word that was utterly inappropriate in decent society yet would be heard a mile away even if whispered.

"I cannot imagine why you should ask me about such a volume," Mrs. de Roye said, but her gaze slid away, as if she knew more.

"Because there are no details of who to contact," Eliza continued in a rush. "And you seem to know all the details about everyone in town." Her voice faltered. "I thought you might know more or who to ask to learn more. It was a remote hope, no more than that, and certainly no reflection of your own reputation."

Mrs. de Roye pursed her lips and rearranged the gloves, adding to Eliza's conviction that she did know more. "Rather an unusual volume for you to seek, Mrs. North." The proprietress met her gaze steadily. "I had understood that you were widowed."

"I am." Eliza lifted her chin. "But I am hopeful that I will not remain so." She swallowed. "And I would like to be more informed when next I…"

"I understand completely, Mrs. North," Mrs. de Roye said briskly, her decision evidently made. "I will make an enquiry for you, though I must warn you that my efforts may prove fruitless."

Eliza understood. Not only did the decision rest in the hands of another, but not every request would be greeted favorably. She could only hope for the best.

"I certainly appreciate your assistance, Mrs. de Roye," she said with a smile, then tried to tip the balance with her purchase. "I will take the kid, thank you. They are exquisite."

NICHOLAS HAD LEFT Haynesdale rather abruptly, using the excuse of too much brandy, but knew Haynesdale was not entirely fooled. He showed an uncharacteristic haste in returning to his aunt's home in Berkley Square, in the hope of winning Helena's agreement to his scheme before his aunt made her appearance for the day.

Two could argue with Aunt Fanny more successfully than one.

He had no sooner stepped into the foyer than he knew he had failed twice in rapid succession.

"I will not hear of such scandalous behavior on your part," Aunt Fanny said primly and there was no doubt to whom this comment was addressed.

A man of less fortitude might have surrendered the field and retreated, but Nicholas was not yet prepared to wave the white flag. He took a deep breath and continued into the breakfast room, casting his hat and gloves on the table in the foyer as he passed.

"Nicholas!" Helena exclaimed with a delight that proved she hoped he would take her side. "Just the person I most wished to see!"

"There is a portentous change," he grumbled, accepting her flurry of kisses.

"You have not shaved as yet," she said, her eyes narrowed as she surveyed him. "Are you only just returning from your night's revels?"

"I am and since each family can only suffer one scandalous member in their company, you will have to behave."

His aunt snorted at that and Helena grimaced before returning to her place. Nicholas bowed to his aunt, whose lips tightened as she surveyed him. She sniffed elaborately, then returned her attention to her breakfast. "I should not have thought there was any brandy left in London at this point," she said, her opinion of that more than clear.

"Very little, in fact. I was obliged to seek a measure at the home of the Duke of Haynesdale." Nicholas helped himself to toasted bread and sat down at his customary place. He heard his aunt's sharp intake of breath and felt his sister watching him avidly.

"Is he as handsome as they say?" Helena asked in a whisper.

"You *know* Haynesdale," Nicholas said with some impatience. "You have known him all your life."

"At a distance, only," she complained. Helena was seventeen years of age, the product of his father's second marriage to a woman much younger than his own mother. Helena had inherited the striking good looks of her mother—in fact, her coloring was so different from Nicholas' own that people were always surprised that they were siblings. Both, he supposed, resembled their mothers in more ways than one. Helena had hair so dark that it was almost black and clear blue eyes with thick dark lashes. Her cheeks were always slightly pinkened and her lips were like a perfect rose. She was tiny and delicately wrought but had an enthusiasm for life that would not have been readily contained in a woman twice her size, or twice her age.

In this, she resembled her mother, Lavinia. That woman had unleashed a tempest in their father's heart and subsequently his life. Lavinia had been a highly excitable woman—of whom Aunt Fanny had heartily disapproved—and Nicholas did not doubt that Lavinia would have exhausted their father in short order. Instead, her insistence upon driving a curricle and racing it rather inexpertly (and, it must be said, their father's indulgence of this) had led to their untimely demises. Helena had been only two summers of age at the time. Another five years had passed with Helena in Aunt Fanny's custody, before Nicholas found it within himself to sell Southpoint and buy his commission.

There were moments when Nicholas found Helena as wearying as her mother had been. He rather fancied there might be a sequence of such moments in his immediate future, unless she was wed and soon.

Then some other unfortunate man would endure those wearying moments. Perhaps the company of Helena in the bed would be sufficient compensation for the trial. Nicholas could only hope as much.

"This is the most vexatious detail about so many years between us," Helena continued as she spread jam thickly on her scone. "I could never dine with your friends before you left for war." She flicked an accusing look at Nicholas as if this convention was his fault.

"I have only the one friend these days."

Her eyes danced. "Fortunately, the Duke of Haynesdale is the most interesting one."

"Helena!" Aunt Fanny said. "You will not be forward with His Grace."

"I would be if I had the chance," Helena said under her breath, judging quite rightly that her aunt would not be able to hear her defiant words. Aunt Fanny was becoming deaf. Nicholas liked to think that she had feigned deafness so many times in the past decade that truth was beginning to resemble fiction.

"What was that?" she demanded sharply of his sister.

"I would dance with him if he asked," Helena said more loudly, her eyes shining with mischief. Nicholas bit back a smile. The last thing his sister needed was encouragement.

"Of course, you would," Aunt Fanny chided, returning to her compôte with purpose. "It would only be polite, though perhaps not a prudent choice. Those Haynesdales cannot be trusted in the least." Her stewed rhubarb began to disappear in a most methodical fashion. "I think you should decline him the first time he asks."

"Aunt! That would be rude!"

"I have always found Haynesdale to be a most trustworthy friend," Nicholas said, fearing his suggestion would be declined before it was even uttered aloud.

Aunt Fanny harrumphed. "No doubt you see him at his best. No doubt his mother contrives to win your support and insists that her son do as she demands. No doubt…"

"I do not believe Haynesdale does anything anyone asks," Nicholas noted.

"I like him better all the time," Helena murmured and Nicholas nudged her foot under the table. She gave him a sparkling smile.

"What did you say?" Aunt Fanny demanded fiercely.

"I like this jam better than last time," Helena said with feigned innocence.

"Good. I advised you to try it daily for a week before deciding upon an opinion," Aunt Fanny said. "You are always too hasty in your choices and blackberries are excellent for the constitution…"

"I had a notion this morning, Aunt," Nicholas dared to say when his aunt had expounded thoroughly on the constitutional benefits of blackberries. She glanced up with suspicion. "The duke reminded me that his sister was recently widowed and has come to live with him in town."

Aunt Fanny frowned at her butter knife as she spread the highly beneficial jam in her turn. "Sister? I don't remember a sister."

"Mrs. Eliza North is several years younger than the duke," Nicholas said, feeling the weight of Helena's bright gaze. "She was married to a pastor some years older than herself."

"Yes!" his aunt crowed, wagging the butter knife. "I recall the gossip well. He had only two thousand pounds a year, but she insisted she loved him." She smiled, savagely spreading the jam. "Love! What nonsense. Her mother was quite disappointed, as I recall." It was clear this memory gave Aunt Fanny a measure of satisfaction. "Two thousand pounds and a duke's daughter! She was not even foul to look upon!" Aunt Fanny chuckled to herself as she recalled her enemy's humiliation and bit into her scone with gusto.

"Haynesdale is concerned that his sister will be at loose ends during the season," Nicholas continued. "He doubts she has any inclination to wed again as yet."

"I should think she would be glad to do so," Helena said softly. "After a *pastor*."

"What was that?"

"How sad she must be," Helena said clearly. "To be without her lord and master."

"Even Eliza DeVries should not be compared to a trained hound, Helena," Aunt Fanny chided. "Mind your manners."

"Yes, Aunt Fanny."

Nicholas cleared his throat, continuing despite the challenges presented. "I had the notion that Mrs. North might make a suitable chaperone for Helena this season." Helena frowned at him, but he ignored her. Aunt Fanny looked skeptical. "As a pastor's widow, she is unquestionably a person of high moral standards and one who could provide an excellent example to Helena. She also had a lavish debut herself so will remember many useful details."

"She did, indeed," Aunt Fanny said, clearly considering this as she chewed. "No expense was spared for *her* first season." She smirked a little. "And to consider the result. Ha!"

"But she married for love," Helena said. "Even if you could not see the merit of her husband, the pastor, she did. I think it is *wondrous* when people follow their hearts."

Aunt Fanny gave her ward a dark look. "It is folly! Be advised that I will not suffer any such nonsense from you. You will marry well if arranging such a match is the last deed I do. Do you understand me, Helena?"

"Yes, Aunt Fanny," she replied so meekly that Nicholas guessed that she had a rebellious scheme.

"Mrs. North could undoubtedly make introductions," Nicholas said.

"If not ensure that Helena encounters the duke at intervals," Aunt Fanny said softly. Helena gave a little squeak of delight but before Nicholas could insist that his friend be left out of the matter, his aunt nodded decisively. "It is a most suitable notion, but I will have *expectations*, you understand. This Mrs. North and I must come to an agreement about decisions."

"I took the liberty of inviting Mrs. North for tea today," Nicholas said. "Knowing that you would wish to discuss any details with her."

His aunt's eyes twinkled unexpectedly. "Did you? There is a new conviction about you, Nicholas, no doubt a result of decisive action in the field. Do not imagine for a moment, however, that you will *ever* guide my choices." She shook the butter knife at him. "I will always decide my own fate, as well as that of your sister. Responsibilities such as these cannot ever be taken lightly."

"Of course not, Aunt," he said, trying to sound dutiful. His sister kicked him under the table, a reminder that he and Helena were not that different.

"You might ask Constance, as well," Aunt Fanny continued. "The dowager duchess, Lady Haynesdale. I have not seen her in years and should like to have the chance to speak with her again."

Nicholas recognized the strategy of the suggestion. Aunt Fanny would confront her old foe on her own turf, when and where she perceived herself to be in a stronger position. Aunt Fanny would see that she was doing a favor for Eliza and thus for Lady Haynesdale. She would surely treat both with condescension and perhaps even pity. He had no doubt his aunt would greatly enjoy the meeting and that the dowager duchess would be insulted.

But then, if he did not invite her, or she did not attend, his aunt would be insulted and he knew that little good would result from that situation.

"I will enquire, Aunt," he vowed without enthusiasm. It was a moment to yearn for the simplicities of war.

"Ask the duke, too," Helena prompted.

Nicholas had no opportunity to speak for his aunt fairly pounced on that idea. "Yes, do!" she said with uncommon enthusiasm.

"I thought the Haynesdales were untrustworthy," Nicholas felt compelled to remind her.

"I would forgive much of what has passed between Constance and myself if the duke saw fit to offer for our Helena," Aunt Fanny said nobly.

Nicholas shook his head with a smile. "You will never manage that, Aunt."

"Never? Helena is a beauty…"

"And Haynesdale is disinclined to wed," Nicholas said flatly, rising to his feet.

"Nonsense! He has a responsibility to his family to do so and I for one would not flinch from advising him as much. You, as his friend, should certainly offer such counsel…"

"If you will excuse me, I must ensure that the dowager duchess knows of your invitation, Aunt." Nicholas bowed and left the room, glad of the reason to leave the house again.

He could only hope that Haynesdale's mother would refuse, given past enmity between the older women. Her presence might undermine his entire scheme.

Given his fortune of the day thus far, though, he was fairly certain she would accept and a battle of words would rage over the tea tray—while he was compelled to witness it.

Not for the first time, Nicholas despaired of the complications of navigating private life. For years, he had simply commanded men, knowing his orders would be followed and the most reasonable course of action would prevail. In society, though, it seemed that even the most minor victory could not be easily won.

All he had desired was the opportunity to talk to Eliza again, but even this quagmire could not make him regret their conversation of this morning.

Yet, the prospect of another made Captain Nicholas Emerson smile.

~

LADY FRANCES DALHOUSIE, formerly Viscountess Hexham, knew that her hearing was not as acute as once it had been. There was nothing wrong with her eyesight, though, much less her wits, and she was beginning to fear that her ward, Helena, might never be respectably wed.

She did not need much imagination to envision how much Lady Constance DeVries would enjoy that humiliation. Indeed, she could readily believe that the dowager duchess might refuse to permit her widowed daughter to chaperone Helena, no matter what appeal Nicholas made to his friend, simply to facilitate Helena's inevitable downfall.

The truth was that the chit was impossible. Lady Dalhousie had dismissed three perfectly decent footmen in the past year, simply for the crime of being too handsome for their own respective good. She had endured eight months of dark glances from her butler,

Pettigrew, who had begun to loudly lament the prospects of finding good help with Helena in residence.

The girl simply could not resist temptation, particularly the allure of a handsome man. It was undoubtedly the influence of her mother, a shadow in her blood that compelled her to wild behavior and the flaunting of every possible rule of society. Lady Dalhousie was beginning to wonder whether her niece kept a list to ensure that she did not miss a single one.

The day before, she had caught Helena smiling at someone else's footman, the lad having been charged to hold the reins of a fine pair of bays. The horses were unimpressed by the young man, but Helena had been fluttering her lashes in a most forward way. Then there had been the clerk at the haberdashery who had carried their parcels to the carriage, never mind the reckless young man racing his horse who had reined the steed in so hard at Helena's wave that Lady Dalhousie had feared injury to rider or beast of burden.

The girl would be the end of her. If Lady Dalhousie could have summoned a suitable man with the snap of her fingers and seen her niece wed that very afternoon, she would have done it. As it was, Helena's forthright manner had frightened two potential suitors—or more likely, their mothers—in a mere fortnight. The season yawned ahead of Lady Dalhousie like an endless abyss, or a valley of torment that no decent gentlewoman might survive.

She welcomed her nephew's suggestion of a chaperone, and liked even more that the candidate of his choice was a parson's widow, a slightly older woman and the daughter of Lady Haynesdale.

Could Helena's fall from grace, if it occurred, be somehow blamed upon Mrs. North? Lady Dalhousie was not so noble that she found the possibility objectionable. She would not be above rubbing salt in the wound of Lady Haynesdale's wounded pride either, in such circumstance.

As a result, she was prepared to accept Mrs. North as her niece's chaperone, regardless of that woman's appearance or attitude.

And yet, she was pleasantly surprised. Mrs. North was an attractive young woman, surely in her late twenties. She dressed modestly as well, her blue and cream dress being neither in the latest mode or sadly out of date. Her dark blonde hair was neatly arranged, her hat was ornamented with the right number of flowers for her station—neither too mean nor too ostentatious—yet she wore a pair of remarkably fine kid gloves, which surely cost more than a parson's widow could afford.

Perhaps they had been a gift from her family.

Mrs. North's posture was excellent, her manner polite without being overly familiar, and her eyes bright. Her smile was present but not encouraging and her manner was attentive. In fact, she might have been ideal.

Helena despised her on sight, which was also an excellent recommendation. Helena despised anyone inclined to refuse her, which was why she adored only Nicholas.

To Lady Dalhousie's surprise, Nicholas also joined them for tea. He never appeared at tea and his presence prompted his aunt's suspicions.

Why had he suggested Mrs. North?

"How sad that your mother could not join us today," she said when the tea was poured. Pettigrew offered a plate of delicate sandwiches to Mrs. North, carefully arranged on the plate to appear more abundant in number than they were.

"She was disappointed to decline," Mrs. North said

smoothly, keeping her gaze on the sandwich she had chosen. "But the planning of her garden is a passion this time of year. I'm afraid she cannot be readily parted from her books."

"I did not realize she took a keen interest in gardening."

"Of course! The roses at Haynesdale are my mother's pride."

Lady Dalhousie silently wagered that they were not as fine as the roses at Hexham Court, tended for centuries by her husband's aristocratic family. "How lovely that she has such an interest to divert her."

"My aunt is also fond of gardening," Nicholas contributed.

"Indeed?" Mrs. North sipped her tea. "I'm afraid that I have little luck with roses myself."

"*You* have a garden?" Helena asked.

"I did. At the parsonage in Cumbria where my husband was pastor. I enjoyed it, though it is the responsibility of another now."

Helena looked confused.

Mrs. North smiled a little. "The parsonage is part of the living, which has been granted to another candidate. Perhaps the new occupants will make more of the rose cuttings my mother gave to me."

"What cuttings did she give you, if I may ask?" Lady Dalhousie said, trying to keep her cup from clattering in her saucer. To give roses to a parsonage was one matter, knowing the living would pass inevitably to a stranger, but to surrender them to someone who did not tend them well was nigh sufficient to make her faint.

"I'm afraid I am not very knowledgeable about roses," Mrs. North said. "There was a very pretty pink one. *Quatre Saisons*, I believe my mother called it. At least, it is pretty at Haynesdale."

"A damask," Lady Dalhousie said with authority. "Possibly known since the 5ᵗʰ century BC, and often considered the twice-flowering rose of Paestum mentioned by Virgil."

"My mother says it was known in the 10ᵗʰ century BC, cultivated on the island of Samos for the ceremonies of the cult of Aphrodite." Mrs. North took an acceptably small bite of her sandwich.

"*'The rose each ravished sense beguiles',*" Nicholas said softly and Mrs. North blinked, obviously recognizing the source.

"I have yet to learn that one," Helena said and Lady Dalhousie's gaze met that of Mrs. North. The younger woman smiled, as if having read her thoughts, and Lady Dalhousie was relieved to find them in agreement upon the works of Sappho.

Yes, she was a very suitable choice.

"You know another," Lady Dalhousie prompted.

Helena stood and cleared her throat to recite. "*The rose the poet's song perfumes, And in each muse's bosom blooms, How sweet to seize the blushing Prey, and snatch it from the Thorn away!*"

"The poet Anacreon," Mrs. North said with approval. "From Ode 51. A much-quoted verse on the merit of the rose. Brava, Miss Emerson." Her smile turned conspiratorial. "I had to learn that one as well." She straightened, her voice clearly resonant in the parlor. "*Before the Rose pale sickness flies; The Rose can ev'n the dead rejoice: 'Gainst Time itself it keeps the field, To Time its odours scorn to yield.*"

Nicholas applauded them both. "Poetry! I am convinced that I have underestimated your skills, Mrs. North."

The lady in question granted him a quelling look. "Are you, Captain?"

Oh, yes, there was interest between this pair. How

intriguing, if unlikely to lead to much result. Perhaps this was why Nicholas never courted any lady.

He aimed too high if he admired this one.

Even if Haynesdale was agreeable, she would put a stop to it herself on principle.

Lady Dalhousie cleared her throat. "Despite your lack of skill in the cultivation of roses, Mrs. North, I am intrigued by your interest in my niece this season."

"I fear, Lady Dalhousie, that my brother and your nephew have conspired in this plot. They would see their responsibilities tended, in Miss Emerson having a companion, myself being urged to attend parties and balls, and yourself having the leisure to remain at home."

"Where I should much rather be, when it rains as it does today."

Mrs. North sipped her tea. "And of course, the arrangement would leave both gentlemen free to do as they wished."

"You have undone me, Mrs. North," Nicholas said and bowed slightly.

Mrs. North smiled at him but Lady Dalhousie fixed her gaze upon the younger woman, clearing her throat for emphasis. She could not exactly treat a duke's daughter like a servant, but she could be haughty. "I hope you understand, Mrs. North, that this would be an informal arrangement."

Mrs. North laughed lightly, proving that she was not witless. "Oh, I have no desire to become a paid companion!"

"I am hoping that you might introduce my niece where possible, and ensure that her decorum is acceptable."

Helena rolled her eyes at this, which was a perfect example of the issue. The two older ladies' gazes met in mutual agreement.

"I fear she may offer a challenge," Lady Dalhousie felt compelled to add, knowing it was an understatement.

Mrs. North smiled with a confidence that was undeserved. "I am certain that Miss Emerson's company will be a joy."

Lady Dalhousie withheld her doubts. "I have vouchers for the ball at Almack's this evening, Mrs. North. Would you be inclined to begin your companionship so soon as this?"

"I should like nothing better." Mrs. North finished her tea and declined another cup. "Shall I collect Miss Emerson at eight in my brother's carriage?"

Both Lady Dalhousie and Helena straightened with interest at the mention of the ducal carriage. "Thank you, Mrs. North," Helena said after a prompting glance from her aunt. "Will your brother accompany us?"

Nicholas seemed to be much interested in the bottom of his teacup.

"I suspect not," Mrs. North said with a smile. "His Grace has been much occupied in the evenings of late, as Captain Emerson can testify. I have been assured for years that the one place he will never be found is Almack's."

Nicholas coughed and his eyes were twinkling in a most wicked way, but Lady Dalhousie let him have his jest—whatever it was.

Mrs. North stood then and took her leave, thanking Lady Dalhousie so graciously that the older lady might have been convinced that she was the one doing the favor. Helena went to the window when Mrs. North left, while Nicholas escorted that lady to her carriage.

Lady Dalhousie sat back and savored her tea, well content with her nephew's solution and her own newfound ability to remain at home, just as she preferred.

The situation was worthy of another iced cake.

CHAPTER 3

*P*ompous woman.

Troublesome girl.

Eliza had a definite sense that in accepting this responsibility, she had made a wager with the Devil.

And that particular devil not only had dancing blue eyes, but was immediately behind her as she descended the stairs.

"You need not show me the way, Captain," Eliza said, keenly aware of Nicholas' presence. His aunt's home in Berkley Square was one of the smallest townhouses there—and the last home in the block with a Berkley Square address—but it was neatly kept. No stranger to frugality, Eliza had noticed that the sandwiches offered for tea were sufficient but not plentiful, and that their fillings had been of more economical varieties. The cakes, while from a fashionable confectioner, had surely been counted out with care and spaced artfully on the plate with plainer cakes in between. Sensing as much, she had not partaken of one.

She would have to ask her mother about Lady Dalhousie's situation.

"What if I feel compelled to do as much?" he asked, his tone playful.

Eliza halted and spun to face him, a move that so surprised him that he took another step before halting. They were very close as a result, a situation she could not find objectionable.

She also realized that the butler had vanished, summoned by Lady Dalhousie's bell.

They were alone for the moment and she chose to savor it.

Nicholas did not retreat, either, a choice that gave her hope for her own dream, though his expression was guarded. Again, she sensed the change in him and wondered at its source. The shadow in his eyes was more difficult to ignore at such close proximity.

What had happened to him during the war?

Nicholas had shaved in the interval between breakfast and her visit, which did not entirely eliminate his air of disreputability. Eliza remembered him being bold but not reckless—indeed, he had been courageous but not foolhardy, always responsible and protective of others. He shared those traits with Damien. There was a resolve to the line of his lips, a hint that he had seen much, and she yearned to touch him, to soften that line with her fingertip.

To coax him to smile again.

He had also changed to another uniform. Though it was neatly tended and fit him trimly, the fabric was a bit worn along the seams. She recalled Damien's comments about his friend's lack of fortune.

With sudden clarity, Eliza understood the need for Helena to marry well—and in the same moment, she guessed why the girl was so lively. It was not in that young beauty's nature, at least not yet, to make a choice for the sake of others. Helena must resent that she would not be able to freely select her own husband. Unless Eliza misunderstood the girl's nature, she wagered that Helena would endeavor to have her choice despite the expectations placed upon her.

In so doing, she might condemn her brother and aunt to a future of austerity, if not more constrained circumstances than that.

Eliza had to help.

"Do you reconsider your choice, Mrs. North?" Nicholas asked softly. "You seem to be solemnly pondering the wager you have made."

"I apologize that I was lost in thought." Eliza retreated a step. "You have granted me a daunting responsibility, Captain Emerson, and I simply wonder at the best course."

"How so?"

"I rather fancy that your sister is inclined to follow her heart when it comes to courtship, independent of more practical considerations."

Nicholas smiled, a dazzling sight and one that made Eliza's heart leap. It was not sufficient to banish the shadows in his eyes, but still she warmed beneath his regard. "You are as perceptive as ever, my lady," he murmured. "What if I were to tell you that I have learned to grant responsibility only to those who can be relied upon to meet it?"

Eliza held his gaze, keenly aware that it was not just roses that beguiled. "Then I might suggest that your assessment was overly generous in this instance. Perhaps you have been away from society for too long."

"That only leaves me and my sister more reliant upon your excellent judgment."

"Was there any hint of a match in your sister's first season?"

Nicholas frowned slightly, considering her question, and she savored the opportunity to study him. "You recognize that I was still abroad, so have no firsthand knowledge of her debut." Eliza nodded and he continued. "And yet, I recall my aunt mentioning in a letter that there was a man." He raised a finger. "Ah, I remember now! In truth, Aunt Fanny wrote to complain to me of my sister's insistence upon accepting the attentions of a man my aunt considered to be highly unsuitable." He shook his head. "I was expected to intervene from the south of France."

"And did you?"

"Of course not. It would have been quite impossible."

Eliza agreed, doubting that Helena would heed any counsel against her own inclinations. "You might have returned to England to object. The war was over."

His expression turned wry. "I could not imagine any horse would be fast enough to keep Helena from a scheme."

"Why did she abandon it?"

"I believe the gentleman withdrew his affections, in what my aunt believed a timely manner."

Eliza nodded, assuming that the gentleman's family had learned of Helena's lack of fortune. Perhaps Aunt Fanny had ensured that they learned as much. "Had he a name?"

"Undoubtedly, but I did not hear it."

"I see." Eliza noted the return of the butler at the top of the stairs, who cast a stern glance upon her, standing so close to Nicholas. Clearly he believed she had departed. She turned and continued toward the door, Nicholas fast behind her. The captain, of course, only desired her promise to assist him. How vexing that he saw her only as another sister or a friend who could be relied upon to aid his cause!

How irksome that she had no desire to resist his appeal.

"Surely you will not abandon the task before you have embarked upon it, Mrs. North?" he asked, a measure of urgency in his tone. He opened the door for her, as the butler was yet descending the stairs. The lack of a footman only confirmed Eliza's suspicions about the aunt's financial situation.

She had to help Helena, but she also wished for the success of her own endeavor—and she realized that would require a change in Nicholas' opinion of her.

If such a feat could be accomplished.

She would need all the time with Nicholas she could contrive.

Eliza turned to him with a smile. "Surely not, Captain Emerson. I am not one to balk at a challenge."

"Excellent."

"But I must insist upon a revision to our agreement."

"Indeed?" He was wary and rightly so.

"I know little of the eligibility of unwed gentlemen in town or your aunt's assessment of them. I have lived for years in a small village in the north, after all." She smiled. Nicholas did not, as watchful as a predator. "In order to succeed in this endeavor, I must have your assistance, Captain Emerson."

"In what way, Mrs. North?"

"I must insist that you join us at any social gathering, that you might advise me." He frowned and she guessed he would refuse. "Your sister must wed well and I would not err in a matter of such importance, sir."

"I see you take your responsibility most seriously, but I am not prepared to spend all of my evenings upon the matter of Helena's marriage." He inclined his head slightly. "One night, Mrs. North. I scarcely have more connections than you in town these days, but I will meet you tonight and share what I do know." His tone was hard and she doubted his will would soften.

Did he pursue the attentions of a lady already? How Eliza wished she knew.

She took a breath, knowing her stipulation had to

be made. "You will be sober, sir," she said quietly. "If you must embark upon nocturnal revels, you will indulge after leaving the company of your sister and myself."

His gaze darkened and held her own. "You are demanding, Mrs. North."

"I pursue the greater good, Captain Emerson, and at your request. If you object to my amendments to our arrangement, I will be obliged to decline this opportunity."

"My aunt believes you have accepted."

"Correcting her view will be your obligation, sir."

Their gazes locked and held. Frederick had often said that those who indulged overmuch—whether it be in the consumption of drink or the cultivation of risk—sought to forget some inescapable truth or painful wound. If that was the case with Nicholas, Eliza only wanted to help him to heal.

Then Nicholas smiled, a slow change of his expression that lifted one corner of his mouth. "Remind me never to negotiate with you again, Mrs. North," he murmured, a welcome admiration in his tone. He claimed her hand and she welcomed his firm grip. "You have made it impossible to refuse."

"I did not mean to do as much," she protested but Nicholas laughed.

"On the contrary, I believe your strategy was artful. Well done, Mrs. North." He bent over her hand, touching his lips to the back of her glove. He looked up then, his expression alight. "I hope that the result is as you desire."

"The result, Captain Emerson?"

Again, his expression was mischievous. "You may not be so glad of my company without my indulgence."

It was a warning and a fair one. If he indulged as

much as she feared he did, the sudden cessation might leave him disgruntled, if not worse.

"I am not afraid of you, Captain Emerson," she said with resolve.

"Is that wisdom or folly, Mrs. North?"

"It is trust," she said firmly, noting the flicker of surprise in his eyes. "I look forward to your arrival at Almack's this evening, Captain."

Eliza returned to Damien's carriage, wondering at the bargain she had made. Thomson called to the horses and the carriage began to move when Eliza looked up at the house. She spotted Helena at the window, watching her departure, that girl's expression inscrutable.

Between the two of them, Eliza's evening might prove a challenge, indeed. But despite that, she could not regret the prospect.

Not in the least.

~

Miss Esmeralda Ballantyne did not, as a matter of principle, incur debts.

To owe money or favors to any other individual was to be beholden to that person, and this she could not abide. In addition, those who made loans had a nasty habit of demanding repayment of said obligations at the most inconvenient moment possible. As a result, Esmeralda bought what she could afford, paid immediately and owed nothing to anyone.

Thus, it troubled her deeply to have a benefactor, even in her current dire situation.

That the identity of this mysterious patron was unknown to her, was simply salt in the wound.

Fleet Debtor's Prison was not the Hulks, but neither was it home. She had nearly despaired on her first day of incarceration, having been required to surrender every penny she carried to avoid being stripped by fellow inmates for her clothes. She had been locked in a cell with a dozen other women, four filthy children and countless vermin, without so much as straw for bedding, much less anything to eat. The crusts of bread cast into the cell and onto the floor were not food in Esmeralda's view, though watching her fellows and their desperate consumption of those offerings gave an indication that her views might change.

She had not slept for two days, simply stood in one corner with her arms folded across her chest, and despised Jacques Desjardins with every measure of her being.

When they came for her, she feared the worst. To be compelled to provide entertainment to a crowd of dirty and desperate men was not a price Esmeralda was prepared to pay, though she feared she would be overwhelmed and forced to do as much. She was shaking inwardly as she left the cell, planning how she would fight to the bitter end.

To her surprise, she was ushered up the stairs and into a room of her own. It was smaller than the one she had left but markedly cleaner. There was even a window, though barred, which emitted both a beam of sunlight and a waft of fresh air. It smelled like the river, but she was hardly particular after the foul odors of the past two days. There was a stool and a small table, as well as a straw mattress in one corner.

"Doubtless your friend will arrive soon for his reward," snarled the jailor, then locked the door behind himself.

She had been bought, evidently, and doubted the sum had been more than a few pounds for the benefactor would have to pay the warden for this privilege, too. She nudged the mattress with one booted toe and vermin did not erupt across the floor, which was some consolation.

"I should like a broom," she called at the door. "And a bucket of water."

The jailor's voice was a growl of irritation. "Your ladyship has expectations," he sneered.

"As will my *friend*," she said sweetly. "I am certain a measure of his generosity goes to your purse so neither of us would wish for him to be disappointed, would we?"

There was a moment of silence instead of a reply, then the sound of the jailor's footsteps faded. It took an hour, but Esmeralda had her bucket of cold water and her broom, though the light filtering through the window had dimmed.

"I will need a light to make a job of it," she said when the sloshing bucket was set on the floor inside the door.

The jailor eyed her. "Then I might have need of a favor myself," he said, but Esmeralda had her limits.

And she possessed a small advantage that she was not adverse to using.

She smiled as she removed her gloves, but knew her gaze was hard. "I would not recommend such a demand," she said with resolve. "Friends, in my experience, do not care to share, particularly with those outside of their social class." She let her eyes widen. "Such a demand might eliminate this ally's interest completely, and that would regrettably leave both of us the poorer."

He muttered a curse and slammed the door behind himself, but Esmeralda had her candle. It was short and made of tallow, the kind that smoked and would soon gut itself, but she was glad of it all the same. She removed her jacket and hat, then set to work, praying all the while that her mysterious benefactor did not abandon her.

She knew only his contribution was keeping her jailor's demands at bay—after this support was withdrawn, her position would be worse than it had been and she would become the lowest victim in the entire prison.

She had best make the most of opportunity. She would also have need of a comb.

Even as she made a list of necessities, Esmeralda endeavored to solve the riddle of who her benefactor might be. Latimer must know, but she had no means of contacting her butler. Less important than the friend's identity was his intention—she could not believe his choice was disinterested, but did he mean to keep her for himself or to destroy her completely?

She could only hope the answer would be revealed in short order. Esmeralda was not a patient woman at the best of times and this interval was far from the best of times.

"THERE IS A DELIVERY FOR YOU, my lady," Higgins said when Eliza returned to Haynesdale House. "From Carruthers & Carruthers." He offered the package to her, which was about the size of a book.

Eliza had neither purchased nor requested a book, but perhaps Damien or her mother had sent her a gift. She thanked Higgins and took the parcel to her room. The house was quiet and she guessed that her mother was in her chambers and that Damien either slept or had gone out. She only opened the package once the door was closed behind herself.

It was no book, but a folio including a sheaf of loose pages with a note atop them.

Dear Mrs. North—

I have heard of your interest in my work The Ladies' Essential Guide to the Arts of Seduction *and hereby enclose three excerpts from this volume, soon to be published by Carruthers & Carruthers. At this point, the publisher seeks impressions of the work from discerning ladies, the better to ensure that there are no great omissions and to finalize the final work. I would greatly appreciate your observations upon these excerpts at your earliest convenience and welcome your suggestions, if any, of additions. You may correspond with me in the care of the publisher. Please note at that time whether you would be interested in reading more.*

Thank you for your interest and assistance.
Sincerely,
Mrs. Delilah Oliver
Author

Eliza was delighted. This was the volume she had been seeking!

Mrs. de Roye had known the author, after all. And the volume was to be published by Carruthers & Carruthers, a most reputable firm. Eliza was thrilled to be granted an early glimpse. She fanned through the loose pages, which had the appearance of letters. The writing was in an elegant and feminine script, but these offerings of advice were clearly not from a single letter. They were separate pages and the text did not continue from one to the next. Sadly, there were only three leaves included in this portfolio, but Mrs. Oliver implied that there were more.

Eliza sank into a chair to read the first page.

Upon the question of absence...

It has often been said that absence encourages the deepening of regard, but in this writer's experience, that is not the case. People in their essence do not change much over time, although there may be superficial adjustments over time—once one has taken the measure of a person's character, that assessment, if correct, should remain true. What often does happen, particularly in question of ladies who are generous of nature, is that time and distance will permit such a lady to forget the irksome habits or inappropriate tendencies in one who was once of close acquaintance. The return of that individual can thus provide a strong and unwelcome reminder of his deficiencies and perhaps make it clear once again why paths parted in the first place. I encourage ladies not to doubt their earlier judgments of former companions, lest they be mistakenly encouraged to offer such persons new opportunities.

It sounded as if the writer was thinking of one person in particular, one who had been a disappointment. As a friend? As a lover? It was impossible to be certain, but this page offered little new beyond compilations of advice Eliza had read before.

She hoped the work improved from this point.

Disappointed but still hopeful, she set the first page aside and read on.

Upon the matter of encouragement...

It is a lamentable fact of our society that men often wed women considerably younger than themselves. This disparity of age is not without its issues in matters of compatibility and quality of conversation, but let us consider the conundrum from another angle. It is not uncommon for a man of eligible age to meet or become acquainted with a female who is yet a child, either through family connections or close friends. There may be fondness between them or even a complete disregard, but if the pair encounter each other a decade (or more) later, they might each perceive the other in a more favorable light. The lady, no longer a child, may be attractive to the gentleman, while the gentleman may be found far more interesting by the lady than when he was outside her sphere. In such instances, it is not unknown for the gentleman to decline to make his interest clear, as he might with any other eligible lady of similar age. There is perhaps a lingering memory of the lady in question as a child and the certainty that any romantic interest might yet be inappropriate or unwelcome.

In such instances, when the admiration is mutual, I believe it is permissible for the lady to offer encouragement to the gentleman in question. She need not be bold or brash, but can subtly reveal her interest that the gentleman might become aware that his own attentions are welcome. A touch of her gloved fingertips upon his arm, for example, even if fleeting, can leave a favorable impression. A confession, delivered in a whisper directly into his ear, perhaps with her lips straying to touch his skin, can be sufficient. Perhaps the most effective method of encouraging the gentleman is to ask for his protection against an undesirable suitor. A man of principle will be honored to provide such service to any lady he holds in regard, but in such an instance as this, the task itself may guide his thoughts in a welcome direction—as well as offering the opportunity of time in each other's company, the better to promote a potential union of hearts and minds.

This was rather more the manner of advice she had expected, though still regrettably vague. Encouragement. Did Nicholas require encouragement? Even if he was disinterested, Eliza thought she had little to lose in being so bold as suggested here.

She considered the specific suggestions and thought she could certainly find a moment to touch his arm at Almack's that evening. She might have done as much earlier in the afternoon. A whisper in his ear was far more daring and she was uncertain when she might find opportunity for that—let alone what she might confess. She sighed as she reviewed the last suggestion.

Regrettably Galveston had been declined already or she might have been able to ask Nicholas to defend her against that man's unwanted affections.

The very prospect made Eliza smile, but she read on.

Upon the matter of secrets...

No deed creates a stronger bond between lovers than the confession of a secret. A secret is often, by its very nature, a matter of tremendous personal importance, so the sharing of it with any other being implies a profound trust. The secret once revealed also creates a bond between confessor and recipient, one that is not readily compromised. Thus, I can only encourage any lady reading this volume to consider the possibility of her beloved having a secret, and thence to contrive to learn it. This is not, it must be noted, in order to use this secret as a threat, for that would be a breach of the entire marvel of love, but instead to gain greater understanding of the hidden depths of the lover's nature. We each have details of ourselves, dreams and visions, history and secrets, that we surrender to few others, if any at all—to become the custodian of another's secret is the sweetest burden of all.

One may be assured that all men and women possess at least one secret, and that in fact, the gaining of trust and intimacy may result in a cascade of confessions, each more profound than the last. A truly deep bond between lovers, one sufficiently strong to last a lifetime if not beyond, can be forged with secrets. What is your beloved's greatest desire or source of wildest joy? What is your beloved's deepest regret or most profound fear? What is the thought or experience that your beloved has never shared with another? Unlock this prize and hold it as if it were your own secret, and this can only bind your two hearts as one. Perhaps the confession of your own will open the door to opportunity...

Secrets.

Sadly, Eliza had only the one and she was not in a hurry to confess it to anyone.

She turned over the three sheets of paper but they were blank on their backs.

That was the sum of the advice.

No matter how she considered it, the promised counsel had been a disappointment.

Eliza would reply immediately to this Mrs. Oliver. That lady had to have more advice to offer on the question of seduction than these mere crumbs from the proverbial table.

If not, her book was surely doomed to failure—or worse, obscurity.

It was unfortunate, for the premise had been most enticing.

ALMACK'S, Helena was convinced, was the most dull establishment in all of London, perhaps in all of England. There was no question that it was more tedious than any place in Europe, where all the most daring and wondrous events occurred. Though she had been to the venerable club three times in her debut season, a year later, she was sorry to discover that its appeal had not increased a whit.

This should have been more remarkable, save that her aunt held Almack's in highest esteem. Perhaps that was a warning of a kind, for Helena had no doubt that there were vouchers aplenty in her future.

Aunt Fanny was always impressed by the most mediocre things. She invariably informed Helena of her remarkable good fortune in even being allowed across the threshold of the club, and had done as much three times between tea and the arrival of the duke's carriage.

Aunt Fanny insisted that it was by dint of her own social influence that Helena gained vouchers, given that their own family connections were modest, but Helena could hardly regard this as a triumph.

Besides, on this night she knew she had been welcomed because her chaperone was the only sister of an unwed duke—not just any duke, either, but the Duke of Haynesdale whose very name lit a gleam of ambition in many an eye.

Mrs. North was amiable and surprisingly pretty, given her advanced age and the fact that she was a widow. Helena thought her new chaperone might even be as ancient as her own brother. Mrs. North's dress was modest but of excellent quality, and her hair was as yet devoid of grey. She had an attractive smile, though Helena had only glimpsed it once or twice.

Perhaps she was happy no longer to be wed to a parson. Helena could not imagine a worse fate. There would be Bible verses and Sunday sermons—she would be obliged to listen if her husband was delivering them —visits to the poor and doubtless a great many other charitable duties. Helena would much prefer to go dancing or shopping.

Mrs. North had been a bit stern in the carriage on their way this evening, insisting that Helena sit with composure and not plague her with questions about her brother, the duke.

Helena supposed that riding in his smaller carriage should have been sufficient to thrill her, simply by the notion of proximity, but it had not been. It would have been if the duke had accompanied them, she was certain.

The difficulty with a second season after her debut was that it all seemed unchanged and dreary as a result. There was no longer any adventure to be had. At least in the previous year, she had been excited for her debut.

She eyed the new crop of debutantes awaiting their dance partners and felt a measure of pity for them—soon enough they would learn that Almack's was not the most amusement they might have in town.

What a shame that it was too cold as yet for a visit to Vauxhall Gardens. Helena had been vastly entertained by Mr. Melbourne there the previous year, warmed by his kisses in the shadows, an adventure that had left her feeling decidedly bold.

Sadly, the dashing Mr. Melbourne was not in attendance on this night.

Helena looked.

Twice.

She liked the ballroom at Almack's well enough, with its mirrors and gas lighting. She did not care that there was no food and orgeat was a beverage she could take or leave. It was the company that she found excruciatingly difficult to bear. It seemed there were only anxious young women—peering toward the door, though each strove to hide her interest in every new arrival—along with their mothers and chaperones. To a one, these were fierce and often plump older women with sharp gazes and bold ambition. Watching her competition made Helena feel wise and fortunate that her chaperone was comparatively young.

With the surety of experience, Helena saw that there were far too few gentlemen in attendance and she guessed that even few of them had much fortune. The way that mothers avoided them and the necessity of introducing their daughters was a telltale sign—if a man in attendance had been eligible, titled and wealthy, any glimpse of him would have been obscured by a veritable hive of ambitious mothers and their charges.

"If ever your brother came to Almack's, they would devour him," she said beneath her breath.

"There is little chance of that," Mrs. North said and

Helena braced herself for a lecture. "For then there would be one less duke in need of a wife. Society could not incur such a loss, could it?"

This sounded like a jest, but Helena knew that no chaperone of merit would find humor in that situation.

"The only males in attendance are younger brothers of the debutantes," Helena complained, unable to disguise her disappointment in that.

"It is early," Mrs. North advised. "Your brother intends to arrive later and might bring a friend."

"Oh!" Helena said with newfound enthusiasm. "Perhaps the Duke of Haynesdale will appear, after all."

"Captain Emerson has other comrades, surely."

"Yet I hear only of his good friend, the duke." Helena smiled at her companion. "You cannot know all of your brother's intentions. I cannot even guess at all of my brother's schemes."

"I know the duke's habits well enough."

"Even though you have been married these past years?"

"And my brother was at war, then in seclusion by his own choice. I doubt his distaste of society has changed overmuch."

Helena turned to face her, curious. "Why was he in seclusion? Was his heart broken?" She immediately imagined any number of romantic sufferings the duke might endure, then envisioned herself healing him with a sweet kiss to his brow. His gratitude would be so immense that he would beg for her hand and she would be showered with gifts as his beloved duchess.

"He was injured in the war," Mrs. North said. "And lamed for a time. His gait seems to be improving of late, however."

A limp! That was almost as romantic as an eyepatch, although it would mean that he did not dance often. Perhaps that was why he retreated from society:

he could not bear to watch others enjoying the pleasure he could no longer share.

Helena sighed at the perfection of her own imagining.

Where were all the officers? Surely there were *some* militia in town other than her brother.

"I understood there was a gentleman of interest last season," Mrs. North said. "Is he the one you seek so avidly?"

Helena's thoughts flew. What did Mrs. North know about Mr. Melbourne? Aunt Fanny might have forbidden a renewed acquaintance, so Helena had to tread with care. "I simply would know who is present tonight," she said with a smile.

Mrs. North studied her. "If there is a specific gentleman of interest, I might be able to ensure that you encounter him."

"So that I can wed with haste and your responsibilities will be done?" Helena shook her head. "If I do agree to wed, Mrs. North, it will be at the last moment of the season. I could not bear to miss a single party."

"And if you do not secure a match this year?"

Helena shrugged. "Perhaps I will elope with a dashing stranger." He would be a handsome man, one with absurd quantities of money, one who had no care for convention and who would see at a glance that she was the sole woman who could ever capture his heart. Helena smiled at the prospect, easily imagining theirs would be a tempestuous and rapid courtship.

Mrs. North shook her head. "Only to find yourself despoiled and destitute in a dirty inn the next morning. You are more clever than that, Helena."

"I thought you had married a pastor," she said, studying her chaperone with interest. "What would you know of affairs of passion?"

"What do you think happens to maidens who embark on such adventures?" Mrs. North asked, then continued without waiting for a reply. "They are quickly wed to whatever man will have them after their paramour has ruined and abandoned them."

"He might not!"

"Dashing men who elope with maidens always do," she said with conviction. "In truth, it is somewhat disappointing that they should be so predictable."

Helena did not believe her for a moment.

"You are skeptical," Mrs. North said with a smile. "And so might I be, had I not wed a country pastor with a living in Cumbria. So close to Gretna Green. Such a man is likely to be the one to perform the office, lest the lady's friends in town witness her humiliation. I have seen it time and again."

Helena felt a chill. "Aunt Fanny would not do that to me," she insisted.

Mrs. North seemingly possessed no doubt. "If your reputation were to be compromised, your aunt Fanny would wed you to a willing suitor so quickly that your head would spin," She fixed Helena with a look. "The sole matter of import to your aunt is her social standing. Do not be so foolish as to give her the opportunity to choose its maintenance over your happiness."

She *was* serious, which only proved that she knew little of how Aunt Fanny indulged Helena. Her warning also proved that she was dour and dull, more so even than Aunt Fanny.

To Helena's relief, a familiar gentleman entered the ballroom and surveyed the occupants. His gaze landed upon Helena, who stood a little taller at the welcome prospect of his company, and he hesitated. Doubtless, Aunt's dire warnings still rang in his ears.

But Aunt was not present, and Mrs. North was a fool.

Helena smiled at Mr. Melbourne with an enthusiasm that could not be mistaken.

His satisfaction was evident as he strode directly toward her. He was every bit as marvelous as Helena recalled, a man well worth her interest in the absence of an attentive duke.

Even if Aunt vehemently disagreed. Melbourne was the younger son of a baronet, that title having been too recently created to win Aunt's approval. The family was not as affluent as Aunt decreed to be necessary and Melbourne's mother was Scottish, a great sin in Aunt's view, which made Melbourne utterly unsuitable. He was highly amusing, though, and had permitted Helena to race his gig, plus he had stolen two memorable kisses at Vauxhall Gardens before his departure from town, entreating her to remember him—even to dream of him.

Helena had done both.

Mr. Melbourne was dressed as impeccably as ever, his cravat perfectly knotted and his dark jacket emphasizing his broad shoulders. He wore boots and breeches and as he tipped his hat to her, she thought her heart might burst for joy. His hair was dark and inclined to curl, his eyes were a merry brown, and he possessed the most delightful cleft in his chin. He smiled at her, made some comment to his companion, then strolled toward her with obvious purpose.

Helena wished she had dampened down her shift more than she had dared.

Mrs. North abruptly cleared her throat.

Helena turned to see that a man approached them, his expression hopeful. He was not unattractive, but he was old in Helena's view, perhaps of an age with her brother. His hair was of a chestnut hue and straight, his sideburns carefully tended, his jacket well-cut but not the first fashion. His smile was a little too broad, as if he sought to ingratiate himself to her. She braced herself for him to grovel at her feet and beg for the honor of a dance.

She would decline him for Mr. Melbourne's hand with satisfaction.

"Mrs. North," he said, bowing low to her companion. He kept his gaze fixed on that lady's features, apparently oblivious to Helena. Was the man blind? No, he had to be trying to win Mrs. North's favor, the better to speak with Helena. "What a delight it is to see you again."

"Mr. Galveston." Mrs. North inclined her head but did not confess to be charmed or delighted. Helena could see that Mr. Galveston was waiting hopefully for some such encouragement.

How strange. She would have expected an elderly widow like Mrs. North to be grateful for whatever masculine attention she could get.

"May I introduce my companion to you, Mr. Galveston? This is Miss Emerson."

Helena smiled, prepared for Mr. Galveston's admiration when he finally looked upon her. Instead, his gaze swept over her without a great deal of interest.

"Miss Emerson. Delighted, I am sure, to meet any acquaintance of Mrs. North." And he turned back to Mrs. North, so enraptured that Helena might not have even been present.

Helena bristled at this.

"Miss Emerson is the niece of Lady Dalhousie," Mrs. North supplied. "I have agreed to escort her to some social events as a favor to her aunt."

"How generous of you, Mrs. North," Mr. Galveston fairly crowed. "Your nature is unfailingly selfless."

Why did they not simply marry and coo to each other in private?

The music began for the next dance with ideal

timing and Helena glanced toward Mr. Melbourne to find him not half a dozen steps away. He smiled and she smiled in return, then Mrs. North cleared her throat with resolve.

Helena realized she had missed part of their conversation.

"Of course, Helena would be delighted to dance with you," Mrs. North said, steel in her tone. "She is not customarily so distracted and I apologize. Doubtless she is simply eager to dance."

Helena recognized a lost cause when she was presented with one. She smiled at Mr. Galveston and took his hand, letting him lead her to the dance floor. She saw Mr. Melbourne's step falter but she cast him a smile of such encouragement that he could have no doubt of her desires. He smiled and watched her, his gaze so fixed upon her that she knew all would come aright between them this season.

Aunt Fanny need never know of his presence in town, then Mrs. North would not know to keep him from Helena's side. She turned her smile upon Mr. Galveston when she met him again in the dance and his step faltered. She liked that he was now suitably dazzled by her and danced with enthusiasm.

It was almost the end of the dance when she spied her brother entering the ballroom. With him was a man so old and infirm that he was leaning upon a cane.

This could not be the Duke of Haynesdale!

But the ripple of excitement that passed through the ranks of debutantes and mothers revealed that he certainly was a man of consequence. The crowd that gathered around him with enthusiasm made Helena fear the worst, no less the way Nicholas and his companion laughed together. They were of an age, and the stranger had a limp. In addition, Mrs. North was visibly surprised by his presence, which meant he *was* the Duke of Haynesdale.

A veritable antiquity.

No amount of wealth could make him a palatable choice for Helena.

It would be Mr. Melbourne for her, if she could contrive it to be so.

And contrive it, she most certainly would.

CHAPTER 4

"Almack's," Haynesdale growled as they approached the door. "This is the last place on earth I wish to be." Despite his objections, Haynesdale matched Nicholas' pace, proof that his complaints were for appearances only.

"And yet you insisted that we pause here." Nicholas could not imagine why that might be, although he greatly wished to visit this establishment. The prospect of another conversation with Eliza would have taken him to any fête, however dreary the guest list. The prospect of pleasing her had even been sufficient for him to decline a brandy with his friend. "Are you suddenly in pursuit of a debutante for a bride?"

Haynesdale scoffed. "I have no plan to wed and you know it well."

"And yet, you have need of an heir."

"The next person fool enough to offer that particular counsel will regret it."

Nicholas chuckled. "Who else has so advised you?"

"Who has not?" the duke replied without interest. "I confess myself surprised that you fairly leapt at the chance to visit this establishment."

Nicholas grinned. "I wish only to ensure that my dear sister has not intimidated yours."

"Eliza is not readily daunted."

"But Helena is a demon."

Haynesdale stopped to look at him. "Then why did you encourage the arrangement? Have you no compassion for my sister?"

Nicholas feared that his friend might spot the truth. "I thought she might find Helena a finer match than my aunt, who seems convinced that only the equivalent of the Prince Regent himself will do."

"Your sister cannot be that pretty."

"Alas, she is a beauty, and I say that without prejudice." Nicholas frowned as they reached the doors. "She is also possessed of an audacity that not all appreciate."

Haynesdale chuckled. "She is willful is what you mean." He sighed. "I yearn already for my library. Let us get this duty behind us."

What duty? Nicholas had no opportunity to ask, for Haynesdale charged onward. He fairly snarled at the older woman at the door who might have protested his lack of breeches and Nicholas feared she might need her smelling salts as a result. By the time the lady in question recovered her tongue, Haynesdale was striding with purpose into the ballroom.

Helena was dancing, predictably, with a man in his thirties whom Nicholas did not know. That man looked rather unremarkable for Helena's usual taste. Eliza stood watching them with some measure of approval, but Nicholas also noted the second young man avidly watching Helena from the far side of the room. His dissatisfaction was clear even at a distance. This young man was a dandy, to be sure, confident and richly dressed, younger than Helena's partner. For some reason, Nicholas disliked him on sight.

Haynesdale had abandoned him, evidently intent

upon speaking to someone at the other side of the room. Nicholas was content to take a stance beside Eliza. "Shall I fetch you a ratafia?" he asked in a low murmur and she cast him a welcome smile.

"I thank you, no."

"You have found her a suitor already? My congratulations to you, Mrs. North, on such efficiency. Is he suitable?"

Eliza laughed lightly. "I have foisted Mr. Galveston upon her, but do not confess that truth to either of them."

Nicholas studied the man in question with new-found interest. The man in question was younger than he might have expected and, while not handsome, he was not unattractive. He danced most attentively with Helena, who ignored him as much as she could manage. "He looks to be a respectable gentleman."

"He is."

"And five thousand pounds a year. Do you hope for more, Mrs. North?"

She cast him a sparkling glance. "You tease me, Captain Emerson. I find him to be admirable but not a man to claim my heart."

"I thought your heart was in your husband's possession."

She flushed and seemed to be fixed upon the dancers. "Of course. I think he might suit Helena well, but I suspect she does not agree."

Nicholas did not want to talk about his sister. "Perhaps she also waits for love."

Eliza shook her head. "Perhaps."

"I am curious, to be sure, Mrs. North. Can a person hope for two such loves in one lifetime or is one grand passion the sum of possibilities?"

"I believe it is uncommon to love twice with vigor."

"Then you are doomed to be a chaperone?"

"Not necessarily." She lifted her chin and smiled. "I will wed again if my heart is captured." She slanted him a glance that was almost coy, though he guessed he saw more in her manner than was the truth.

But then she placed her hand upon his arm and leaned closer, her breast almost against him. She looked up at him, her voice a husky whisper, her eyes filled with stars. "What of you, Captain Emerson? Would you not wed for love?"

"Assuredly," he said, transfixed. "But my expectations of that happy event are low."

"They should not be," she said and let her gloved fingertips trail down his arm before she turned to watch the dancers again.

Nicholas felt as if his very blood was on fire. She could not have meant to caress him. She simply had not considered her action. He swallowed and strove to make coherent conversation. "And Mr. Galveston? Is his heart engaged?"

"I think him too sensible a man for such inclinations. I did not fear to break his heart with my refusal."

"How so?"

She took a deep breath. "I knew him while I was married. *We* knew him. His land was near Frederick's living, but not in the same parish. Whenever we met socially, Mr. Galveston was unfailingly charming." She smiled in memory of something, the expression giving a wrench to Nicholas' heart. "The village ladies were always trying to contrive a match for him. It was quite amusing how he evaded their schemes."

"So, you know something of him."

"I know he has a good reputation and is much admired by his friends and neighbors. His holding is prosperous and well-managed, his tenants are content, and his horses are well-tended." She cast him a look. "I am aware of other men whose properties are not in such happy condition."

"And yet you declined him."

"As I said, my desires are different this time."

Nicholas frowned, unable to make sense of that claim, but Eliza hastened on.

"He would make a good match for Helena," she said.

"But he would have to stop gazing at you for such a match to have a chance, Mrs. North. Are you convinced that he has abandoned his suit?"

"Of course." She changed the subject, her tone bantering. "I cannot believe you convinced Damien to come. Your powers of persuasion must be far beyond my expectation."

He laughed. "Would you believe that he was the one to insist upon coming here this night? I know not why, but he seemed a man intent on some purpose."

"Then you intended to break your word to me?"

"Of course not, but I was spared the need to contrive my arrival here."

She looked across the floor. "And he speaks with Lady Wentworth. I wonder why."

Nicholas considered the older lady seated on the far side of the dance floor beside Haynesdale. "Do you know her well?"

Eliza shook her head. "She and *Maman* are acquainted, to be sure, but I would not have thought Damien had cause to seek her out. He must be awaiting someone else."

The music ended and Mr. Galveston led Helena toward them. Nicholas recognized that his sister's mood was triumphant, though he could not imagine why. The music changed abruptly, the new rhythm sending a flutter of consternation through the ranks of those gathering around the perimeter of the dance floor. Before the couple reached them, the dashing young buck smoothly intervened, claiming Helena's hand and leading her back to the floor as Mr. Galveston stared after them.

He gaped, in truth, like a fish gasping for air.

Helena fairly skipped beside her partner, her satisfaction undisguised.

A waltz. Nicholas was certain that Eliza would never have permitted such choice and her startled expression supported his conclusion.

"Who is he?" he asked Eliza, who made a sound of vexation beneath her breath.

"I do not know, and this is a *waltz!*" she said. She smiled coolly at the approaching Mr. Galveston and walked past him, leaving that man obviously bereft as she strove to reach Helena and intervene. Helena's partner seemed to be aware of Eliza's pursuit, for he swept Helena toward the far side of the room with a flourish.

There was only one thing to be done. His sister had to be supervised, and the best place to do that was from the dance floor.

Nicholas strode after Eliza with purpose, capturing her elbow in his hand. She looked back at him with surprise. "Mrs. North. Shall we provide an example of how it is done?"

"But...."

"We shall never catch them otherwise," Nicholas said in an undertone. He offered his hand and watched relief fill Eliza's gaze.

"Thank you, Captain. I should be delighted." She placed the slight weight of her hand in his and he led her to the floor, leading her steadily to closer proximity to Helena and her partner. "I would never have allowed a waltz," she murmured with obvious annoyance. "And with a man to whom I have not been introduced."

"She knew it, I wager."

"Does she know *him*, do you think?"

"I cannot say," Nicholas replied with quiet heat. "But rest assured, we will find out."

DAMIEN MADE his way around the perimeter of the dance floor, pausing to exchange greetings with those he knew. He was besieged by enthusiastic older women and presented to a dizzying number of maidens in white. He pretended to tire, leaning more heavily upon his cane, until it appeared he could bear no more and appeared to collapse into the chair that had been his destination all along.

Lady Penelope Wentworth snorted delicately behind her fan, a sound of skepticism made purely for his own benefit. "So tragic when a young man becomes feeble," she said, her eyes sparkling even as she spoke. She had to be in her seventies, but was as spry and alert as a woman half her age. Damien had not spoken directly to her in years, but he knew she had supplied valuable intelligence during the war about activities in London, committed under the guise of society. The aunt of the Duke of Inverfyre, she was a baroness, a widow and a fixture upon the most exalted guest lists in town.

"While you in contrast, Lady Wentworth, have not aged a whit since last we met. How many years has it been?"

"Easily a dozen, Your Grace. I do not care to consider actual numbers beyond that."

Damien smiled.

"May I assume you seek my companionship for a reason, Your Grace?"

"You are as astute as ever, Lady Wentworth, and I hope as informed." He watched as she inclined her head slightly, the way her gaze flicked over the dancers failing to disguise how intently she listened. "I seek tidings of a certain lady," he murmured.

"Who is not a lady, by many accounts," she replied in kind.

He met her gaze to find understanding there.

"We can debate the question of whether nobility is defined by birthright or by character," he said and she smiled.

"There would be little debate between us on the matter, Your Grace. I believe we are in agreement. This particular lady has found herself in a most dire circumstance. Your interest would be considered inappropriate by some but not by me. It is perhaps unexpected."

Damien chose to ignore that. "She is innocent."

"I suspected as much all along. Do you know her location?"

"Yes."

Lady Wentworth watched the dancers for a long moment. "I had heard that a chimney sweep visited her abode after her...departure from those premises."

Damien smiled. "It is said to be good fortune to encounter such a tradesman."

Lady Wentworth almost smiled though she did not look at Damien. "Doubtless, the lady's butler would agree. This one brought sufficient funds to buy an improvement in the lady's situation."

"How can you know this?" Damien demanded, a little vexed that his ploy had been discerned. He thought he had been so circumspect and clever.

Lady Wentworth's smile broadened. "My butler's son is married to the niece of that lady's cook."

Damien shook his head in admiration. "Do your servants have connections in every household in town?"

"Not quite, but we are always trying to repair the

omissions." She turned to him, eyeing him over her fan. "I assume you seek a specific detail from me."

"Where to find a particular man in France," Damien admitted readily. "He is the key to proving her innocence."

"I note you omit to call him a gentleman."

"It is no omission. He is a thief, if not more."

His companion nodded acknowledgement of that. "Sadly, I do not know," she admitted. "I know only that he was cast from our shores and forbidden to return for a year. There was some mention of Paris, but that might be solely speculation."

"Do you know the history between himself and the lady?"

"No, but I could wager a guess."

Damien met her gaze and arched a brow in silent query.

Lady Wentworth pursed her lips. "Women seldom embrace her trade willingly. They are coerced or even deceived, often by men of this one's ilk. I cannot help but note that the arrival in London of the lady in question coincided with the start of the war."

"And his appearance coincided with its ending," Damien concluded. "I had noticed the same." He considered that Miss Ballantyne must have begun her days or at least learned her trade in France, and that only the war had kept her safe from Jacques Desjardins. "Why would she cede any assistance to him with such a shared past?"

"I would guess that there is some detail he holds over her. A secret that puts her in his power, perhaps, or a possession she will pay any price to regain."

Desjardin's decision to leave the stolen gems in Miss Ballantyne's house meant that she would be incarcerated while he was banned from England's shores. She would not be executed for theft, though her time in prison would be unpleasant. Damien had done his best to appease that situation by giving money to Latimer, her butler, to be spent on improving her situation. Everyone knew that jailors were susceptible to bribes.

But this did not strike at the root of the issue. Miss Ballantyne was still imprisoned and Jacques Desjardins remained at large, if in France. Likely she would not be released before he could return to Britain.

He suspected that had been the fiend's plan.

"I wonder where he might be found," Damien mused.

"You would have to ask the lady in question," Lady Wentworth said softly. She turned to consider him. "I must say that I am surprised to find you of all men taking an interest in this matter."

"And why might that be?"

"Because your views upon such ladies has been ardently expressed on more than one occasion. I would have expected you to be gladdened by her fate, or at least content that justice had been served."

Damien turned to meet her bright gaze. "But justice has not been served, Lady Wentworth. Indeed, it has missed the mark, because I erred in my haste. The only honorable solution is to correct the result of error."

She smiled a little. "So, it is a question of honor."

"You might say as much."

"I am relieved, to be sure," the baroness said, turning to watch the dancers again. "I had begun to despair that Constance's influence upon you was rather less than might have been hoped."

"I beg your pardon?"

"Your father was deeply concerned with principle and morality, to the point of being quite rigid in his views. Your mother, in contrast, was always one prepared to act in what she perceived to be the greater good, regardless of expectation. I had hoped that since

Luke's demise, Constance might have had greater sway over her surviving son."

"You wish me to be inconstant?"

"I hope you might become the kind of man who is not bound by convention, but makes his own choices." She smiled at him. "In this matter, I find great encouragement for your future happiness, Your Grace."

Damien was startled. "I cannot see why that would concern you unduly."

"Because I like your mother very much. It is one matter to lose a husband who is many years one's senior, but quite another to also lose two sons, never mind in rapid succession. In such moments, I am glad to have no children myself, for the loss of even one might be too much to bear. I feel great sympathy for your mother."

"I suppose you are also going to advise me to wed." He knew he sounded weary.

"You suppose wrongly, Your Grace. I was advised to wed repeatedly but did not accept such counsel until I encountered a man I could not bear to live without. We wed late, we had no children, but we were aboundingly happy. That was well worth whatever sacrifices I might have made in not wedding at a younger age." She granted him a pert glance. "And so, I advise to seize happiness wherever you find it. Pay no heed to those who criticize you or your choices. If ever a woman makes your heart sing with joy, let nothing keep you apart, certainly not your own assumptions and opinions. Such encounters are rare and should be cherished."

Damien held her gaze for a long moment, seeing the truth in her advice. There had never been a woman who had so fascinated and stirred him as Esmeralda Ballantyne could. There had never been anyone who had challenged his opinions or dared him to reconsider them. There had never been a woman who haunted him as she did. And in so realizing, he knew that it was not merely justice at stake in the question of her unwarranted incarceration.

"I had thought to remain an anonymous benefactor," he said, gripping his cane as he rose to his feet. "But I will visit her."

"In disguise?"

"No."

Lady Wentworth's smile was brilliant. "Good," she said, reaching out to pat his hand. "I fancy your mother will like her, whenever they meet."

"I am not so certain of that, Lady Wentworth, but I shall take your advice and not concern myself with such details."

She laughed with pleasure. "Do give my regards to your mother."

"She arrived in town just three days ago."

"Then I will call tomorrow. Good evening, Your Grace, and good luck to you."

Damien bowed then turned to leave, once again leaning heavily on his cane that there might be no insistence that he dance. He waved to Emerson, though he was not at all convinced that man noticed, and left his friend in Eliza's company.

Truly, he could not regret the prospect of another encounter with the formidable and beautiful Miss Esmeralda Ballantyne. That she almost certainly despised him for his part in her arrest would only add a certain fire to their encounter. How would he convince her to forgive him for his error? Would she confide the location of Jacques Desjardins? Damien would do anything to ensure her safety and only hoped he could convince her of it.

The lady, he knew, was not inclined to accept a

claim simply because it had been uttered aloud. Damien would persuade her, one way or the other.

Indeed, he was so intent upon his quest that he forgot to limp as he approached his waiting carriage.

~

OF COURSE, Nicholas would be present to witness Eliza's first failure in defending the chastity and reputation of his sister.

And as a result, what should have been a wondrous experience—that of dancing a waltz with Nicholas—could not be savored because of her wretched responsibilities.

That those were duties she had willfully undertaken, and done as much in order to spend more time with Nicholas, was vexing indeed.

Eliza's luck was unfailingly bad on this particular evening, even without the realization that Mr. Galveston clearly intended to continue to pursue his suit.

Who *was* Helena's partner?

Nicholas tightened his grip slightly on Eliza's hand, drawing her attention back to him. "I know we are mere allies in the matter of Helena's future, but my pride will suffer great indignity if you spend the entire dance watching my sister." He lifted a brow when she met his gaze and Eliza knew he would tease her. "Or perhaps the gentleman is the object of your fascination."

"You must know *something* of him," Eliza said worriedly.

Nicholas spared the man in question a glance over her shoulder. "His tailor is excellent. His valet might be indifferent, as I fancy he could have encouraged a brighter gloss from his boots." He sobered. "It may in fact be a question of the age of the boots themselves, and given their condition, no greater gloss may be had." His gaze locked with hers, a wayward twinkle in their depths. "I should require a closer inspection to be sure, and there are much more pleasant occupations than a scrutiny of any gentleman's boots."

Eliza found herself smiling. "Do you dare to confide the nature of these other temptations?"

"If I did, you would surely be astonished." He eased closer to the couple in question and cleared his throat with vigor before Eliza could ask. "Helena, I trust you are enjoying your waltz."

"Nicholas!" The maiden in question jumped in a most satisfying way.

Nicholas spun Eliza out of his embrace, but continued to support her hand as he surveyed the other man with obvious expectation. "I do not believe we have been introduced."

Helena gave him a poisonous glance but moved away from her partner dutifully. That man did not manage to immediately hide his irritation. "Nicholas, this is Mr. Ethan Melbourne. We met last season before he was called away to his family home. Mr. Melbourne, this is my brother, Captain Emerson, recently returned from the Continent, and Mrs. North, who is kindly escorting me this evening."

Bows were made and pleasantries exchanged as the dancers swirled behind them. Helena fairly tapped her toe in her obvious urge to step back into her partner's embrace.

Nicholas had other plans, to Eliza's relief. "I have been advised, Helena, that it is not appropriate for you to dance a waltz with a man to whom you are not engaged or otherwise related, which means we shall be obliged to change partners."

"But..."

"The next is an *allemande*," Eliza said, as if that

would reassure the girl. "As you do not have a commitment as yet, perhaps Mr. Melbourne would be your partner."

Mr. Melbourne, clearly seeing his lack of options, bowed. "I should not dream of bringing any taint upon Miss Emerson," he said. "I was simply overcome with delight to see her again and would have escorted her to whatever dance they played."

"Of course," Nicholas said, offering his hand to his sister. Her eyes flashed and her smile was a little bit tight, but she ceded—and Eliza found herself dancing with Mr. Melbourne.

They danced in silence for some moments, a perfectly decorous distance between them. In contrast, Nicholas had already prompted Helena's laughter. Mr. Melbourne's interest was clearly in his former partner and he did not even trouble to make conversation.

Eliza cleared her throat. "How pleasant that you should encounter an acquaintance again so early in the season."

"Indeed, I was very pleased to see Miss Emerson. She is an excellent dancer." He turned them so that he could watch Helena and smiled at the view.

"So, I noted. I hope it was not bad news that compelled you to leave town last season."

Mr. Melbourne sobered and flicked a wary glance at Eliza. She sensed that he was going to tell a falsehood. "I fear it was. My father had suddenly fallen ill and I was summoned to his bedside." The younger man shook his head and though he appeared to be chagrined, Eliza had the definite sense that he concocted a tale. But why? "Alas, I arrived too late to speak with him one last time."

Her sense of his dishonesty grew, despite her inability to find a cause for it. "How disappointing for both of you."

"It was." He smiled a little. "My inheritance is scarcely a consolation compared to his wise counsel."

Mr. Melbourne did not appear to be the manner of man who relied upon the counsel of older gentlemen, much less heeded it, but Eliza saw no cause to comment. "I offer my condolences for your loss."

"And I thank you."

They danced again in silence and Eliza could not recall that a waltz was typically so long.

Mr. Melbourne frowned. "As you chaperone Miss Emerson, might I entreat you for a favor? You must be within the circle of her aunt's trust."

"Perhaps I am."

"My father was a most excellent judge of financial matters, far better than I am myself," he said with a smile that Eliza did not trust a whit. "Do you think that my income of six thousand a year would be sufficient that Lady Dalhousie might find my suit acceptable?" He hurried on before she could ask. "I know she did not approve of my interest last season, for my income was granted solely by my father's indulgence. I can only hope that the change in my circumstance might alter her view."

"I should be surprised if it did not," Eliza said, wondering anew at her sense that all was not as this young man insisted.

He smiled with evident relief. "I have no desire to interfere, if Lady Dalhousie has greater plans for Miss Emerson." He cast a glance across the floor to the maiden in question. "I wish only for her happiness, wherever it might be."

Oh, he lied.

Eliza knew it to her marrow, but she could not tell whether the sum of his confession was a fabrication or whether just one element was a fiction. "Perhaps you should call upon Lady Dalhousie and declare yourself."

Alarm lit the younger man's eyes. "Oh no! She was most resolute last season. I could not do as much, not without surety that I would be received well."

Eliza did not note that his ardor appeared to have definite limits, though she was tempted. She would never accept a man who refused to endure a difficult interview on her behalf.

"I may have occasion to speak to Lady Dalhousie," she said instead as the music finally drew to a close.

He bowed, giving her the sense that he was as relieved to part ways as she. "I will be utterly in your debt, Mrs. North, if you might manage as much."

"I believe we go to the theater on Friday evening. Perhaps we might encounter you there."

He smiled wolfishly and Eliza thought she glimpsed his truth in that avaricious expression. If Helena had been an heiress, his choices would have made sense, but as it was, Eliza was mystified.

"I believe that can be arranged, Mrs. North."

And then he was gone, strolling across the floor to where Helena eagerly awaited him. He claimed her hand as the first notes of the *allemande* sounded and led her to a spot on the floor. Eliza's gaze flew to Nicholas, but he was watching his sister, a slight frown between his brows.

A cough sounded in close proximity and she found Mr. Galveston bowing before her, his expectation obvious.

Eliza could not see a way around his invitation. She smiled and placed her hand in his, letting him lead her to a spot immediately beside Helena.

Perhaps Nicholas was right and the best way to supervise his sister was to dance.

As the dance began, Eliza realized her brother was no longer seated by Lady Wentworth. In truth, there was no sign of him. Where had he gone at such speed?

Why had Damien come to Almack's at all?

～

"THE HEIRESS of Hexham will never wed the worthless likes of you!"

The words of Lady Frances Dalhousie echoed in Mr. Ethan Melbourne's thoughts, as they had since she had first hurled them in his direction. Summoned to a meeting at her townhouse, he had scarcely expected such affrontery—but given her objections, he had been compelled to abandon his pursuit of the delightful Miss Emerson the previous season.

That had been doubly irksome, given that Miss Emerson had wealth.

The tale of being summoned to his family home had been a fiction, intended to keep Miss Emerson from learning of her aunt's instruction.

As was so often the case with convenient fictions, it had served Mr. Melbourne well. Here was Miss Emerson, as lovely as ever, without a suitor and in the custody of a chaperone who clearly knew nothing of that past interview. Even the brother was oblivious, which meant there was a moment of opportunity for Melbourne to act before it was too late.

The tale of his inheritance, surrendered to Mrs. North, was also a fable, a scheme to ensure that the chaperone did not forbid his presence. Melbourne had only his debts to his name and he had need of funds soon, making the amiable Miss Emerson the obvious solution.

He had to tread lightly, though, and he had to move quickly. His lies would not withstand much perusal: they could only gain him sufficient time to convince Miss Emerson to elope with him. As soon as the chaperone conferred with Lady Dalhousie, he would be revealed. He could only hope that revelation would not occur quickly.

On this particular evening, he chose to take his leave of Almack's. Captain Emerson did not appear to be a man Melbourne would like as an enemy. A military man, both larger and older than Melbourne, Emerson certainly would know how to fight. Melbourne preferred to cultivate a bruise only when he could capitalize upon it to soften a lady's objections.

With Miss Emerson, he did not imagine any such encouragement would be required. His usual tactics of flattery, stolen moments and seductive touches should be more than sufficient: she was nigh already his.

Ethan was by nature a gambler, but he had a healthy respect for Dame Fortune. So much had gone well already this night that he would not press on. Instead, he would give the appearance of leaving the field. That would diminish any sense of urgency in the chaperone to speak to Lady Dalhousie.

Melbourne lifted his hat to Miss Emerson, catching her eye from the other side of the ballroom, and watched her countenance light. She even waved to him, careless of convention, and he smiled to himself as he departed. He did not have to look to see the widow or the brother glare at him. Let them be as dour as they liked. His campaign was resumed and Melbourne was determined that this season, it should succeed.

Haste was key.

CHAPTER 5

*H*is strategy was doomed to failure.

Nicholas could not believe he was dancing at Almack's, abandoned by Haynesdale, utterly sober yet enjoying himself, simply due to a short interval of dancing with Eliza again. He had chastised Helena during the waltz to no discernible effect but was relieved to see Melbourne leave the gathering. There was something about that man that convinced Nicholas to neither like nor trust him, and he could not wait to compare his observations with those of Eliza.

That was not the only reason he wished to talk to Eliza. That caress of his arm, that fleeting touch that was of much longer duration than expected, haunted him. He would have an explanation—or more.

When the second waltz of the evening began, Nicholas saw his opportunity. He led Helena directly toward her chaperone, smiling when he saw Eliza's eyes light from across the floor. "Why look, Mr. Galveston is approaching Mrs. North," he said for his sister's benefit.

"You will not condemn me to dance with someone as ancient as yourself," Helena complained under her breath. "You are supposed to be my ally in this, Nicholas!"

"I *am* your ally."

"Nicholas!" Helena hissed his name through her teeth.

He spared her a quelling glance. "I am certain I have a year or two upon him." His sister's eyes flashed, but she had her way often enough in Nicholas' view. He bowed before Mrs. North, whose gaze flicked to Helena. "I believe you owe me a reward, Mrs. North," Nicholas said, offering his hand.

Eliza hesitated and Nicholas knew why. Who could guess what trouble his sister would find if left to her own resources?

Galveston stepped forward in that moment, as if his arrival had been planned. "Mrs. North, might I be so bold as to invite Miss Emerson to dance? I know it is a waltz, but I appeal to you with my pledge of the utmost decorum."

Relief lit Eliza's gaze. "Mr. Galveston, I am confident that you will be a perfect gentleman."

"Miss Emerson?"

Helena seemed to draw upon some inner strength, sparing a last overly-long glance around the room before accepting Mr. Galveston's hand.

Nicholas grinned as he whirled Eliza away onto the floor. He watched as Eliza ensured that Helena and Mr. Galveston were dancing in an appropriate manner.

"Whatever you said to your sister, Captain Emerson, it was taken into consideration," she said. "There is a great increment of space between them."

"Then my reward has been doubly earned," Nicholas said, pulling her slightly closer. He expected her to retreat but instead Eliza cast him a smile of satisfaction. He had not been mistaken about that caress! "Do I recall correctly that you like to dance?"

"You do and I do. You are a very good partner, Captain. My toes are beguiled."

"There is praise offered in the tone of a woman who has known less good partners."

It was bewitching to be so close to her, to feel the indent of her waist beneath his gloved hand, to inhale of her scent and savor it. "Frederick could not abide dancing," she confessed, as if it was unkind to even utter such a truth. Nicholas felt a surge of pride that was utterly unworthy of him. He could not be jealous of a dead man, but he was.

Ten years with Eliza as his wife. Nicholas could not even imagine such good fortune.

He smiled down at her, encouraging her to continue.

She did. "I believe he contrived to do it badly that he might be less often compelled to participate."

Nicholas feigned dismay. "How churlish not to be inclined to indulge his wife!"

"I could not complain if he was remiss only when there was dancing." Eliza dropped her gaze, and he wondered whether that had been the case.

"And was he?" He prompted her as he should not have done.

Eliza met his gaze again. "I call you churlish for encouraging me to speak poorly of the dead," she said lightly and Nicholas smiled.

"I seek only to understand the limitations, if indeed there are any, to a match made for love alone. I had assumed that such a partnership would be filled with bliss and harmony in all matters at all times."

Eliza smiled in her turn. "Love does not mean complete agreement in all matters," she chided gently. "Only in the greatest one."

"Being?"

"That hearts and minds are joined together, never to

be put asunder. Of course, there will be moments of disharmony. No one's temper is always steady."

"I confess myself astonished. Do those couples who are madly in love ever find cause to argue?"

"Of course. Where there are strong opinions, there may be disagreement."

"But I suppose the subsequent reconciliation is all the sweeter for the moment of discord?"

"Indisputably."

Nicholas could not resist the urge to tease her. "And I must imagine that any physical demonstration of a newfound accord must be sweet, indeed."

Eliza blushed in the most delightful manner, her cheeks becoming suffused with pink even as her lips parted. He wondered whether she looked thus in her moment of release, and everything tightened within at the prospect of discovering that truth.

If, of course, he had been capable of doing as much.

The truth of his situation tempered his spirits.

"Of course," she said, her throat working. He drew her a little closer before he thought the better of it and she caught her breath but did not move away. It was sweet torment to have her so close and his heart thundered when she moved so that her hair brushed his jaw.

"And how are such disputes resolved?" he asked, striving to keep his thoughts upon their conversation when he wanted to carry her away from this place. "Must one party surrender unequivocally and abandon his or her position, or is there negotiation?"

"You make a marital dispute sound like a war, Captain Emerson!"

"I have no other source of comparison, and if I am to pursue a love match, I should like to be aware of any potential pitfalls." She stole a glance at him through her lashes, her smile making his chest tighten. "Indeed, Mrs. North, I should be obliged if you took advantage of our alliance to tutor me that I might make the best choice possible when such a decision must be made."

"I cannot believe you have need of my advice, Captain."

"When entering unfamiliar territory, every prudent leader seeks tidings of the challenges that lie ahead," he informed her solemnly. "Reconnoiter is an under-appreciated tactic."

"I see. How might I so advise you, then?"

They danced for a moment while he considered the question.

"I suppose one must begin with the most basic of information," he said finally. "How does one know when one is in love?"

"One knows," Eliza said with assurance.

"But how?"

"The heart leaps at the first appearance of the target of one's affections."

"I feel thus when my commander appears to inspect my troops. Surely that cannot be love?"

Eliza laughed. "You know it is not."

"I suspect as much, surely. There must be a more accurate measure."

"One's mouth goes dry in the presence of the heart's captor, and words are elusive. Even coherence can be a challenge."

He nodded. "Then I was in love with my first tutor of mathematics, for that was my reaction each time he demanded my solution to a query."

"You know that was not love!"

"I have no means to be certain as yet."

"You cannot bear to be separated from the one you hold in esteem and yearn to be reunited whenever you are apart."

"I feel thus about my horse, to be sure. Perhaps I

should leave this gathering and check upon Sterling's welfare."

Eliza laughed, her eyes dancing in a most delightful way. "You mock me, sir."

"Perhaps I tease you in this, but my desire for knowledge cannot be denied." He smiled and shook his head slightly. "I am utterly at your mercy, Mrs. North. Please do instruct me."

Their gazes locked for a moment during which he dared not blink, then Eliza, against every expectation, drew closer. She dropped her voice to a whisper, her lips almost against his skin, her breath sending shivers through him. Nicholas could scarcely recall the steps to the dance, and he did not even take a breath lest she move away.

"Love is consuming," she whispered. "Love claims one's every thought and every moment. Love insists that one be with one's beloved, even if just in their presence and unable to speak openly. Love demands that one do whatever is necessary to bring about that happy proximity, no matter the price to one's pride. Love urges one to put the interest of the beloved before one's own interest, no matter the expense." Then she touched her lips to his flesh, bestowing the lightest of kisses.

It could have been no accident.

Nicholas was stunned.

He looked down at her in awe and watched her smile. "Love is humble, then," he managed to say, though his voice was husky.

"Indeed." She fairly glowed with the assertion and Nicholas regretted that the music ended.

He led her from the floor, not wanting to release her hand or relinquish her company. "I fear I have no capacity for humility, or so I have been told. Perhaps my pursuit of love is doomed."

"It is true," Eliza acknowledged with a playful smile. "You have always been infernally confident, Captain."

"But is such confidence unwarranted?"

"You seek a compliment from me, sir, which is unworthy of you."

"Once again, you outwit me, Mrs. North. It seems that a love match cannot be for me. I fear I should only disappoint the lady in my shortfalls." He made a show of considering the matter deeply, but shook his head in apparent defeat. "No, it will be solitude for me, I fear, unless I encounter an heiress who cannot survive without my companionship."

"Solitude and brandy," his companion corrected. "Have you consumed anything this day that was not delivered in a glass?"

Trust Eliza to be unafraid of declaring his truth.

"Not a morsel," Nicholas acknowledged cheerfully. "It has been a day to excel all others."

"But you cannot live on brandy!"

"I assure you that I have seen it done," he said, hearing that his tone had become a little harder.

She persisted, as fearless as ever, and he could only admire her. "But why?"

Nicholas bowed before her, surprised to find himself answering her. "Because then I do not dream, Mrs. North," he murmured. "And that is the best possible situation." He swallowed to find Eliza watching him, her eyes dark and her expression filled with compassion. He dropped his gaze, feeling that he had revealed too much, and kissed her gloved hand. "And now, to consider the heiresses," he said, winked at her, then excused himself.

Nicholas knew he should take Haynesdale's example and leave before he made a fool of himself. He should find some revels of less sedate variety than dancing at Almack's. He should recall his own objectives and his father's advice, and depart.

But he could not go.

Eliza North had kissed him, perhaps deliberately, perhaps on purpose, and Nicholas needed to know why.

No, he wanted more than one fleeting kiss, to be sure.

NINE DAYS after the stolen gems were discovered in Esmeralda's house, the key turned in the lock of her cell. It was late in the evening, the time when she was most wary. She stood, putting her back to the wall opposite the door, the hard-won comb in her fist and hidden behind her back. Her heart was leaping with fear. In a way, waiting for the worst might be more terrible than enduring it. She was exhausted from worry and fear.

"There you are there then," announced her jailor, who coughed lustily after his words. He then stepped aside to allow another to pass.

Esmeralda could only stare at the familiar silhouette of a man leaning upon a cane. He carried a lantern in his other hand and his lips were drawn to a taut line. The Duke of Haynesdale's eyes glittered coldly as he appraised first her prison cell and then her.

Esmeralda knew she looked far from her best. Her dress, which had once been a spritely green and black stripe, was smeared with dirt. The cuffs of her jacket were soiled and her linen was in desperate need of a change. She had abandoned all hope of tending her own hair and had simply combed it out, leaving it in a single braid that fell down her back. She did not doubt that the lack of sufficient food had hollowed her cheeks and put shadows beneath her eyes–her stays were looser than they had been in years. But she stood and held his gaze, prepared for his indictment.

Doubtless he came to gloat. It was easy to recall both his words about women in her trade and his disdain. Regrettably, it was also simple to feel the thrill of his presence again. He was tall and broad, fiendishly handsome, undoubtedly ruthless, clever and the most desirable man she had encountered in years. Esmeralda was aware of the heat that slipped over her flesh when their gazes met.

"Fifteen minutes, Your Grace," the jailor said.

Haynesdale granted that man a withering glance. "I will summon you when you are needed," he said, a welcome steel in his tone.

The jailor considered this, blinked and retreated, after locking the door behind himself.

"I suppose it is too much to hope that you might have him thrashed," Esmeralda said when the silence had stretched too long between them.

The duke smiled ever so slightly. "I am glad to see your fire has not been doused," he said softly, then placed the lantern on the small table. Its light filled the chamber with a gold glow, making it look markedly better than Esmeralda knew it was. His gaze locked upon her again as he braced his cane against the chair. "I am certain you know the reason for my presence." He began to untie his cravat, his gaze unswerving, his expression one of resolve.

Esmeralda would have retreated a step if the wall had not been immediately behind her. "*You* are my benefactor?" she asked in shock.

"Your astonishment is hardly flattering, Miss Ballantyne." He cast his cravat onto the table, shedding his jacket immediately afterward.

Esmeralda felt her mouth work. He meant to possess her? Here? She was disgusted and dismayed—and yet, she could not keep herself from watching as he disrobed. He pulled his shirt over his head, revealing his tanned and muscled shoulders as well as the expanse of his chest. A part of Esmeralda yearned to touch him, to feel the hard heat of him beneath her hands, and another was appalled at his presumption.

"But you have made your opinion clear..." she protested.

He gave her a hot look. "Can a man not change his thinking?"

"You!" Esmeralda spat as he took a purposeful step toward her. "What manner of vermin are you to take advantage of me in such an ungentlemanly way?"

"I believe there is no reasonable reply to that query," he said, so utterly untroubled that she raised her hand to slap him. He caught her wrist in his hand, then rubbed his thumb against the soft skin on the inside of her wrist, his eyes fairly glowing as he bent to press a kiss to her flesh.

No doubt he felt the wild flutter of her pulse against his lips, because he smiled, a predator content with the situation. Esmeralda tried to lunge past him but he caught her easily, lifting her off the ground and holding her captive against his chest. She beat on his shoulders with her hands, hating that her strength was so diminished.

"I shall fight you every moment," she threatened in a whisper.

"I do not doubt it," he replied. He kept one arm locked around her waist, as invincible as a band of steel, then raised his other hand to grip her nape. His fingers slid into her hair slowly, his touch sending an unwelcome shiver through her, and Esmeralda could not tear her gaze from his mouth.

"I will bite you," she whispered and his smile flashed.

"Oh, I hope so," he murmured, then captured her mouth with his.

She had expected a fierce kiss, a claiming that showed no regard for her feelings, so the tenderness of his touch caught her by surprise. She failed to bite him, much less to fight him, for his lips moved against hers with a reverence and a persuasiveness that she could not deny.

His kiss was an homage. A salute and a tribute.

It was utterly seductive.

Esmeralda's hands landed on his bare shoulders as she surrendered to temptation. For years, she had admired him, wondered about him, even dreamed of him —and now he kissed her with a reverence and a passion that was her undoing.

He made a sound of satisfaction at her capitulation and deepened his kiss. The heat rose between them with dizzying speed, leaving Esmeralda clutching at him as he held her captive and feasted upon her mouth. She closed her eyes, reasoning that she owed him at least this kiss, then forgot all her objections in the haze of pleasure he conjured.

She was short of breath when he lifted his head, when his fingers moved against her in a slow caress, when he blazed a line of kisses to her ear. His warm breath made her shiver as he whispered. "There must appear to be a liaison," he murmured and Esmeralda's eyes flew open. "But there will not be one." He pulled back slightly, his gaze boring into hers with intensity. "I give you my word of honor."

Esmeralda frowned and shook her head, uncertain of his meaning, but he kissed her again before she could speak. He braced her against the wall, trapping her between the bricks and his hard strength, his hands moving to her waist.

"No one will see clearly in this pose," he whispered

against her throat. "You must convince them of the truth of our supposed union."

Esmeralda looked toward the door with its small window and realized that the duke was aware they had an audience. Her objections to him began to melt that he would hide her from view and preserve what modicum of privacy she yet possessed.

He had some purpose and it required her assistance to succeed.

Esmeralda chose to trust him.

She gasped and let her head fall back, her lips parting in apparent ecstasy as she pushed a hand through his hair. She framed his face in her hands and kissed him hungrily, holding him as captive to her demands as he had held her to his own. She felt his smile and was not surprised by the glimmer in his eyes when she broke their kiss.

"Even I might be convinced," he murmured with satisfaction.

She nipped at his mouth. He had a marvelous mouth, ideal for kissing, both firm and responsive. She kissed him again, glad of the opportunity. "Why?" she whispered.

His jaw set. "I led them to you, but was deceived. This matter must be set to rights."

"So, justice can prevail?" she murmured. "There are those who would say it has been done by my incarceration here." She might have expected him to be amongst their number but the duke's eyes flashed green fire.

"And they would be wrong. Esmeralda." He said her name like a caress, vehement and yet with an admiration that only fed her desire for him. She wanted him in her own bed, in her house, on smooth clean sheets when she was fresh from a bath, her skin scented with rose petals, the taste of brandy on his mouth. "I will repair my error," he whispered fiercely and she could only regret that his apparent seduction was for the sake of principles alone.

What would it be like to have such a man desire her for herself?

Esmeralda was certain she would never know.

His grip tightened on her waist, his fingers flexing. "Have you lost weight?"

"The rations are not generous," she whispered, sparing him a slightly smile. "And the fare seldom to my taste."

"I will see that amended as well," he vowed and continued before she could thank him for that. "Lift your skirts. It has been too long."

Esmeralda thought at first he referred to his own satisfaction, then realized he referred to the jailor watching them, a man who would surely expect a quick union. She lifted the front of her skirt, glad again that the duke's figure hid details from view, then wrapped her legs around his hips. Even feigning intimacy with him was thrilling, even in this circumstance. His thighs were powerful and his buttocks tight.

She held fast to his shoulders, winding herself around him, and he crushed her into the wall. He was so large and hard that Esmeralda caught her breath with yearning. He smiled and ground his hips against her, the sensation so satisfying that she wondered whether she truly would have to pretend to find her release. Even with the layers of cloth between them, there was something utterly satisfying about the feel of the duke against her.

He claimed her mouth in another kiss, one more passionate than the last, driving her to distraction with his tongue. She writhed against him, wanting more than she was likely to have, and her fingers dug into his shoulders. "More," she commanded, aware of their audience and he chuckled darkly, moving against her with a wondrous resolve.

She gasped, not feigning her pleasure in the least, and wonder of wonders, the Duke of Haynesdale smiled. He watched her as he rocked against her and their gazes held, some undeniable force taut between them. She saw resolve in his eyes and an increment of wonder that could only feed her confidence.

She rolled her hips, imagining that they were together in a finer circumstance, that he had come to her for more earthy reasons than his noble justification. Just the notion fed her desire and she felt the quickening muster within her. She watched his gaze sharpen as the tide rose, then her pulse leapt as he claimed her mouth again, kissing her with such fervor that she could only savor the ride. And when the crescendo broke, she cried out in pleasure, well aware that he only pretended to have found his as well.

He leaned his forehead against her shoulder, tension emanating from him in waves, and she could only admire his struggle for control. "Where do I find him?" he whispered, both his words and his urgency unexpected.

"Who?" she asked, although she thought she knew.

The duke looked up, his face close to hers, his gaze fairly burning. *"Jacques Desjardins."* He mouthed the name but her heart skipped all the same.

She shook her head, refusing his aid even though the offer touched her heart.

"What does he hold over you?" he whispered, nuzzling her ear as if they cuddled in the aftermath.

Esmeralda blinked back her tears and shook her head minutely.

"You cannot resolve this alone," Haynesdale whispered. "I will see this matter concluded in your favor. Do not be such a proud fool that you decline." She looked up, then touched her fingertips to his face, shaken by his fierce expression.

But Esmeralda had never had a champion and she could not believe in her heart that she had one now. She knew without doubt that the price of Haynesdale's assistance would prove too high for her to pay.

She bowed her head so he could not see in her eyes how close she had come to believing him. "Send Ophelia Pearl, the actress, to me, please."

She felt his shock that he had been denied anything he asked, that she had dared to decline his offer. Then he moved abruptly away from her, dressing with savage efficiency. She watched him in profile through her lashes, surprised that she had been able to affect him so, and ashamed that she had done as much.

"Your gait is stronger," she said when he turned toward the door, cane in hand, hat on his head. She could not let him simply leave her with such tension between them.

Haynesdale cast her an inscrutable glance, his eyes dark. "A lady recommended the benefit of exercise to me," he said with heat, biting off the words. Then he spun and departed, leaving the lantern.

He was gone before Esmeralda realized he had referred to her as a lady.

～

WHY WOULD Nicholas not wish to dream?

The evening passed pleasantly, though Eliza could not set aside the question. She might have asked outright, but she did not dance again with Nicholas. She wondered whether he contrived as much to ensure that she had no such opportunity.

Or perhaps he had been offended by her boldness in chastising him about brandy.

Perhaps she had erred in following the advice of Mrs. Oliver's pages.

In truth, Eliza was impatient with the evening's festivities. What would she have given to simply be able to talk to Nicholas! Instead, she was occupied in ensuring that Helena danced with suitable partners. The girl was an excellent dancer and drew many admiring gazes. After Melbourne's departure, her conduct was laudable.

Nicholas danced with every debutante present, by Eliza's accounting, ensuring that none were neglected. This she might have viewed with less favor, save that he came to her for the last dance before supper was served. It was another *allemande*, leaving little opportunity for conversation, but she did manage to ask him to accompany them home in the carriage.

"I have a matter I would discuss with you," she confessed, when she could think of at least three such topics.

He considered this without surprise and replied when the steps next brought them together. "With Helena present or not?"

"Afterward, if you do not have other obligations."

Their paths parted for the dance again and it seemed an eternity before she met him again. "I will walk home from Haynesdale House readily enough," he agreed and she sighed with relief. "My other obligations, such as they are, can wait."

Helena chattered about the evening all the way home, then fairly raced into the house, purportedly to confess all to Lady Dalhousie. Perhaps she simply understood that her presence was not required.

"Will she tell your aunt about Mr. Melbourne?" Eliza asked Nicholas when they were underway again, though Helena's partners and confessions were the last thing she wished to discuss.

Nicholas had resumed his seat opposite her, apparently ignoring the space vacated by his sister. Had he taken no encouragement from her swift kiss? Had he even noticed it?

"Who can say? I suppose I will have to join them for breakfast to learn more."

"Do you know anything of him?"

Nicholas shook his head. "Do you?"

"Only what he told me and I fear it was not all true."

Nicholas' attention fixed upon her. "What falsehood did he tell?"

"I do not know. I simply distrusted him." She sighed, discontent with her own answer. "I regret that I have no firmer reply than that."

"I do not trust him either, though I cannot say why."

Their gazes met again and she saw that he shared her confidence that their views were the same.

Eliza took a chance and moved her skirts closer to her thigh in silent invitation, making space for Nicholas to sit beside her. His gaze fell to the bench beside her, then he met her gaze again. She smiled and he moved across the carriage immediately, settling beside her. The strength of his thigh was pressed against her own but she did not move away.

"Perhaps such confidences require quieter tones," he murmured and she shivered with delight.

Eliza dared to place her hand upon his knee. "I believe they do," she said, her heart leaping when his gloved hand covered hers. She leaned closer and whispered. "He said he had six thousand pounds a year."

"Mrs. North," Nicholas said softly and she looked up, seeing that his eyes were dark and his expression was not shocked. "I have no desire to discuss Mr. Melbourne in this moment."

"Nor do I," she admitted.

"And Mr. Galveston, it seems, has not abandoned his suit. Did you mislead me about his intentions?"

Eliza moved her hand down Nicholas' thigh, hearing him catch his breath. "Perhaps you might defend me from his attentions," she dared to say, then looked at his face again.

He might have been turned to stone, so impassive was his expression, though his eyes glittered like sapphires. "Is that what you truly desire, Mrs. North?" he asked so quietly that the words were barely audible.

"No," she admitted, feeling audacious beyond all. "I wish for you to kiss me, Captain Emerson."

An eternity passed before he replied. "Why?"

"Because you dance as Frederick did not. I can only wonder whether you kiss as Frederick did not. He had little interest in demonstrating physical affection and I wonder at the omissions in my knowledge." She smiled up at him. "You did offer to corrupt me, Captain Emerson. I confess that I find myself willing to accept."

She had no opportunity to reconsider her audacity or regret her words, for Nicholas raised his free hand to her cheek, tipped her chin upward and captured her lips beneath his own.

And just as Eliza had always anticipated, Nicholas' kiss was a marvel.

~

NICHOLAS WAS SEDUCED.

He was snared.

He was a fool and a rogue, yet he could not keep himself from kissing Eliza senseless. She was so welcoming and sweet, precisely all he had ever desired—and yet a woman he never could or would possess. Even as she melted against him, encouraging him beyond expectation, Nicholas knew this passion was ill-fated in more ways than one.

Still, he could not turn away from temptation. Still,

his hand slid into her hair, his other arm eased around her waist to bring her closer as he deepened his kiss. He was drowning in sensation, his heart racing when she laid her hand upon his shoulder and sighed contentment. She was utterly enticing, compliant and seductive, though he doubted she realized how powerfully she affected him.

If there was to be one kiss between them, he would make it one to remember.

Nicholas was about to end it, when Eliza opened her mouth to him and he could not believe his good fortune. When he felt the flick of her tongue, he thought he might die of pleasure and when her fingers curled in his hair, gripping it to pull him closer, there was nothing Nicholas wanted more than to bury himself within her. He would spend the entire night coaxing her pleasure, if not the next day as well, and that was the realization that ended the moment for him.

He could not grant what she desired of him.

It might have been tempting to offer Eliza a dalliance, and if his condition had been other than it was, he might have surrendered to that opportunity. As it was, he could only disappoint her and he knew his own limits.

Indeed, he felt them in this very moment. There was not a stir of response, though his heart and mind wished for it thoroughly. What more evidence did he need?

Nicholas broke their kiss with reluctance, forcing himself to move back to the other bench, across the carriage. He felt Eliza's gaze upon him, and knew his fist was clenched, but he looked resolutely out the window, his throat working.

They were not fifty feet from Haynesdale House.

He burned for Eliza, but he could not embarrass

her. He strove to recall his own carefully laid plan to secure his own future, a plan which had no allowance for a mistress or a wife, much less the conundrum of Eliza DeVries, but could think only of that kiss.

And how much he wished for another.

"Why do you not wish to dream?" Eliza asked just as the carriage halted. She might have read his thoughts and Nicholas was startled, but he did not immediately reply.

He stepped past her as soon as the footman opened the door, and offered his hand to her. Even with his awareness of the possibilities—or their lack—he could not surrender the chance to touch her gloved hand one last time. Her hand was a sweet burden in his own, one that made him regret all that had been and all that never could be.

He could give her an answer, but it would be only part of the truth.

"I spoke out of turn, Mrs. North, and I do apologize," he said formally. He kept his tone curt, intending to discourage her questions. He did not doubt that she had many, and given any opportunity, that she would ask them. Eliza was fearless. Nicholas could not hold her gaze, keenly aware that he confided less than she wished of him.

How he wanted to give her all of her desires!

How he hated that he could not. If nothing else, he was a man who would not promise what he could not provide.

"There is no need to apologize, Captain Emerson. A gentleman always fulfills a lady's request, by my understanding."

"All the same, I trust that you will no longer require my presence when you chaperone my sister." He dared to look at her face in time to see her lips part. She would argue with him and he would be lost again.

Nicholas bowed instead. "Good evening, Mrs. North." He briskly pivoted, walking down the street and into the night. He was well aware of her gaze following him.

Enough.

Eliza was not for him and he was not for her. How could he fail to understand this simple truth? A dalliance would only tarnish her reputation and diminish her chances of future happiness—even if he could have provided one.

He was a fool, an optimist when there was no cause to be one, a man who always kept his vow. He would protect Eliza with all in his possession, expecting naught in return.

He would even deny her invitation to lead her astray, for her own good.

Nicholas turned his steps at the corner, intending to head for White's instead of his aunt's house. They would admit him to the club thanks to his association with Haynesdale, and there, he would most assuredly find a brandy and soon. The same was not true of his aunt's abode.

The last thing he desired on this night was to dream.

He feared, though, that he might have no choice.

He halted then, considering. He had to face his demons sooner or later. He would not be able to indulge when Haynesdale took him to Brooks's. Perhaps he should accept Eliza's challenge and forgo the brandy on this night, the better to take the measure of what haunted him.

Nicholas had never been afraid to face the worst, and on this night, he knew a wise notion when he heard it. He pivoted and headed for his aunt's abode, determined to take the measure of his nightmare.

That might well be the first step to conquering it.

CHAPTER 6

*E*liza watched Nicholas stride away, her fingertips rising to her lips in wonder after his glorious kiss. Had he ended their embrace because the carriage had reached the house? Had he meant to protect her reputation? Or had she done something wrong in responding with enthusiasm?

She did not know.

She did not care.

She only wanted more. She had never felt such an ache before, or experienced a yearning left unsatisfied. She had never been discontent with the sum of physical union, but on this night, she burned for another kiss, if not more.

Clearly, Mrs. Oliver's advice had merit. Eliza turned toward the house with a light step, telling herself to be content to have a kiss to dream on.

Such progress would suffice for this night, at least.

Then she paused and turned to the driver who had been with the family for decades. Nicholas had mentioned his horse. "Thomson, does Captain Emerson not have a horse?"

"Indeed, my lady, he does. A fine stallion to be sure."

"Does Lady Dalhousie have a stable?" It seemed unlikely that a modest townhouse would have a stable.

"Not so far as I know, my lady. Sterling is in our stable, at His Grace's insistence. Captain Emerson was going to board him, but the duke would not hear of it."

"Just the one horse then?"

"The one as carried him safely through each battle, my lady. The others, I believe, were palfreys and such, sold on the Continent or lost in the war. Sterling, though, has a fine lineage and the captain would not surrender him, though he did not like the ocean passage either time."

"I remember that Captain Emerson's horses were always the best trained at Southpoint."

"A right gift of it he has, my lady. I always said that the Emerson boy knew what a horse would do before the horse began to think of it."

Eliza laughed at that.

"You might remember Sterling being born at Haynesdale, my lady. He was maybe six years of age when the Captain took him to war and as fine a horse as ever you saw."

Eliza sobered, remembering that Nicholas had taken only one horse with him from Southpoint. There had been mingling of stock between the horses at Southpoint and Haynesdale for years, and one remarkable stallion had been the product of it. That had been the horse Nicholas had taken, at Eliza's father's insistence.

"I do remember," she said. "Papa insisted that he take that horse, though I had forgotten the stallion's name."

"Aye, the old duke knew that a military man needs a horse he can rely upon, to be sure. You should have a look at him one day, my lady. Finest stud I've seen in years."

"Captain Emerson studs him?"

"'Tis how Sterling's board is paid, my lady, though perhaps Captain Emerson means to make more of him than that." The old driver smiled. "But he knows horses, that lad. Always has."

"Thank you, Thomson. You have made me curious. I will come to see Sterling one day." Eliza nodded as the driver bowed, then turned to the house. She liked that Nicholas kept his horse at Haynesdale and was curious to learn of his future plans.

But mostly, she savored the memory of that kiss and wondered as she climbed the steps how she might encourage him to lead her yet further astray.

If only Mrs. Oliver would reply favorably to her request.

And soon.

~

IN THE MIDDLE of the night, when the house was utterly silent, Nicholas heard the explosion. Fire burned against the darkness of the night and men screamed in close proximity. Shot whistled through the air and the smell of blood rose to choke him.

He clutched the sheets and writhed, knowing he was snared in his nightmare yet again, but powerless in its grip. He groaned in his sleep, and struggled to awaken, to no avail.

Nicholas knew the nightmare as well as he knew his own name. It was always the same. It was always exactly as that night had been. He heard the race of his heart pounding in his ears, and wished he could look away.

That wish was not to be granted.

He saw the silhouette of the fortification above him, etched against the night, and his agitation grew. The darkness was so complete that even the stars were obscured. The fortified wall and castle that loomed above them was only a darker shadow against the night. Nicholas sat in silence with the others, terror tying his innards in knots as they waited the signal. Only Haynesdale was utterly composed.

There was only darkness, dread, and the sound of the frogs in the stream behind them.

In his sleep, Nicholas stirred restlessly, wishing he could change what followed.

When the attackers began to move in silence, he moaned, wanting to warn them. They reached the base of the walls, unchallenged. They placed the ladders against the wall, with only a single musket shot from above in response.

He saw Haynesdale again gave him a triumphant wink and head for the ladder, intending to lead his men to triumph. Nicholas shook his head, battling against the sight of what he knew would follow.

But he could not awaken, so he was compelled to see it all again.

Suddenly, light exploded on all sides. The air was filled with the sound of musket fire and the cries of injured men. There were flashes of light around and between them, grapeshot at every turn, and the very earth seemed to rock beneath their feet. In a heartbeat, the darkness had been shattered and they stood within the heart of a fireball.

In the midst of that terror, Haynesdale stumbled and fell—then did not immediately rise again. Nicholas forced his way through the chaos to his friend's side, panic filling him just as it had then. Haynesdale tried to wave him off, rising to one knee, but he was struck again, and this shot took him to the ground. Nicholas cried out and reached for the duke.

Men were falling on all sides. All had gone awry

with lightning speed. The night was lit by flashes of light from explosives in a fiendish scene of torment worthy of the innermost circles of Hell.

Haynesdale was not dead but he could not walk. Nicholas tasted that relief again, then hefted the duke to his shoulders. He carried him to safety, feeling again the weight of his friend again. He felt his feet sinking into the ditch filled with fallen men. Terror rose when one clutched at his boot in a plea for aid.

It was impossible to help them all. He had to save Haynesdale. He stumbled on, falling to his own knees more than once, desperate to reach a measure of safety.

Nicholas barely felt the shot in his own shoulder, so intent was he upon his task.

He finally lowered Haynesdale's body on the east side of the Revillas stream. He heard the duke land in the mud; he realized his shoulder was on fire; he looked back at the fiery Hell they had escaped. The smell of burning flesh and blood assailed him and he was physically ill in the stream, appalled by the price their forces had paid. He was kneeling in muck, water halfway to his elbows, filth all around him...

Nicholas' eyes flew open and he was startled to find himself in a small bedroom. He could taste his own bile and smell the smoke, but he was not in Spain. The room was utterly familiar, the small one he favored on the third floor of his aunt's house where he could see all the corners. He sat up, panting, desperate to verify his location and realized his shirt was damp with perspiration.

He was in London.

The war was over.

It had been his nightmare again, more vivid than ever—perhaps even more vivid than the battle itself.

Nicholas rose and shed his nightshirt, then washed in cold water in the darkness. By the time he pulled on a clean linen, his heartbeat and breathing had slowed. He listened, but the house was still silent.

At least he had not awakened anyone.

He crouched down and lifted the floorboard he had loosened when first they had come to this house. His aunt had always been curious to the point of nosiness and as a young man, he had been accustomed to more privacy.

The bundle of letters from his father, sent to him at school, was still there.

As was the money he had saved. Nicholas counted it out, knowing the sum but reassured by the feel of the bills in his hands. He caressed the letters from his father, recalling how they were filled with jests and encouragement, as well as a measure of pride.

He held his past and his present, both in this room.

It was time to take a chance upon his future.

Haynesdale would see him admitted to the gaming hell at Brooks's this very night, where the stakes were higher, and Nicholas would win.

He knew it well.

His father had left Nicholas with debts to pay and no funds, as well as an aversion to games of chance. That man had also taught Nicholas from boyhood how to play every game. They had jested once that Nicholas possessed all the luck in the family, for it seemed he could not lose. He would put aside his abhorrence of gambling for one night and one night only, to change his circumstance.

On this night, the high rollers at Brooks's would fund Nicholas' future. Even though he had to remain sober to win, he now knew he could endure the full onslaught of the nightmare for that reward.

Eliza North had given him that gift of certainty, though she had not realized as much, and it was a precious one.

~

DAMIEN DEVRIES, Duke of Haynesdale, was not accustomed to having any offer of his assistance declined. He had spent the night at White's though nothing there had provided satisfaction. He was still vexed when his carriage arrived at his home just before dawn and did not immediately descend to the street. He knew he would not sleep soon. He could not tolerate one of his mother's endless lectures about the history of her beloved roses on this day, nor could he face the solitude of his library. The last thing he needed was a brandy.

How could Miss Ballantyne be so stubborn?

He refused to consider how this woman, of all women, should be the one to so fire his blood, to stir his desire to a fever-pitch and to arouse a nobility of purpose within him that she appeared to think misguided.

How could she refuse him?

Within hours, it would be known in every drawing room that he had visited the notorious courtesan in prison and speculated widely that he was her anonymous benefactor. There was no telling how the tale might be embellished from there, but what irked Damien was that any taint to his reputation had been incurred to no purpose.

He still could not believe that she had denied him. Did she not desire assistance? Did she not trust him with the task of aiding her? Damien could not credit it. Miss Ballantyne might possess many traits both enchanting and irksome, but she was not a fool.

She had a reason.

And if he was going to right the wrong he had created, Damien had to discover what that reason might be. He resolved to visit Miss Ballantyne's home and see what might be learned from her servants. There was no point in subterfuge at this point, but he believed there might well be a justification for haste. Doubtless they would recognize him from his feint as a chimney sweep.

The hour was, sadly, too early for such an errand.

It was not, however, too late to deliver Miss Ballantyne's message to the actress at the theater.

~

A LETTER WAS BROUGHT to Eliza during her solitary breakfast. To her surprise, it was from Helena Emerson. Evidently, the younger woman wished for her company to collect a new dress from the dressmaker that afternoon. Helena was very precise about the time, which was odd.

Why was Eliza's presence necessary or even requested? If the dress was completed, the fittings would be done. It could be delivered if Lady Frances did not feel inclined to an outing on this particular day.

Eliza frowned, remembering her questions the night before about the financial situation of Lady Frances. With Damien absent, it was a good moment to consult with her mother.

As usual, the dowager was in her chamber, where she invariably remained until after luncheon. Constance DeVries was a tall and slender woman, as well as a pretty one. When they stood together, it was clear that she and Eliza were closely related, though Eliza recalled that her brothers had favored the duke more than the duchess. Her mother's once lustrous chestnut hair had always turned blonder in the summers, but now it was a silver corona. She had it arranged when she rose in the morning, with the result that she always looked as if she was in the midst of changing, when in fact, she had not yet dressed.

She was prowling around the perimeter of a large table that had been in her chamber in London for as long as Eliza could recall. Spread upon the table's surface was a large drawing, a map of sorts, of the rose garden at Haynesdale. The names of the varieties of roses were on small cards, like those that might mark the seating of guests at a large dinner party. In fact, the cards were supported by small silver stands often used for precisely that purpose.

When the dowager was not in her garden, she did not fail to think of it constantly.

Eliza's mother wore a dressing gown of periwinkle blue silk and barely glanced up from the table when Eliza appeared. She murmured a greeting, then frowned and moved one placard to the left, wincing at the result. "But then, the *Great Maiden's Blush* will be slightly compromised, for the *Celeste* will cast a shadow upon it. Such a majestic rose. I cannot bear when it suffers in the least bit." She moved the card back with dissatisfaction, and Eliza knew she had arrived during one of her mother's debates with herself about the garden.

"I wondered, *Maman*, if you could tell me about Lady Frances Dalhousie."

"Formerly the Viscountess Hexham," her mother said, propping one hand upon her hip. Her vexation, however was reserved for the rose garden. "Why did Damien feel obliged to add to the kitchens? The new wall and its incursion in the gardens put my entire scheme awry."

Eliza guessed she would have little interest from her mother before they discussed the roses and went to the table. "The kitchens were ancient, *Maman*. Damien only does the right thing. That is why the servants are so devoted to him."

Her mother harrumphed. "He could spare a thought for his mother."

"You know he does."

Her mother pointed. "You see the shadow it casts here, and this bed has been completely upended. The plants are safely bedded down for the winter, but they must be re-planted as soon as the frost is gone from the soil, and I have no plan for them! Mr. Marchand awaits my instruction."

The only person who shared her mother's passion for roses was the head gardener at Haynesdale. If a single plant did not survive, the two of them would commiserate together and likely weep buckets.

"You have less garden space," Eliza noted.

"Yes, dear, and that is the conundrum. Some of the older roses had even suckered into the border, so we have more plants and less space." She heaved a sigh. "Kitchens." She seized her teacup and drained it, though the tea was likely cold.

"What about the pavilion?" Eliza asked.

"What about the pavilion?" her mother echoed with disinterest. "There are no gardens around the pavilion."

"And I have always wondered why," Eliza said, prompting her mother to look up. She took a piece of paper and drew a circle to indicate the pavilion, a tribute to Greek architecture that existed in solitude in an area adjacent to the rose garden. "Do you remember the reflecting pool at Hampton Court?" She drew an-other larger circle around the first one.

"Lilies," her mother said. "Water lilies grow within it."

"And there is a path around it and a hedge. A most tranquil place."

"Is there not a fountain?"

"We have a pavilion instead," Eliza said. "And there could be a border of roses either immediately around the pool or on the other side of the path, inside the hedge."

"No hedge. The deer will consume it. A wall!" Constance swept away the placards with a gesture and turned over the large sheet of paper. She surveyed the room, then seized the saucer from her cup, inverted it and drew a circle around it. Eliza, well accustomed to these planning sessions, was already looking for a larger circle to trace. She removed a small mirror from the wall, one with a simple round frame, and placed it on the paper. Her mother adjusted the position before tracing around it, then nodded satisfaction when Eliza returned the mirror to the wall. They both scanned the room without finding what they sought.

"A dinner plate," Eliza said.

Her mother rang the bell and Higgins appeared shortly. "Yes, my lady."

"I need round plates," she said. "Larger than a saucer but smaller than this mirror." She considered her own words. "Or even larger than the mirror, if we plan for a truly splendid border."

The older man blinked, then peered at the paper on the table. "A new garden, my lady?"

"Perhaps around the pavilion," Eliza contributed. "With a reflecting pool."

"Like the one at Hampton Court, except with a pavilion and a rose border—if not two—and a wall instead of a hedge, but otherwise precisely the same."

Higgins bowed. "An excellent notion, my lady. I will bring plates shortly to assist."

"Have you had breakfast, *Maman*?"

"I have no time for such fripperies! This notion will change all." Her mother was arranging the placards in rows. Eliza joined her, knowing they had to be sorted by height of the plant and color of the flower.

"Perhaps breakfast at the same time, my lady?" the butler prompted.

"An excellent notion, Higgins," Eliza said, because her mother was murmuring to herself.

"An entire border of *Apothecary Roses*," the dowager mused with obvious excitement. "Completely surrounding the pool. They would be magnificent. And the scent!"

Eliza worked with her mother until Higgins returned, and the butler aided in the arrangements of the various plates so that they could be traced. He vanished with them as soon as the plan was completed.

"This is north," the dowager said. "Which means the *Great Maiden's Blush* can be against the inside of this wall, sheltered from the wind and in full sun. It will do splendidly there." She looked up suddenly, changing topics with her usual swift unpredictability. "I should invite Lady Dalhousie to visit when it is done. She will be vexed beyond measure." The dowager chuckled a little.

"That is unkind, *Maman*," Eliza said, realizing in that moment that her mother only spoke thus about the lady in question.

"She is the one who made trouble for me. Beware jealousy, Eliza. It drives women to harsh deeds."

"But she has a rose garden of repute of her own, at Hexham."

Constance shook her head. "No longer."

"How can that be?"

"Hexham was entailed. Her husband's nephew, the child of his younger brother, is the viscount now and his wife, the viscountess."

"But Lady Dalhousie goes to Hexham after the season."

"To visit as a guest," her mother said with surety. "And I would not be surprised if Hexham was no longer her destination since her nephew's wife bore their second son."

"And the house in Berkley Square?"

"From her own family, but she has only the property, such as it is. The money was all on his side and bound to Hexham." Her mother shook her head. "No, Fanny must be in considerable debt by this time. Alas, I cannot be glad of that. To be without money is a terrible situation, Eliza, and no one is deserving of it."

Eliza thought of the sandwiches and the lack of a footman and realized it all made sense.

"That was why she took the girl, of course," her mother continued easily. "It was not a gesture of affection to be sure."

Eliza blinked for she did not understand. "Helena?"

Constance looked up, eyes bright. "Of course, Helena. It was quite a coup on Fanny's part, to be sure."

"How so?"

"There is no blood between them. Frances was the sister of Captain Emerson's mother, but Helena is the daughter of Nicholas' father and that man's second wife. In many families, Frances would not have been able to take Helena, but there was no one to fight her for that ward." She shook her head. "The girl was only two when her parents died, though she must have been seven or so by the time Captain Emerson settled his father's estate and bought his commission. The debts were frightful." She frowned at the drawing. "Doubtless Frances was familiar by then."

"I do not understand," Eliza said. "If Lady Dalhousie's finances were diminished, why would she voluntarily take a ward?" She moved the yellow *Rose de Turcs* to a sunny spot on the proposed wall on the layout.

Her mother immediately repositioned it further along. "I cannot bear its deep yellow against the pink of the *Quatre Saisons*," she confided. "It should be amidst the white Albas." Then she took a breath, straightening to survey the evolving plan. "The child was always pretty. Doubtless, Frances thought to make a good match for the girl and secure her own future. She may live decades yet, you know. I certainly intend to do so, but I wed rather better."

"Is that the source of the rivalry between you?"

"Rivals? We are not *rivals*, Eliza. Frances despises me because I claimed what she desired. It is that simple."

"Papa? Because he was a duke?"

Constance smiled, forgetting her plan for the moment. Her eyes lit as they always did when she mentioned the late duke. "I did not even realize Luke's consequence when I met him. I scarcely even heard his name. I just looked into his eyes, and I knew that I had just met the man who would hold my heart forever."

"That quickly?"

"It was immediate, and later he told me that it was the same for him. We had such a great love, Eliza, and the only thing I have ever wanted for any of my children was that they would know the rapture of that bond." She came around the table and embraced Eliza. "I would never have anticipated that Frederick would be the one to claim your heart, but I am glad he did. Even though it is hard to be without one's beloved, it has to be better than never having loved thus before."

Eliza found a lump in her throat. She nodded agreement. "What about children?"

"Oh, Eliza. There is such joy in children, but there can also be such pain." Constance lifted her chin and looked into the distance, a suspicious shimmer in her eyes. "I remember when James was born. Our first and a boy, as perfect as could be, and your father's pride." Her throat worked and she blinked rapidly. "Then Reginald, so quick to make his debut in the world, to my relief, and in a hurry for all his days and nights. They were so different and yet so much the same, and I could see Luke in them in different ways. Then Damien, always inscrutable and so loyal. I was blessed to have three fine sons, and even more blessed to then have a daughter as good and true as you are, but that did not diminish the anguish of losing two of them in rapid succession, right after your father." She shook her head and her tears fell, her words husky when she continued. "Then Damien came home, wounded and I feared we would lose him, as well."

"You do not urge him to wed?"

"He will wed or not as he chooses."

"But the duchy..."

Her mother waved a hand. "I have one son and one daughter left to me, and I will love you both and defend you both until my dying breath. If you choose to marry for love, I will bless your match with all my heart. If you have children, I will pray at their christenings and spoil them at every opportunity. But I will never insist that you make any choice for my satisfaction or the sake of the duchy. I have you both and that is a treasure beyond price."

Blinking back tears, Eliza embraced her mother, feeling the dampness of her mother's tears upon her own shoulder.

"What did Lady Dalhousie want with you yesterday?" Constance asked.

"Captain Emerson asked me to chaperone his sister. I believe he thinks the task taxing for his aunt and he says that I will make a better match for Helena."

"The girl is difficult, I hear," her mother said, returning to her plans. "Be sure Fanny does not leave you to take the blame for some wild choice on Helena's part."

"She would not, surely."

Her mother looked up. "She was the first debutante to dance with your father and intended to wed him.

Then he and I met and he forgot her completely. That is the source of her enmity: she insists I stole him from her."

"But he loved you."

"Indeed. Fanny has never been interested in that detail." Her gaze strayed over the plan with enthusiasm. "Can you not escape the arrangement?"

Eliza could not lie. "I do not want to, *Maman*."

Constance looked up, her gaze locking with her daughter's, and eventually she nodded. "Because Captain Emerson was the one to ask for your assistance," she said softly. "I always wondered."

"*Maman*, it is not as you think..."

"Is it not, Eliza?"

"There is no impropriety."

"Perhaps there should be."

"*Maman!*"

"Eliza, for more than twenty years I have noticed how you looked at him. You are a widow, my dear. The rules of your debut season no longer apply." She smiled. "I wish you happiness, wherever and however you find it," she added, then appeared to be lost in the planning of her garden again.

Eliza was leaving her mother's room when that lady called after her. "If you might see to the menus, Eliza, that would be of tremendous assistance. Damien would eat beef at every meal given his choice, and Mrs. Jones would indulge him, but I would rather not begin to lo before the end of the season."

Eliza smiled, glad of the task. "I will see to it, *Maman*."

~

BERT LATIMER WAS SO ASTONISHED to find the Duke of Haynesdale at the door that his characteristic impassive expression might have been compromised.

"I have been to see her," the duke said grimly, stepping past him into the house. He halted in the foyer, leaning on his cane, his gaze assessing and his manner expectant.

Latimer closed the door and invited the duke into the front parlor with a gesture. "Your Grace?"

"I come in search of information," the duke said crisply. "Miss Ballantyne refused my assistance and I must know the reason why."

Latimer stood straight. "I would not compromise my lady's trust…" he began but the duke made an impatient gesture.

"Then she may spend years in that prison cell, and for no just cause. I know she is not a thief and I take responsibility for my part in her being charged as one. But you must perceive that the sole way to correct my error is to prove the identity of the true thief before Miss Ballantyne's hearing." He paused while Bert considered his options. "It will be on May 6, a Tuesday, and unless action is undertaken now, it will be short and she will be found guilty."

"But the true thief has left England, Your Grace."

"And his name is already known. I see no reason for Miss Ballantyne to defend him, which means there is a detail I do not know."

"She would not defend him!"

"She refused to tell me where he might be found."

"Perhaps she does not know, Your Grace."

"Perhaps there is another risk she would avoid." The duke's gaze was so steely that Bert had to drop his to the carpet. He was torn between his duty to his mistress and his desire to ensure that her best interest was served. He, too, felt the lack of information.

"I cannot breach her confidence, Your Grace."

The duke harrumphed, the noise disguising the sound of an approaching footstep. Doris was in the parlor before Latimer could stop her.

"Don't be an old fool, Bert," she chided, then curseyed to the duke. "I am Miss Ballantyne's house-keeper and cook, Mrs. Nelson," she said. "And I have heard things."

The duke smiled a little. "As all clever servants do, Mrs. Nelson. I have never thought it a betrayal of duty to confess such details when doing so would assist one's mistress or master."

"Nor do I, my lord. He came, that fiend, and I was certain she would cast him out. Anyone could tell that he meant ill to my mistress."

The duke braced both hands on his cane to listen. "Yet she did not cast Jacques Desjardins out of her home?"

"She was afraid, Your Grace."

"Doris!" It appalled Bert to admit to anyone that Miss Ballantyne possessed any weaknesses.

"She was, Bert, and you know it. He was a bad 'un, that one, wicked to his very marrow. Any woman of sense would be afraid of him. I was." Doris paused and Bert hoped she might not say more. "But she was not afraid for herself, Your Grace, though that would have been reasonable."

"Doris," Bert whispered, knowing it would come out now.

"Then for whom?" the duke demanded and Doris, typically, nudged Bert, leaving him to make the final confession.

"The first day, I was certain she would refuse to let him remain in her house," Bert admitted. "I listened, for I already despised him and I wished to hear his humili-ation." The duke nodded once in understanding, his eyes bright as he waited. "He said he had found Sylvie and that, my lord, changed all."

"Who is Sylvie?"

Bert shrugged and felt Doris do the same. "I never heard the name before, sir, but Miss Ballantyne recognized it very well. She was much more afraid after that confession."

"She defends someone, someone she perceives to be more vulnerable than herself," the duke murmured. He lifted a brow, which made him look diabolical. "Have you any notion where this Sylvie or tidings of her might be found?"

Bert shook his head, but Doris stepped forward. "She writes a letter each Christmas, Your Grace. I notice it because she is always a little upset when it is ready to be dispatched."

"To whom?" the duke demanded.

"She mails it herself, Your Grace," Bert said. "I have never seen the address."

Doris cast him a sly glance. "She left it in her chamber last year when a visitor called. It was sealed but addressed." She produced a piece of paper from the pocket of her apron and presented it to the duke. Bert was shocked. "I felt quite bold in copying the address, sir, but I feared that one day it might be of import. Secrets like that have a way of causing trouble, if I may say so, Your Grace."

"And so they do, Mrs. Nelson. You are a wise woman to anticipate as much." The duke studied the piece of paper. "A convent?"

"It looks like it, sir."

"And in France." The duke placed the paper in his pocket. "How long has she sent these annual letters? Do you know?"

"As long as we have been in her service, Your Grace," Bert replied, seeing no cause for delicacy at this point.

Anticipating his next question, he continued. "Miss Ballantyne employed both Mrs. Nelson and myself when she took her first residence in London in December 1805."

"There was a letter that first year," Doris said.

"She had been in England at least a year at that point," Bert continued. "Though I have no notion whether the letter Mrs. Nelson noticed our first Christmas was the first one dispatched to that address."

"Twelve years," the duke murmured. "That indicates a considerable obligation. Was there ever a reply?"

Bert exchanged a glance with Doris, noting the minute shake of her head. "Not to our knowledge, Your Grace," he admitted.

"Perhaps an elderly relation whose care Miss Ballantyne secured," Doris offered. "She was much concerned with the financial security of others in their later years."

"Doris!" Bert said under his breath.

"He should know, Bert. Miss Ballantyne has been uncommonly good to us, and I see no reason to hide the truth."

"Indeed," the duke said softly. "I would be honored by your trust."

"She purchased annuities for both of us several years ago, Your Grace, and often augmented them at Christmas. She said no one should be fearful of hunger in their later years."

Again, Bert caught a glimpse of a half-smile on the resolute countenance of the duke. "Indeed," he said quietly again, but this time, there was admiration in his tone. "I am fond of giving annuities myself, for much the same reason." Evidently having decided upon some course, his manner changed. He inclined his head crisply and turned toward the door. "I thank you both for your assistance.

Miss Ballantyne has asked that an actress named Ophelia Pearl should call upon her. I sought her at the theater, but without success. Do you know how to find her?"

"We do, Your Grace. I will ensure that the message is received."

The duke evidently had anticipated as much. He continued to speak as he headed for the front door. "I will be leaving London shortly, but Miss Ballantyne's continued comfort remains a concern of mine. I will leave word with my solicitor, Mr. Greene, that you may be required to contact him for assistance and ensure that he is prepared to offer same. He will also be advised of how to reach me if you recall any other detail that you believe to be helpful."

"I thank you, Your Grace, for your assistance," Latimer said, unable to keep an increment of relief from his tone. It could not hurt to have a powerful man upon Miss Ballantyne's side.

Doris showed no such restraint and for once, Bert could not fault her for that. She seized the duke's hand and dropped to one knee before him, kissing his ring as if he were the Pope himself. "I thank you, Your Grace," she said, her voice tremulous. "She is the best mistress and kinder than anyone knows. She does not deserve this fate."

"And that is why we must see the matter repaired, Mrs. Nelson," the duke said smoothly. He urged Doris to her feet and held fast to her hand as he smiled at her. "I will see it done. You may rely upon me."

They stood together and watched the duke stride toward his carriage, his gait distinctive for the way he favored one leg. Bert closed the door only after the duke had vanished into his carriage, feeling that the house echoed with the absence of their mistress.

"I believe him, Bert," Doris said with fervor.

"As do I, Doris. As do I." Bert took a shaking breath. "I will send word immediately to Miss Pearl."

Doris frowned. "I think, Bert, you should write to that address. Miss Ballantyne will not be able to do as much, I wager, and His Grace should find a ready reception if he is to help."

Latimer considered this. It was not in his nature to meddle where he should not, but there was good sense in the suggestion. "I will," he bowed.

Doris smiled. "And I will put the kettle on. We both have need of a strong cup of tea, to be sure."

CHAPTER 7

*N*icholas was tired, having slept poorly, but more importantly, he could not locate Haynesdale. He wanted to verify their arrangements for the evening at Brooks's. So much rode on this evening's success. He had called early at the duke's home, only to be told that Haynesdale was not in. He had not even seen Eliza, though he thought he had heard her voice from the upper floors of the house.

He stopped at White's, but Haynesdale had not been seen there since the night before. Where the deuce was the man? Again, he considered the possibility of Haynesdale having taken a new mistress and wondered where he might find the woman in question, if she existed.

On the way out, he paused at the betting book, since there had been a cluster of laughing men gathered around it on his arrival. What was the bet of the moment?

There was one that had solicited a great deal of activity, which was remarkable since it had only been added that morning.

Mr. Anthony Davidson wagers £10 that Mr. Ethan

> *Melbourne will be married to Miss Helena Emerson before Easter Sunday.*

Below it was a long string of additional wagers, either in agreement or in dispute.

Nicholas was startled by the claim, not just because it involved his sister but because Easter Sunday was less than three weeks away. As far as he knew, no offer of marriage had been made by Mr. Melbourne. If there was to be a wedding, then banns had to be called three Sundays in a row in advance of the wedding.

Surely, he could not have missed the publishing of the banns for Helena's wedding or the news of her pending nuptials?

Ten pounds was a considerable sum to wager on a comparative trifle—at least, it was a trifle for those other than Melbourne and Helena. This Davidson either had little doubt of his triumph or was reckless with his money.

Perhaps it was a cruel joke at his sister's expense, and one that Melbourne either knew about or supported. Indeed, Melbourne's wager in favor of Davidson's assertion was on the list, as well.

Did Helena know? Or did this rogue make sport of her?

Fortunately, Nicholas had been forced to endure the tale of the dress to be collected this very afternoon, and Helena's insistence upon the timing of that errand, and knew precisely where to find his sister on this day— who would be in the company of Mrs. North.

He refused to give credence to the immediate improvement in his spirits, just at the prospect of seeing Eliza shortly.

Whatever Helena confessed, Nicholas would ensure that this travesty of a tale was removed from the betting book at White's. He was not reluctant to offer encouragement or even a challenge to Mr. Melbourne either.

~

Dear Mrs. Oliver—

I thank you for entrusting pages from your book manuscript to me for my perusal and review. I think the subject a most broad one, but find that these provided excerpts barely touch upon the subject of seduction. I should hope that there is more detail in the remainder of the book and would be delighted for the chance to review it.

In addition, I am aware from my years as the wife of a parson that many wives currently struggle with the hidden legacies of war left with their husbands and lovers. It is hardly my place to guide your work, but I believe it would be very helpful to have some advice in overcoming such injuries —or even healing them—in the men who so valiantly served Britain in recent times. When meeting with such ladies in my previous capacity, I would have welcomed a more specific guide to offer them consolation and assistance.

I look forward to your reply and thank you for your confidence.

My regards,
Mrs. Eliza Worth
Widow of Reverend Frederick Worth

"SHE WANTS MORE DETAIL," Catherine said, after reading the reply.

She and Eurydice Montgomery were in Catherine's father's office at Carruthers & Carruthers. Catherine had retreated there with the portfolio returned from Mrs. North, having recognized it immediately. Eurydice had arrived shortly thereafter, purportedly seeking a new book. In truth, she had visited the shop daily since they had heard of Miss Ballantyne's arrest. The floor vibrated with the beat of the printing presses so there was little chance of their conversation being overheard, but the women kept their voices low all the same.

"Of course, she does," Eurydice replied. "Miss Ballantyne is always right about such matters."

They looked as one at the sheaf of pages the lady in question had surrendered to them when last they had seen her.

"Have you shown them to your father?" Eurydice asked.

"Not yet," Catherine admitted. "I showed them to Rhys and he was greatly entertained by their content." She felt her cheeks heat, for he had also been determined to try some of the suggestions provided there.

Eurydice smiled, clearly reading her thoughts.

"I would have a lady's view before presenting them to my father, the better to argue my case," Catherine continued.

"Here is your opportunity."

"Should we send them all? She might be overwhelmed by the detail."

"She is a widow, and she has consoled women married to returning soldiers. I cannot imagine that any intimate detail will surprise her."

Catherine nodded and put the newer sheets into the portfolio. "I suppose I will have to feign Mrs. Oliver's hand again."

"You did it very well," Eurydice said cheerfully.

But Catherine barely heard her friend's words, for she was astonished to spot a new arrival at her father's shop. At first glimpse, it appeared that Mrs. Oliver had come Carruthers & Carruthers, though that was impossible while Miss Ballantyne was incarcerated. Catherine led the way from the office, portfolio in hand, Eurydice fast behind. "Mrs. Oliver! How might we be of assistance?"

On closer scrutiny, there was something not quite right about that woman's appearance. It was Mrs. Oliver, yet not quite. Could Mrs. Oliver have an imposter? That any person should disguise herself under a disguise was difficult to believe.

The woman who appeared to be Mrs. Oliver looked up, her eyes gleaming, and made her way toward Catherine. "I should say so! Have you my books?" she demanded, her voice rising above the subdued sounds of conversation in the shop. "Has service improved in this establishment, or are matters as slack as ever they were?" The barest ghost of a smile lifted the corner of her mouth as she dropped a parcel onto the counter. "And I can only hope that the quality of your offerings has improved. The pages fell right out of these volumes most recently borrowed by me. Such workmanship is appalling."

Catherine opened the satchel and smiled in relief to see the number of handwritten pages within. Whoever this woman was, she had been in contact with Miss Ballantyne—who evidently was well enough to continue with her book.

"And yet, you return as regularly as the sun rises in the east, Mrs. Oliver," she said sweetly. "We are honored by your custom."

"And so you should be, Miss Carruthers," she replied, her imitation so good that Eurydice snorted audibly.

This had to be the actress who had aided Miss Ballantyne with the disguise in the first place.

However she had come by these pages, Catherine was vastly relieved.

~

HELENA'S VISIT to the dressmaker with Mrs. North might have been a military mission for all the precision of its execution. They did not even use the duke's large carriage, but a small one, and the handsome footman who had smiled at her the previous evening was not with them.

Helena had a feeling Mrs. North had ensured that.

She could have endured all of this, if they had not progressed so quickly that she might miss the planned encounter with Mr. Melbourne. She could not bear it if she lost the opportunity to see him again! She had planned the meeting with care and it might all go awry. Mrs. Worth seemed bent upon collecting the dress with haste and returning Helena to her aunt's house with speed. Indeed, the older woman appeared to be distracted by some other concern.

Until the carriage halted at the dressmaker's shop and the door was opened by none other than Nicholas. Helena watched Mrs. North's expression light and guessed that there were other reasons for that lady undertaking this task.

Then she saw her brother's hard expression. His disapproval was fixed upon her. Helena forgot Mrs. North in the face of greater concerns.

If Nicholas was angry, she could lose her sole ally in all the world and that could not be endured. She would say whatever was necessary to placate him, whether it was true or not.

~

NICHOLAS! As delighted as Eliza was to see him again so soon, his forbidding expression was unexpected. Gone was the man whose eyes sparkled as he teased her. The man framed in the doorway of the carriage was deadly serious and fairly simmering with outrage. Eliza hoped fervently that she was not the one who had prompted this response. His lips were drawn to a taut line and his attention was fixed upon his sister.

Helena flushed and lifted her chin with familiar defiance, evidence that she at least guessed the reason for his appearance.

"Captain Emerson," Eliza said.

"Mrs. North," he said, polite despite his mood, inclining his head to her. "I would speak with my sister, if you do not mind the intrusion to your errand."

"Of course not."

Helena clutched Eliza's hand. "Mrs. Worth must remain, as she is my chaperone at your own request, Nicholas."

His eyes flashed blue fire, then he stepped into the carriage, closing the door behind himself and taking the seat opposite them. It seemed the interior of the carriage was vastly diminished and that Nicholas fairly filled the space. The air crackled with tension. Eliza felt Helena's hand tremble but the girl was undaunted.

Nicholas spoke quietly but with heat. "There is a wager upon the books at White's that Mr. Ethan Melbourne will be wed to Miss Helena Emerson before Easter Sunday."

Eliza caught her breath at these tidings but Helena's lips merely set.

"What do you know of this?" Nicholas demanded. "The odds appear to be in the gentleman's favor, yet I know of no such match having been made."

"Nor do I," Helena said, her words breathless. Eliza wondered whether she told the truth. "Do you think I should have been dancing at Almack's last night if I knew myself to be betrothed?"

Nicholas settled back, his gaze simmering. "And yet you are not completely surprised."

Helena opened her mouth and closed it again. She

pulled her hand from Eliza's and smoothed her skirts. "I have suspected his regard."

"Easter is less than three weeks away, Helena. If this match were to be made in such a timely matter, the banns should have been called."

Helena shrugged, feigning indifference. "Perhaps Mr. Melbourne has a special license." It was clear that even the possibility pleased her greatly.

"Does he?"

"I do not know."

"Helena," he growled. "This is no jest! It is no small thing for your name to be listed in the wager book..."

"No, it is rather exciting."

"Miss Emerson!" Eliza could not disguise her shock.

Helena, though, was watching Nicholas. "What will you do if I tell you I know nothing of this?"

"What do you imagine I will do? I will defend your honor as is right and just."

"A duel?" Helena paled. "You might kill him."

Nicholas was resolute. "If he has so tainted your reputation by choice and my honor by association, then that may be the price he pays for such indiscretion."

"And what if I knew of it?" the girl asked quietly. Again, Eliza had no notion of the truth.

"Then I shall abandon you forever to Aunt Fanny's care," Nicholas said firmly. "Once she hears of this outrageous wager, she may well lock you in the cellar for the duration."

"She would not," the girl insisted, but there was a thread of doubt in her tone. "You would not!"

"Did you know or did you not, Helena?" Nicholas demanded, his tone so hard that his sister flinched.

Eliza watched the girl weigh her options. She could not fathom how much Helena knew, but the girl knew something of Mr. Melbourne's intention. She was not fully surprised, and unless Eliza missed her guess, Helena was thrilled by this development.

She supposed that many a maiden inclined to romance would find the idea of a duel being fought over her to be romantic. She might think less of the result, for Eliza would not have wagered against Nicholas.

Evidently Aunt Fanny's cellar was the more fearful possibility, for Helena straightened.

"I did not know of it," she said.

"Then the assault upon your honor is clear and must be avenged," Nicholas said. He left the carriage with purpose, offering his hand to Eliza. His stance was straight and his manner commanding.

When she was beside him, Eliza dared to look into his eyes. He was as determined as she had ever seen him. "Never in anger, Captain Emerson," she murmured.

"Never," he agreed crisply, his gaze cool. "In matters of war, passion is a poor companion."

Their gazes held for a moment and she glanced at his mouth, recalling his kiss and yearning for another. She saw him catch his breath and his eyes narrowed, then he turned to offer Helena his assistance. She was achingly proud of his honor and integrity, had no doubt of his skill, but feared for him all the same.

It would be wrong for him to be injured in a duel after he had survived the war.

The street was quite busy and crowded with the bustle of shoppers. More than one halted to take a view of the ducal carriage, doubtless seeking a glimpse of Damien. Several ladies surveyed Nicholas with admiration and more than one dandy smiled at Helena. Eliza could only think of Nicholas' intention and her fears for him.

For her part, Helena did not have the wits to keep silent. She appealed to her brother despite the surrounding activity, apparently oblivious to those who stopped to look and listen. "Promise me, Nicholas, that you will not..."

"I promise only to see your virtue defended," he said, interrupting her firmly. He closed the door of the carriage and Thomson clicked his tongue to the horses. Nicholas then looked over Helena's shoulder, his expression revealing that he recognized someone. His brows rose. "And it appears the matter shall be resolved soon."

Eliza spun at the same time as Helena, only to find Mr. Melbourne himself strolling toward them. The younger man was swinging his walking stick with such a confident swagger that she could not believe he had happened upon them by coincidence. Helena's pleasure only confirmed her suspicion.

Somehow, Helena had arranged that they should encounter the young man while on this errand. They must have contrived the meeting during their dance the night before.

"This is why you insisted so closely upon the time," Eliza said in an undertone.

"I have no idea what you mean, Mrs. North," the girl protested, then smiled a welcome at the approaching young man. Mr. Melbourne began to lift his hat and a smile curved his lips.

Nicholas, however, intercepted Melbourne's path before he could speak.

~

THERE WAS nothing Nicholas despised more than a cocksure scoundrel, except perhaps one who had fooled Helena into supporting his offense. If this fop meant to take advantage of Helena or damage her reputation, even if she was a willing participant, Nicholas would see that Melbourne understood the magnitude of his error.

Melbourne surveyed him with a measure of disdain, as if finding something lacking in his appearance, then smiled slightly. "Captain Emerson. I did not expect to meet you on this day." He reached out and brushed an imaginary piece of lint from Nicholas' shoulder. "I can recommend an excellent tailor if you seek one."

Nicholas felt his jaw tighten. He liked fine clothing as well as any man, but his current situation was one that called for frugality.

"You must have expected to meet me at some point when you supported the lie that dishonors my sister," he said calmly, instead of taking the bait.

The other man was visibly startled. "What lie?"

"There is a wager on the books at White's that you will be wed to my sister by Easter." Nicholas watched Melbourne's gaze slip away. The man was a veritable eel. "Do not suggest that you are unaware of it. I saw your wager listed beneath. Doubtless this Mr. Davidson is an acquaintance of yours. Who had the idea?"

Melbourne paled slightly. "You did not tell her?"

"I thought it better that I did than someone else. My aunt will doubtless hear of it at some point. She is a great collector of tales of scandal and I would prefer to have the matter resolved before that unhappy day."

Melbourne dropped his voice to a confidential tone. "But you are not a member of White's, Captain Emerson. How can you have seen this?" He smirked a little. "Are you entirely certain of your claim? Or do you repeat a rumor without conviction?"

"I saw the bet myself this morning. I have been invited to White's of late as a guest of a member, the Duke of Haynesdale," Nicholas replied, bristling that this dandy would try to diminish him. "At least you might have the honor not to deny your offence."

"It is no offence! It was but a jest!"

"I confess I find myself offended but not amused. Your jest is a failure, sir."

Melbourne shook his head. "There is no need for such trouble, Captain," he said in a soothing and patronizing manner. "I will speak to Davidson about its removal this very day as you did not find the jest amusing."

"As you wish. I will see you at dawn tomorrow, at Wimbleton Commons."

The younger man's shock was clear. "You cannot mean to duel over this."

"I most assuredly do." A group of pedestrians had gathered around, listening, doubtless drawn by the word duel. "I challenge you, Mr. Ethan Melbourne, over the honor of my sister, Miss Helena Emerson, against the insult you have made to her."

There was an outburst of chatter from those gathered around and one gentleman shouted "Hear, hear!"

Nicholas inclined his head to the astonished Melbourne. "I leave the choice of pistols or swords to you. The Duke of Haynesdale will be my second."

Melbourne's lips tightened. "Anthony Davidson will be mine."

"Excellent. I will see you before dawn." Nicholas pivoted, his challenge delivered and his blood fairly boiling.

"But you cannot mean this, sir," Melbourne protested.

"As you surely meant to impugn the reputation of a lady, I do mean this." Nicholas tipped his hat and retreated.

Helena's eyes were round with wonder. She might have reached out to appeal to him, but Eliza pulled her back.

"It is too late for that," Eliza whispered to his sister,

and alarm finally dawned in Helena's eyes. Eliza, though, was solemn, a glow of pride in her gaze. "I wish you the very best of fortune in this endeavor, Captain Emerson."

He bowed to her. "I thank you, Mrs. North, and would not delay your errand any longer." With that, he retreated, knowing that he had need of a walk and a ride to calm his temper.

In point of fact, Sterling had been neglected of late.

ELIZA ARRIVED home to find Lady Wentworth taking tea with her mother. She had a vague recollection of that lady and was glad to renew her acquaintance. The two older women were in the midst of an intense review of the situations of former friends and acquaintances, leaving Eliza to simply enjoy her tea and listen.

Her thoughts were still churning after Nicholas' challenge to Mr. Melbourne. Helena had fairly worn her out with questions and speculation at the dressmaker, despite her admonitions for the girl to hold her tongue, and Eliza was certain that all of London knew more of the matter than they should by this point.

It had been a relief to cancel their planned outing to the theater the next evening.

She was terrified for Nicholas, though she supposed it would have been more reasonable to be fearful for Melbourne.

Her mother turned to her with a smile and Eliza hoped she had not missed some critical detail in the conversation. "I have invited Lady Wentworth to join us for dinner on Saturday evening," she said. "Do you think, Eliza, that you might oversee the arrangements?"

"I would be delighted to do so, *Maman*. Do you wish to have any other guests?"

"You might invite Miss Emerson, since you have taken a responsibility for her." Her mother considered this. "And her brother, of course. We cannot have her making the journey alone and Captain Emerson is a better choice than Lady Dalhousie."

Lady Wentworth smiled into her tea. "Was it Miss Emerson you escorted to Almack's?" she asked.

"Yes. It is her second season and the family would like to see her settled."

"Very pretty girl," Lady Wentworth said.

"She is a beauty," Eliza agreed.

"And sufficiently bold to accept a waltz." Lady Wentworth sipped her tea, her gaze knowing. Eliza should have guessed that the incident would be noticed.

"I was grateful for her brother's assistance in intervening."

"That was neatly done," Lady Wentworth noted with a small smile. "And what of that partner?"

"Mr. Melbourne," Eliza said. "I am a little puzzled by him, to be sure."

"And so you should be," Lady Wentworth said almost beneath her breath.

Here was a person Eliza could ask for advice. "I understand by his own confession that Lady Dalhousie did not approve of his attentions to her niece last season, though Miss Emerson seems to welcome them."

"Fanny is many things, but she is not a fool," Lady Wentworth said.

"Mr. Melbourne asked me whether the change in his circumstances might influence Lady Dalhousie's view of his suit."

Lady Wentworth put down her teacup. "What change?"

"His inheritance, after the death of his father." Eliza was confused by the older woman's sharper tone. "I should think a greater measure of financial security might alter her view..."

"His father is not dead," Lady Wentworth said with authority. "I saw the baron at Bath not a fortnight ago and he was as hale as ever." She shook her head primly. "As for an inheritance, I have heard of none. Indeed, his father is as much of a spendthrift as his sons, of which Mr. Ethan Melbourne is the youngest. I doubt there will be a shilling for them to share once the baron leaves this sphere."

It was Eliza's turn to rattle her teacup in the saucer. "It was *all* a falsehood, from one end of the tale to the other," she whispered, continuing when her mother's expression turned questioning. "I sensed that there was some untruth in his confession, but I assumed it was a detail, perhaps the sum of his inheritance, not the entirety of the tale."

Lady Wentworth took a cake with a composure Eliza could not emulate. "How much did he claim to have inherited?"

"Six thousand pounds per year."

Lady Wentworth was startled into laughter. "There is an audacity about him, to be sure."

Eliza set her cup and saucer aside, recalling Helena's claim.

"What is it, my dear?"

"Helena told me that she would elope if her aunt did not find any of her choices to be suitable."

Lady Wentworth finished her cake, shaking her head wisely. "You have nothing to fear on that account, Mrs. North. Your charge is penniless or close to it. Mr. Melbourne will choose an heiress, for he has only his debts to recommend him and no taste for economy."

But Eliza thought of the wager Nicholas had seen at White's and could only wonder at Melbourne's choice. She told the older ladies who chut-chutted into their tea. "There is no accounting for the folly of young dandies," her mother said.

"Doubtless Mr. Melbourne has wagered to his own advantage," Lady Wentworth said, reaching to pat Eliza's hand. "Your charge has no fortune, my dear, and is utterly safe as a result."

"Imagine if she was the heiress of Hexham!" her mother said and they laughed together, well assured of the improbability of that.

All the same, Eliza was not entirely reassured.

Perhaps she was simply afraid for Nicholas.

IF THIS WAS to be the last night of Nicholas' existence, he could find little fault with it. The cards came to him with perfect ease: indeed, he only had to think which card would be best to welcome it to his hand. The gaming room at Brooks's was full but not crowded, many of the gentlemen being regular visitors to that establishment. Wine and brandy flowed with abandonment, but Nicholas avoided both. His thoughts were clear, his playing decisive and his success worthy of note by all.

Haynesdale had accompanied him, of course, but sat with his back to the wall, avidly watching the play. He had taken a single brandy but swirled it in his glass, sipping of it so slowly as to make it last all the night long.

Nicholas lost track of time. There were only the cards and the game—and the thrilling sense that his winnings were mounting steadily. He was vaguely aware of Haynesdale's murmured comments.

"Always thus."

"Truly remarkable."

"From boyhood."

And the cards came to him as if summoned.

By midnight, he had won two thousand pounds, but the game was in its infancy as yet. The gaming room was windowless and dark, the shadows deep in the corners. It was sufficiently warm that many had shed their jackets. Nicholas remained in his full attire, his attention locked upon the game.

Players came and left, many of them known to Nicholas only by name. Lord Standish offered to buy him a brandy when that gentleman left the table after losing a thousand pounds, mostly to Nicholas, but Nicholas politely declined. Not a drop would cross his lips until he left the table.

Perhaps not even then.

He had the unbidden thought that Eliza would be pleased by his progress, then wondered whether—or if —he would see her again. He and Haynesdale had agreed to leave Brooks's for Wimbleton, and there was a chance that Melbourne would have a lucky shot.

Nicholas dared not consider it in this moment.

There could only be the cards.

The Earl of Queenston seemingly could not bear to be defeated by a mere soldier, even one of gentle blood. That man settled opposite Nicholas, determined to regain his early losses. He should have stepped away from the table, but the gleam was in his eye and Nicholas guessed that the earl would play until he was penniless.

Nicholas' next four thousand pounds came all from the earl. The other players had left the game but lingered to watch. The earl had shed his coat and his vest, then pushed up his sleeves. His brow was damp and his hand shook when he reached for his wine. He played with a reckless abandon that he should not have trusted, repeatedly declaring his conviction that his luck would change.

It did not.

Nicholas was aware of the tide of emotions in the

room. There were those, assuredly, who did not like the earl and actively wished for his defeat. There were others offended that a mere officer was not only in their club but daring to win. There were whispers of the earl's familiarity with the moneylenders of Howard and Gibbs, and Nicholas half-heard a mention of the wager about his sister at White's. Of course, someone mentioned his challenge to Melbourne, which was viewed as either an excellent endorsement of his character or an example of a soldier reaching beyond his place. The air fairly swirled with innuendo, but Nicholas kept his eyes on the cards.

Finally, against every expectation, the earl cast down his hand with disgust. He had lost again, and Nicholas had won nine thousand pounds in the course of the evening. The earl was teased by his fellows that his jacket was of some value and scowled at them for that. The hour was late, or early, and Nicholas thought it a timely moment to leave the club.

"Not so quickly as that, sir," the earl protested. He drew himself up taller in his seat, his expression belligerent. "I play for Greenhaven."

"Greenhaven?" Nicholas repeated, not knowing the name.

"The manor at Queenston and my family home. You will not win that from me, sir. My ancestors would not permit such affrontery."

"I have nothing of such value to wager against it."

The earl smiled. "I will accept every penny you have won on this night as your wager."

A manor!

Nicholas was sorely tempted, but took a moment to consider his course. It was greed that destroyed the futures of players, an obsession with gains that kept them from leaving the table when it was prudent to do so. His father had often lost his way in the tangled pathways of avarice and honor, and Nicholas had lived with the result. But his thoughts were clear on this night, and if he lost, he would lose only what had not been his mere hours before.

It was a risk to take.

"I accept," he said and gestured for the cards to be dealt.

For this match, the room was silent, tense with the interest of those who gathered to watch. No one so much as coughed and play proceeded quickly. Even the earl seemed to have regained his wits: he played with a surety he had not shown earlier. But still the cards loved Nicholas. The game tended steadily in his direction, gaining vigor with each passing moment. The earl laid down his final hand with a flourish and a dare in his expression.

And Nicholas bested him readily.

The gamesroom broke into cheers and guffaws. The earl's face turned ruddy and he might have charged from the table, but Nicholas spoke. "A moment, my lord."

"I go to arrange your payment, as befits a gentleman," the earl said with acrimony.

"And I cannot accept Greenhaven," Nicholas said, seeing relief light the older man's eyes. "I know what it is, sir, to surrender a beloved holding and I will not bring that plight to any other man."

"But I have lost and you must have your gain."

"I could not accept more than nine thousand pounds, which was the sum of my own wager."

The earl smiled and offered his hand across the table. "I accept your offer, sir, and salute your gamesmanship."

The room dissolved into murmurs of satisfaction and Nicholas' hand was shaken by every member of the club present. But thirty minutes later, he was leaving with Haynesdale, matching his pace to that of the duke. The night was quiet and the air cool. A fog was rolling in from the river and Haynesdale waved down the sole hackney on the street.

"Well done, Emerson," he said once they were in the cab and en route to Haynesdale House. "I never saw a man so fortunate as you at cards." He shook his head. "Eighteen thousand pounds. What shall you do with such a sum?"

"I have a notion," Nicholas admitted. "But first there is a task to be done."

"Ah yes, the unfortunate Melbourne."

"He is not unfortunate as yet."

"I have little doubt that he soon will be. Will you aim to kill or simply to maim?"

Nicholas smiled. "I thought to give him a warning."

Haynesdale nodded approval. "Of course, he is likely to be more serious. I wonder what his skill might be."

"We shall learn soon enough."

Haynesdale regarded Nicholas with a smile. "You are never daunted, are you?"

"Fear serves no purpose. It is better to consider the matter, make a choice and proceed. One must accept that the result may be otherwise than one hopes." He shrugged. If he were to die this morning, he at least had the satisfaction of one kiss from Eliza.

Haynesdale consulted his watch. "We should leave in an hour or so. Will you have a drink with me?"

Nicholas shook his head. "I would brush Sterling, if you do not mind."

"Of course, I do not mind. He is your horse."

"But in your stable."

Haynesdale waved off this detail and they continued in silence. Nicholas knew he had to ask. "Will you take the money for me?" he asked softly. "If all goes awry, it must go to support Helena. She cannot hold it herself, you understand, for I fear she inherited my father's inability to have a penny without spending it."

Haynesdale smiled. "You may rely upon me."

"There is another thousand pounds in my room at Aunt Fanny's," Nicholas confessed, then told his friend where to find it. He surrendered the notes he had won and Haynesdale tucked them away before the cab halted before the house.

"I have every confidence that I will be returning these to you shortly," Haynesdale said and Nicholas smiled. They shook hands, agreed to depart in an hour, and he strode to the alley at the back of the house. An hour to gather his thoughts was more than sufficient, and he would be glad to spend that time doing a task he favored above all others—grooming a horse.

ELIZA COULD NOT SLEEP.

She could not cease to fret about the pending duel. As confident as she was of Captain Emerson's abilities and as much as she understood his justification, there was an uncertainty about the result that agitated her. What if Melbourne won? What if Nicholas was injured?

What if either of them were killed?

She ate a light supper with her mother and retired early, her own interest in the arrangement of the new gardens utterly exhausted. She tried to read, but could not concentrate. She had no patience with her needlework. She had no letters to write, and no gloves to mend. Instead, she stood at the window, the light extinguished, watching for something she could not name, her thoughts spinning.

And so it was that she was at the darkened window when the cab arrived. She saw Damien and Nicholas descend to the street and shake hands heartily. Damien approached the front steps and she heard his greeting to Higgins when he was out of her view. Nicholas, however, marched down the street to the corner, then turned crisply down the next.

Was he walking to his aunt's home?

It could not be long before the two men departed for Wimbleton. Perhaps Nicholas went to the stables. The access to Three King's Yard was directly behind the house, on Davies Street. The captain could walk around the block and head toward the house in the back route to reach the stables. Would he do as much?

Eliza reckoned he would.

She left her room, darting down the silent hall and into the guest chamber at the back of the house. She crossed the room in darkness and looked out the window. The entrance to Three King's Yard was visible from this window and she saw the distinctive silhouette of Captain Emerson as he entered the alley.

He was going to the stables, where his horse was boarded.

This granted her an opportunity to speak with him.

And though she hoped for the best and believed in his abilities, there was always a possibility of ill-fortune. Given that, there was one confession Eliza had to make while yet she could.

CHAPTER 8

Eliza fairly flew back to her room and dressed quickly. Though she had no desire to summon a maid at this hour, she had dressed without one before. She fastened the back of a dress that was slightly too large and wriggled into it, rolled up the braid of her hair, and seized a heavy cloak that would ensure her modesty. She carried her boots and crept down the stairs, only donning them in the shadows at the back door of the house.

It was ten feet to the stables, which glowed with golden light. She could hear Thomson snoring, for his room was over the stables, and Tupper, the stablemaster, was awake late and pacing. A boy sat at the door, keeping watch, and nodded at her appearance. Another was sweeping out a stall, pushing straw and manure into the alley with a broom. Both carriages were in the shadows at one end of the stables, and she could hear the low murmur of a familiar male voice.

Nicholas!

"I have a message for Captain Emerson," she told the boy and he pointed down the length of the stables.

"Just there, my lady. With Sterling."

Of course.

Eliza could see a light in a distant stall, the golden glow from the lantern spilling into the central corridor of the stables. The stables were warm, smelling of straw and horseflesh, a welcome reminder of days in the country. Nicholas had shed his jacket, for she saw the distinctive red of his regimentals cast over the end of the stall, and he was talking to his horse in a low murmur. When she reached the stall, she simply stood and admired him for a long moment, taking advantage of the fact that he was unaware of her presence.

The stallion was a magnificent beast, larger than many with a proud lift to his head. His coloring was striking, being so pale a grey as to be almost luminous, with black hooves, mane and tail. He was of the strain of dapples from Southpoint, which had always been vigorously healthy steeds, and much sought-after for their appearance. The stallion was trim and perfectly muscled, the very image of an ideal horse.

Nicholas himself was just as fine to Eliza's view. He had rolled up his shirt sleeves and she saw the tanned power of his arms. His dark blond hair was tousled and he worked with purpose, brushing down the horse. She smiled as she watched him work, liking the economy and grace of his movements, that he was both gentle and firm with the horse. Indeed, the creature clearly trusted him. Nicholas took the horse's foreleg between his own as she watched, bending over to clean and polish the hoof, as a farrier might. In so doing, he unwittingly granted her a glimpse of his bare chest down the front of his chemise.

Eliza caught her breath and Nicholas looked up at the sound, his gaze darkening when it locked with her own. "My lady," he murmured, releasing the horse's foot to straighten, then bowed. He pushed a hand through his hair and she sensed that he was discomfited. "I did not think to see you here."

"Would you prefer that I was not?"

"No," he replied with gratifying speed. He looked toward the stable boys then back at her. "But I would not see any taint upon your name on my account."

"And I could not have you depart for a duel without seeing you again."

Nicholas said nothing then, simply watched her as if she was a vision that might suddenly vanish. Around them the horses made their quiet night sounds, shuffling in the straw, snorting, shaking their heads. Sterling gave an impatient stamp, attracting Nicholas' attention again, and that man returned to brushing the steed's sides.

"Are you afraid?" Eliza asked.

He smiled at the very notion. "Of Melbourne? I think not."

"But you could die before the dawn."

"And how is that different from every other moment of every other day?"

"I suppose it is not," Eliza ceded, moving to the end of the stall. Nicholas evaded her gaze, working with purpose, even moving to the other side of the horse so that Sterling was between them.

"Tell me a secret, Captain Emerson," Eliza invited, feeling bold.

He eyed her over the horse's silver back. "A secret?" She nodded. "Whose secret?"

"One of yours, of course."

"What if I have no secrets?" He turned his attention to his labor in this moment, as sure a sign that he would deflect her interest as there might be.

"Everyone has a secret." She spoke with conviction and knew he noticed.

"Even you, Mrs. North?" He glanced up, his expression teasing.

"Oh yes." Eliza smiled. "I have a very big secret, one I have never shared with anyone."

Nicholas met her gaze openly, propping one hand on his hip. "I confess myself astonished. I thought you of all people were precisely who and what you seem to be."

"Oh, I am, but nonetheless, I have a secret."

She could see that he was intrigued.

"Yet you do not confess it."

"It would hardly be a secret if I did as much."

"Is it a wicked secret?"

"Some might say as much," she ceded, to whet his appetite. "But I was enquiring after *your* secret."

He bent to examine the hoof of the other foreleg, vanishing from her view. "Why would you imagine that I should have a secret?"

"Because I suspect everyone does."

"And they should all surrender those secrets to you?"

Eliza shook her head. "Not everyone. I'm not interested in their secrets. I am, however, interested in yours."

"Why?"

She pretended to consider this. "Because I fear this morning's events, Captain Emerson, and I would have truth between us, for once and for all."

He stood abruptly, his gaze dark. "Why?"

"Because some secrets should not be kept forever. I understand your reticence, so I will go first and surrender my secret to you."

"I am listening, Mrs. North."

"All the same, I must whisper it, lest another overhear it." She pursued him around the horse, thinking he might contrive a way to evade her, but Nicholas stood watching her, an intriguing light in his eyes.

"You are bold in the shadows, Mrs. North," he murmured and she wondered whether she was the only one thinking of that kiss in the carriage.

"Indeed, I am," she agreed, a little breathless, then laid a hand upon his arm. Nicholas did not move away, so she let her hand slide from his elbow to his wrist, his skin warm beneath her fingertips. He might have been struck to stone, but he did not evade her touch, and when she looked up, she saw that his eyes had darkened to indigo.

She watched him swallow and leaned ever closer, stretching up to whisper in his ear. "My secret, Captain Emerson, is that I did not wed for love." He drew back slightly, looking down at her in confusion, his expression so intense that she did not even wish to blink. "I never loved my husband, not like that. I was fond of Frederick, to be sure, but ours was not a match of the heart."

Nicholas blinked, visibly shocked. "But you said…"

"I did. I lied," she confessed. "I lied to my father that he would allow the match."

"You lied?"

He was so incredulous that she could only smile and nod.

Nicholas shook his head. "But why?"

"Because my heart was broken." Eliza took a breath, fearful of his reaction but knowing she had to continue. "The man I loved with all my heart did not hold me in similar affection. I chose to wed Frederick, who professed to admire me, in the hope that I might at least have children." She felt her tears rise and bowed her head. "But that was not to be. Frederick was not interested in fathering children. He believed he had sufficient work to do in the world without bringing more souls into it." She lifted her head and dared to look at Nicholas. He had not moved and she could not read his expression. She swallowed. "So, now he is gone and I am alone, without either husband or children."

"You might yet have both."

"I might. But if I wed again, I will not compromise. It will be true love or solitude, as simple as that." She slid her hand up Nicholas' arm, certain he had understood her implication, but he turned abruptly back to the horse.

"I can only wish you luck, Mrs. North," he said crisply.

Vexing man! Despite her hopes, Nicholas clearly still did not hold her in affection.

And what infernal advice from Mrs. Oliver. The confession of a secret had been of no merit in her campaign at all. Why would he not simply seduce her and give her that satisfaction at least?

In annoyance, Eliza took a step closer. "I thank you for that, Captain Emerson. I would give you a kiss for luck this morning before I leave you to your task."

He glanced up then, his interest abundantly clear. Perhaps he only desired her. Perhaps that could be sufficient.

Eliza gave him no opportunity to speak but backed him into the wall and boldly reached up to touch her lips to his. Nicholas stood utterly still for a moment, then she heard the brush land upon the floor and his arms were locked around her. He lifted her to her toes and turned to crush her against the wall as his mouth claimed hers in a triumphant and potent kiss, one that thrilled her to her very marrow.

Perhaps he would give her the satisfaction of his touch, after all.

Eliza would not protest in the least.

~

OF COURSE, only Eliza could awaken both hope and despair within Nicholas in the same moment. The woman made an art of tempting him with what he knew he would never possess. Her confession that she had not loved her husband, but another man instead, had filled him with hope that he might be the fortunate one. He had a moment to wonder whether his newfound fortune and his luck of the night so far might extend into his future to make all come aright.

But Eliza's confession of her desire for children shattered his hope before it had fully taken shape.

He would father no children and Nicholas knew it well.

He could not, then, court Eliza at all. It mattered little whether his situation might change and his future might be improved. He still would be aiming high but the greater import was his inability to give her what she desired most. There would be no children, and he would not be witness to her disappointment.

Indeed, he would not be the *cause* of her disappointment.

Nicholas would never willingly fail Eliza DeVries.

All the same, he could not deny himself the pleasure of her kiss. He would touch her this one last time. He would let her believe it was lust on his side and no more than that. He would taste her sweet passion one time before he rode to the duel.

And if he was to die upon the field, he would have naught in his life to regret.

Even her kiss taunted him, firing his blood with a desire beyond what he had felt before, yet leaving a part of him hauntingly unresponsive. There was no evading the truth of his situation, not with a willing Eliza fairly devouring him with her kiss and his body failing to respond to the summons.

He was but a shadow of the man he had been, and the truth of it was wrenching.

Nicholas broke their kiss with an effort, placing a distance between them with deliberation. Eliza was flushed and disheveled, as fetching a sight as he had ever seen, yet he might have been dead beneath the waist.

He reached out and touched her cheek with a fingertip, unable to resist one last caress. "Go," he whispered, feeling his resolve crumble when she might have nestled her cheek against his hand. He did not know how to send her away without injuring her feelings but he knew she had to leave before anyone in the stables noted their doings. He let his tone harden and cursed himself for what he was about to say. "Only Sterling earns his way as a stud, my lady."

Eliza's eyes flashed with predictable fire and she glared at him. "You are crude, Captain Emerson."

"I am a mere soldier. It is our way."

"You are not and you know it, but I will not argue with you." Eliza inhaled sharply and retreated. "All the same, I wish you success this morning, Captain Emerson."

He inclined his head as she spun on her heel and could not deny himself the sight of her furious retreat. It was no moment to regret the past or even to dream of a future he had not yet assured, but Nicholas did both as he returned to the grooming of his horse.

THE MIST WAS RISING from the common at Wimbleton when Nicholas dismounted. Haynesdale had ridden in the smaller of his carriages and his footman held the door as he descended. He surveyed the field and the sky as if they embarked on a hunting expedition, then continued toward Nicholas. At his nod, the footman took the reins of Sterling.

"You will wait, Thomson," Haynesdale said to his driver.

"Of course, Your Grace."

The common was deserted, save for a curricle just ahead. A lively pair of bays stamped with impatience to run and Nicholas guessed that Melbourne must be a skilled driver, if nothing else. That man stepped forward, an auburn-haired stranger following him.

"Davidson, I assume," Haynesdale murmured and Nicholas nodded.

Melbourne's second was markedly nervous, while Melbourne looked resolute and pale. The pair approached Nicholas and Haynesdale, and introductions were made. Davidson offered a case and Haynesdale leaned his cane against his hip as he opened it. The sun crested the horizon just then, sending a pale light over the land. A pair of matched dueling pistols reposed inside the case, their barrels gleaming.

"Pistols at dawn," Haynesdale mused, then reviewed the condition of the weapons with his usual efficiency. Nicholas stood by, trusting him completely. Haynesdale ensured that both pistols were clean, taking his time with the task. He then loaded them with familiar efficiency as the other men watched. He offered the choice to Nicholas, who selected one, testing the weight of it in his grip. It was a fine weapon, with chasing on the barrel and mother-of-pearl inlay.

Melbourne lifted the other and Haynesdale returned the case to Davidson.

The four men turned as one and walked to the middle of the commons with purpose. A cock crowed as the morning mist swirled around their ankles. Nicholas was filled with a resolve, calm before the battle.

If nothing else, it would be of short duration.

He stood back-to-back with Melbourne at Haynesdale's direction, then both seconds retreated to safety. He could smell Melbourne's fear and took note of it, bracing himself for some unpredictable action on the younger man's part. The duke, taking ascendance due to both his nature and his rank, began to count and Nicholas paced away from Melbourne.

At the duke's command, Nicholas pivoted then flinched as a ball shot past his ear. Melbourne had fired early and wide, perhaps deliberately. He now stood, arms at his sides. Even at a distance, Nicholas could see the other man's terror as he lifted his own pistol and aimed.

He could have killed him, but Nicholas saw the growing stain on Melbourne's breeches as that man soiled himself. He aimed for his opponent's left arm instead, for the bone instead of either joint. He would influence Melbourne's driving skill for a short period as a lesson and that would suffice.

There was no cause to inflict a greater injury in peacetime.

To his credit, Melbourne did not cower or run, but he roared when the ball tore through both his jacket and his arm. He fell immediately to his knees in apparent agony. He gripped his injured arm with his other hand, the blood flowing between his fingers with vigor. Both Davidson and Haynesdale went to him, as did Nicholas, the duke arriving last and leaning on his cane to observe. Davidson pulled away the jacket of the anguished man to expose the injury and Melbourne whimpered in pain.

"A mere flesh wound," Haynesdale said and the younger man looked up at him in outrage. Haynesdale smiled coolly. "So close to the heart and yet sufficiently far away. Did you taste your demise, Melbourne?"

Without awaiting a reply, he turned to Nicholas and shook his hand. "Artfully done, Emerson. It takes skill and mercy to grant a lesson without a lifelong injury."

Melbourne sputtered in outrage but was ignored.

"Thank you, Your Grace." Nicholas returned the pistol to Davidson. "It is a fine weapon. I hope you never see occasion to use this pair again."

Dull color rose on Melbourne's neck. "The wager has been removed from the betting book, sir," he said, his tone a little less than conciliatory.

"Excellent," Nicholas said. "Of course, my sister will no longer be able to welcome your attentions after this incident."

They bowed to each other, Melbourne's mouth a taut line—either from pain or discontent, Nicholas did not care—and Haynesdale turned to shout to his driver. "The gentleman will need a doctor, Thomson, though his injury is minor. Will you rouse one?"

"Of course, Your Grace." Thomson dispatched the footman toward the slumbering village, doubtless having ascertained the location of the doctor's abode in advance.

Haynesdale and Nicholas walked back to the carriage and horse together. "I have in mind a hearty breakfast," the duke said. "Join me?"

Nicholas shook his head, having no inclination to see Eliza again in this moment. "It has been a night, Your Grace. I would sleep this morning."

"And a rest well-earned to be sure. You must meet me later at White's for dinner, and tell me of your scheme for your winnings last night. I have no doubt that you possess one and I admit to my own curiosity."

"I will," Nicholas vowed and shook his hand beside the carriage. "Thank you. Never has a man had a better friend than I in you."

"You are mistaken, Emerson," Haynesdale said as he

stepped into his carriage. "For I am the most fortunate of men in my friendship with you." He rapped on the roof of the carriage as Nicholas smiled. He looked back over the commons, waiting for the footman to bring the doctor, and bade himself believe that his future would have sufficient promise to render him content.

He did not believe it, not truly, but perhaps that conviction would come in time. A man had to make his peace with those matters he could not change, after all.

~

To Eliza's satisfaction, Damien was at breakfast by the time she came down. Her brother looked his customary disgruntled self, which assured her that he was both sober and content.

"Captain Emerson?" she asked from the doorway, already guessing the answer.

"Hale as ever," Damien said, turning the page of his newspaper calmly. "Melbourne deloped, though it might be unfair to suggest that he fired wide and early on purpose. The man's skill is decidedly lacking and he has all the audacity of a rabbit. Fine dueling pistols, though. I thought them admirable." He turned another page and she detected a smile of satisfaction. "Emerson is as excellent a marksman as ever. I suspect he struck his opponent within an inch of his intended target, despite the fog this morning."

Eliza smiled with relief as she took her place. Nicholas was unscathed. Her relief was sufficient to weaken her knees.

"You doubted his success?" Damien asked, obviously having noted her reaction.

"I feared that his opponent might cheat."

Her brother nodded. "I shared that concern, I must admit, but we were both mistaken."

"Where was Melbourne struck?"

Her brother touched his upper left arm with a fingertip. "Sufficient to frighten him, but not to kill or even maim him. The bone was even untouched. He will have a scar and I have no doubt that he will make much of it with the ladies." Damien nodded. "I confess that it was highly satisfactory to watch Melbourne weep like a child. Unworthy of me, I know, but I found great delight in the sight."

Eliza smiled, guessing that she might have enjoyed it as well.

"There is something about that young buck that tempts me to a kick. You will want to claim some sausage, Eliza, before I eat it all. There is nothing like an early run to Wimbleton to encourage the appetite. I regret that you will have to wait to read my newspaper this morning."

Eliza smiled. "That is no trouble. I appreciate that you always refold it neatly."

"As do you, though still I know you have read it."

"Do you disapprove so much?"

"Not a whit, but do not tell mother of your bluestocking impulses. She will hire a dancing master for you without delay and we shall be cursed to listen to the music all day long."

Eliza appreciated that this was the worst torment he could imagine. "Surely my days for a dancing master are long behind me."

Damien put down his newspaper. "You must guess that she wishes to see you wed again and quickly, if only for the promise of grandchildren."

"That is not what she said."

He granted her a look. "And you believed what she said to be the sum of the truth? How long have you known our mother?"

Eliza smiled. "Unless suitable men have taken it

upon themselves to visit her rose garden, I cannot imagine how she will contrive such a match."

Her brother smiled slightly. "She believes you need a husband to be happy."

"Yet she has been widowed almost five years and has shown no inclination to wed again."

Damien's brows rose. "I am informed that it is the existence of children that makes widowhood bearable for her, while you have no such consolation." He sighed and returned his attention to his newspaper. "Which proves, of course, that her concern is truly for her own lack of grandchildren and not for your future happiness at all."

Eliza poured her tea, marveling at the variation between her mother's advice to Damien and to herself. "You could wed, sire a brood of children and ensure the future contentment of all of us."

Damien snorted and refrained from comment upon this prospect. Evidently, he found it unlikely.

"True," Eliza said, buttering her scone. "What woman would have you?" She felt his gaze upon her but continued blithely. Having grown up with three older brothers, Eliza had learned young how to tease them best. "Should there ever be a woman so foolish as to consider the possibility of accepting you, I must give warning that I will confess all of your dark secrets to her."

Damien chuckled. "And what is your plan for learning them?" he asked in a low rumble.

"I know," Eliza said, but he shook his head.

"You have not even begun to imagine the darkest of them," he said, utterly at ease with the burden.

Eliza reasoned that she might have no better opportunity and dared to ask her question. "Why would Captain Emerson not wish to dream?"

Damien set aside his newspaper. "He said as much?"

"I asked him why he was consuming so much brandy and that was his reason." She shook a finger at her brother, whose expression had turned thoughtful. "You should not aid him in this pursuit, Damien…"

"I have little choice," he said flatly, interrupting her.

"Because he cannot afford such indulgence? Perhaps it would be better for him not to so indulge!"

"There is the parson's wife. I wondered when she would appear at my table and must confess, Eliza, that I am disappointed to see her so soon."

"Damien! Captain Emerson is your friend. It is irresponsible for you to so indulge him, and I cannot understand why you should be so short-sighted in your choice…"

"Because I owe him my life," Damien said in a tone that brooked no argument. "And such a debt demands more than mere friendship."

Eliza was shocked to silence. "I knew nothing of this."

"It was not your concern. It remains a matter that is not your concern. But if Emerson had not hauled me out of the…mire at Badajoz, you would have lost three brothers in rapid succession and I would have more than a limp to show for my military service."

Eliza could not consume another bite. "Tell me," she insisted, pushing her plate slightly away from her.

Damien studied her, his expression unfathomable, then nodded once. "I will not tell you of it, for the taking of Badajoz is not a tale fit for a lady's ears. Know, however, that we lost five thousand men in a single night in that battle and I was nearly one of them. It was Emerson who saw me pulled from the pit where so many breathed their last, and I am forever indebted to him for that." He snapped his newspaper. "He can ask me for anything and if it is in my power to bestow it upon him, I will do so without hesitation. Similarly, if he declines an offer of mine, I will not press it upon him." He frowned. "I am curious to learn his plans for the future."

Eliza crumbled the remainder of her scone "Could you not return Southpoint to him?"

Damien gave her a quelling look. "Do you imagine I have not offered? He declines such *charity* from me—that is his choice of word. I cannot force him to undertake a responsibility."

"What will he do?"

"I hope to hear as much this very day. He won last night at Brooks's, and won quite handsomely."

"Damien! First you indulge his taste for brandy and then you take him gambling. You are a poor friend."

Her brother chuckled. "Emerson is infernally lucky but determined not to repeat his father's errors. He was as sober last night as I am this morning, and he won eighteen thousand pounds."

Eliza gasped.

"He even won Greenhaven from the Earl of Queenston but declined to take it, for the sake of honor."

Eliza considered the remains of her breakfast, marveling at these tidings. Would Nicholas be tempted to return to the tables to add to his gains, and lose it all—if not more—following in his father's footsteps? "I still cannot understand why he would not wish to dream," she said, almost to herself.

"*'To die, to sleep—to sleep, perchance to dream,'*" Damien recited quietly. "*'Ay, there's the rub! For in that sleep of death, what dreams may come, when we have shuffled off this mortal coil, must give us pause.'*"

She stared at her brother. "He can't believe he will die if he falls asleep."

"He must have nightmares, just as I do, though I expect Emerson's are rather worse than mine."

"Why?"

"I do not recall much of that night, save the pain. I believe he remembers every second of it. You will not be aware of this, Eliza, but the sleep that comes after brandy is no true sleep. It is dreamless oblivion and because I suspect that this is what Emerson desires above all else, I have indulged him." His tone softened. "Do not judge harshly what you cannot understand."

"It was awful?" Hers was not truly a question.

"Well beyond every expectation, even in my partial memories."

"But that was five years ago. Will he not forget?"

Damien shrugged. "I fear that he may also have suffered disappointment in love."

Eliza looked up with curiosity. "You do not know?"

"It is not a matter we have discussed. The fact remains, however, that it took him almost two years to return from the Continent after the ending of hostilities. I can only imagine that a man with Emerson's appetites had found *companionship* in that time. I suspected that a specific lady detained his return and that he would bring home a wife." Her brother fixed her with a look. "He told me that ladies in these times were sensible. Doubtless his lack of fortune was a deterrent to her acceptance of his suit."

Nicholas had come home because the lady he loved had spurned him.

What a fool that nameless woman was!

What a fool Eliza was to hurl herself at a man who loved another.

IT WAS late afternoon when Higgins cleared his throat at the door to the chamber of Eliza's mother. Eliza looked up in hope of relief from the endless review of the gardens.

"A gentleman to see you, Mrs. North."

Certain that Nicholas finally called, Eliza hurried to the front parlor, careless of the hour. There she found Mr. Galveston looking out the front window. After they greeted each other, he bowed. "Your brother's friend was most fortunate at the gaming tables last night. All the town is talking of it."

"I thought they might be talking of the duel at dawn."

Her visitor laughed lightly. "A fortune gained is more compelling than a duel with no deaths, Mrs. North. These are the sad times in which we live."

"I see." She perched on a chair, wondering whether she should call for tea. She did not wish to encourage her guest to linger, though.

"I thought only to confirm with you, Mrs. North, that you have not changed your mind about my proposal." He eyed her hopefully. "I understand that some ladies do prefer to decline before accepting, so I have come to request the honor of your hand again."

"No, sir, I have not changed my thinking, though it is most kind of you to offer again."

"I feared as much, to be sure, once I saw you dancing with Captain Emerson. Perhaps his winnings have changed the situation between you, though I cannot be glad of anyone wedding a gambler."

"I am aware of no change, Mr. Galveston."

"Ah." He glanced out the window again, seemingly choosing his words, then inclined his head to her. "I will return to Cumbria then, departing this very day."

"You need not leave London, sir, because we have not made an arrangement."

He smiled. "But my sole purpose in coming to town was to court your hand, Mrs. North. The city holds little inducement for me to stay now that I have been declined. I hope that your own stay will be most pleasurable and wish you every success, should you choose to wed again." He bowed then and Eliza curtseyed.

She watched from the window with relief as he returned to his carriage, not sparing so much as a glance at the house, then exhaled when the carriage vanished from view. She was glad to have no obligations on this evening, for a quiet dinner with her mother would suit her well after the night before.

"A parcel, my lady," Higgins declared, offering said package to her.

It was from Carruthers & Carruthers, which meant that Eliza could scarcely wait to peruse its contents. She thanked the butler and retired to her room, hoping to learn much more from Mrs. Oliver. At this point, she had to abandon her hopes of Nicholas, but still, she wanted to know all that Mrs. Oliver had to teach.

Eliza was curious and there was no harm in that.

NICHOLAS HAD the nightmare during the day for the first time. He awakened with his heart leaping and his chemise drenched in sweat. He sat up abruptly, smelling the burning flesh more vehemently than usual, and realized it came from his aunt's kitchens.

By the light, it was late afternoon, and he was due to meet Haynesdale.

And his nose told him that someone had been in his chamber. He smelled a feminine scent that made the hair prickle on the back of his neck.

But nothing was awry. Perhaps a maid, nothing more troubling than that. The floorboard that hid his treasures was in place and he breathed a sigh of relief.

Jenkins had obviously been in the room, for Nicholas' boots were polished and standing at attention, his jacket brushed and awaiting him. There was a pitcher of water that was still warm, so he washed and dressed, meeting the valet at the door to his chamber.

"You should have called, sir," the older man chided, then fussed over Nicholas' attire.

"I became accustomed to being without a valet on the Continent, Jenkins. I apologize for any slight."

"No slight at all, sir, none at all, but your circumstances may change in a most welcome fashion."

"Might they?" Nicholas wondered whether the gossip belowstairs was about his gambling or his dueling.

"Indeed, sir. The Earl of Queenston visited while you were unavailable and left a message enquiring as to whether you would care to rent a manor called Greenhaven." The valet's expression was expectant.

"Did he?"

"He left a note, sir, presumably with the details."

"Thank you, Jenkins. I shall have to read it."

Nicholas no sooner reached the stairs than his sister assaulted him, demanding every detail of Mr. Melbourne's valiant efforts that morning. She followed him down the stairs, persistent as she could be, and Aunt Fanny hailed him from the parlor, in search of tidings about that morning's adventures. It was close to an hour before he could extricate himself—and then only because he insisted the duke waited upon him. Nicholas congratulated himself upon confessing very little during that time and strode for White's. It was a reasonable distance, but he was in the mood for a bracing walk. It was a fine day to be alive, to be sure.

Haynesdale awaited him in a private chamber and was studying a map of Paris. He wore a vest Nicholas had not seen before, a silk jacquard of red and black that was most striking, and there was a newfound sense of purpose in his manner.

"Are you planning a trip?" Nicholas asked, accepting a glass of wine and settling into a chair.

"I leave tonight for Dover and will sail on the first tide," his friend said, then folded up the map so decisively that Nicholas understood the subject was closed. He leaned back in his chair and stretched out his leg with a wince. "Tell me of your own plan."

"Where is it writ that I have a plan?"

"You always have a plan, Emerson. It is one of the traits I admire most in you. Tell me of this one."

"It is little more than a notion at this point."

"I do not believe it. You were always excellent with horses and you have been putting Sterling to stud since the end of the war." Haynesdale shook a finger. "You have already embarked upon this *notion*."

Nicholas smiled. "But I could not continue for lack of funds. I thank you for the suggestion of how they might be found."

"Of course, you succeeded. Do you feel a lust to return to the tables and better yourself yet more?"

Nicholas shook his head. "Of course, there is a temptation, but I walked away and will not return again. I know too well the siren's song to which my father succumbed, and its potential price."

"Indeed." Haynesdale's approval was clear. "And so?"

"I mean to rent an appropriate property, with suitable barns and fields, ideally with a small house in reasonable condition. What do you know of Greenhaven?"

"The property you declined to win last night?" Haynesdale waited for Nicholas' nod. "Only that you would be the tenant of the Earl of Queenston and I would wish no man in that situation. The earl is a notorious womanizer and often suspected of cheating. I doubt the rent would be fair, he would assuredly try to tempt you to gamble with him that he might regain his losses of last night, and if ever you did wed, you could not be assured that your wife and daughters would be un-touched." He shook his head. "Without so much as a glimpse of the property, I find little to recommend it."

"Nor do I with that summary."

Haynesdale sipped his wine. "You will not take Southpoint, but will you rent it?"

Nicholas looked up with surprise. "I doubt I could afford it."

"It sits empty and brings me no revenue," Haynes-dale said. "I would be prepared to offer a good price for a reliable man to take it under his care. You know the stables and fields are excellent. The house, I confess, has need of some repairs."

"Has it been empty all this time?"

Haynesdale nodded.

Nicholas' thoughts flew. Southpoint was ideal, not least because he knew it so well. The house was too large for him alone, but he imagined he could divide it, perhaps even rent part of it to another family. It would not be all bad to have his friend as his landlord, for he knew Haynesdale to be fair in all matters. He might glimpse Eliza on occasion, which would be painful, but perhaps it would be better to see her when she was happily settled than never at all.

He looked up, still doubting he could afford it, but Haynesdale named a laughable sum. "You jest!"

"I would have the property occupied." His friend smiled. "And I might appreciate first pick of any new foals." The duke offered his hand and much relieved, Nicholas shook upon their agreement.

"I did not bring your winnings with me tonight."

"I would ask you to keep them for me, as they will be more secure with you than beneath the floor of my room."

Haynesdale laughed with him over that. "Fair enough. I have ordered the best of tonight's offerings to celebrate your triumph. There will be beef and plenty of it. There will also be many wishing to congratulate you, and some of them might be interested in your new endeavor—but they can wait until we have dined."

Nicholas could not argue with that.

CHAPTER 9

Helena was outraged by the injustices heaped upon her by her various wardens. She expected little tolerance or understanding from her aunt, who was so removed from youth to have forgotten what it was like to feel any emotions at all—but still, it was irksome that no one had troubled to tell her Mr. Melbourne's fate in the duel that morning. She had been compelled to interrogate Nicholas when he finally appeared in the afternoon, after hours of anguish and uncertainty. It was appalling to be treated thus.

That said duel had been instigated by her brother, a person she had formerly trusted to defend her best interests, was vexing beyond measure. How could Nicholas issue such a challenge? How could he have fired with any attempt at accuracy? Ethan might have been killed!

The only mercy was that she had her wits about her, and had confided to Ethan that he might contrive to send messages to her with the aid of one of the kitchen maids. Kitty had brought her a note at noon—one with a drop of blood upon it!—and Helena had fairly devoured the instructions from her loyal courtier. He, too, had provided little detail, but the note proved that he was yet alive at least.

There was no question that she would meet Ethan as requested.

There was no doubt that she would flee her captivity to be with him forever. Gretna Green would be their destination and their future would begin with all haste.

Then neither Aunt Fanny or Nicholas could dictate Helena's situation any longer.

The sole detail was that she had to escape the house without arousing her aunt's suspicions. Aunt Fanny was going deaf and she was insensible with age, but she was not a fool. Helena's escape had to be artfully contrived.

She took the bank notes that she had found in Nicholas' room without remorse. He had betrayed her first, to her view. Helena had known for years that he kept letters from their father hidden there, and she often indulged herself in reading them. Though she had little memory of her parents, there certainly were days in Aunt Fanny's care that Helena imagined how much better her life would have been if her parents had survived longer. She liked her father's letters to Nicholas. They were filled with advice and amusing tales, and reading them conjured a clear vision of both the man and what her life might have been beneath his care. She had found the money two days before and left it in place, wondering about its origin and Nicholas' plans for it—until this very day.

She knew, of course, that Mrs. North had cancelled their expedition to the theater that night, but Helena also knew that Aunt Fanny was unaware of the change of plans. There was a moment of opportunity, which Helena intended to use to advantage.

After supper, she put on her new dress and had

Kitty arrange her hair, then descended to the front parlor where her aunt was writing letters. Helena's heart in her mouth but she contrived to hide her agitation.

She would have to lie, but it would be a falsehood for a good cause, for Ethan and freedom.

Aunt Fanny looked up, her expression shrewd as she surveyed her niece. "The new dress favors you well," she said. "Where does Mrs. North take you this evening?"

"To the theater," Helena lied. "We are to see *Much Ado about Nothing*."

"A most suitable play for a young lady," her aunt said with approval, putting down her pen. She rose and circled Helena to inspect her as was routine, tugging up her long gloves a little higher and tucking the stole around Helena's shoulders so that it covered more of her neck. "You look very pretty, Helena."

"Thank you, Aunt Fanny. I very much like this dress."

"How unusual for you to be content with any garment," her aunt said with a chuckle. She settled into her chair again. "Have you met Mrs. North's brother yet, the Duke of Haynesdale?"

And there it was, the perfect idea.

"Very briefly, Aunt Fanny, but he did smile at me. I would not wish to sound vain, but I thought his gaze lingered upon me."

Her aunt nodded approval. "Good."

"I wish he were going to the theater with us tonight. I should like very much to have the chance to talk to him."

"Is he not?"

"I have not heard as much. It sounded as if Mrs. North and I would be joined only by Nicholas."

"How trying," Aunt Fanny said. "You might endeavor to change her view on that."

Helena dropped to a stool before her aunt. "I had a notion, Aunt Fanny, though it is daring beyond all."

"And this from you," her aunt mused.

"I thought that instead of waiting for Mrs. North to collect me here, I might go to Haynesdale House myself. Once there, I might contrive to see that the duke joins our party."

"You cannot ride alone to Haynesdale House!"

"It is only a few blocks to Grosvenor Square, Aunt Fanny, and will take mere moments. You need not summon the carriage. I could take a hackney, and Pettigrew might accompany me..."

"A hackney cab!" Aunt Fanny blustered. "A young girl unescorted in a public vehicle? No! I will not hear of it! Pettigrew!" She bellowed this last and Helena held her breath. The butler appeared, bowing in the doorway. Before he could speak, Lady Dalhousie gave her command. "Order the carriage, Pettigrew, to take my niece to Haynesdale House. She is to meet Mrs. North there, and you will escort her."

The butler's typical impassivity was disturbed, his expression reminding Helena of a ripple passing over a monolith of stone. He was skeptical but would not challenge her aunt. "Yes, my lady." He departed without saying more, and Helena was one step closer to her objective.

"Thank you, Aunt Fanny. I will be as charming as I can be."

"Of course, you will be. A match with the duke would be most advantageous, even if he is a Haynesdale. We shall have to trust in your brother's endorsement of his merit."

"Yes, Aunt." Helena turned to leave the room. She had Nicholas' money in her small evening bag and would wear her heavy cloak. She and Kitty had packed a small valise, which Kitty would ensure was in the custody of the footman.

"Wait!" Aunt Fanny declared just as Helena was crossing the threshold and she feared that all would go awry. She stopped and turned, striving to keep her expression untroubled. Her aunt smiled, always fair warning of trouble. "Your mother's pearls would be a fine addition," she decreed. "I had planned for you to wear them first at your wedding, but perhaps they will bring you good fortune in contriving one. Come here, girl. I will fasten them for you."

~

IT WAS A CLEAR EVENING, but cold. Damien was still out, presumably with Nicholas, so Eliza had dined with her mother. Both ladies retreated to their private sanctuaries, Lady Haynesdale to read about the best additions to the soil when moving roses and Eliza to peruse the pages from Mrs. Oliver which had arrived too late to be useful.

It could not hurt to be informed, all the same.

Upon the merit of patience...

In our times, many gentlemen have returned from war with wounds, both those that are healing and those that will never heal. Such an assault upon a man's vigor can influence other areas of his life. A man with an injured leg, however, might be convinced that his limp makes him undesirable to the ladies. One who has lost an eye might not believe that a lady will bear to look upon him. In my experience, men tend to see such newfound shortcomings to be more dire than their feminine companions.

Indeed, to my view, such physical souvenirs give a man an air of mystery and also indicate an appetite for life that is most beguiling. Further, a scar always hints at a story and I am most fond of men who offer more than meets the eye.

If the gentleman who draws your attention is in possession of such an injury or scar, you may find him uncommonly reticent in matters of affection. The key is to offer encouragement that cannot be mistaken for anything else and also to be patient. Time is the greatest healer of all wounds, and it will take time for an injured man to become persuaded of his amorous prospects again. Persistence and patience will conquer the most reluctant of lovers.

Eliza supposed that counsel was reasonable, but she also found it somewhat vague. She set aside the first leaf with a sigh and read the next one.

Upon the merit of audacity...

When a lady seeks the earthy attentions of a gentleman, a weekend at a country house can provide ample opportunity for a liaison. It is imperative to ascertain which chamber belongs to the desired gentleman, as a visit in the middle of the night, in darkness, may not leave additional opportunities to verify his identity. This, in truth, is part of the appeal of an unexpected visit and subsequent seduction. The illicit and secret nature of it is frequently alluring, if not exciting, for both parties.

The forthright lady might 'mistake' her room, entering the gentleman's assigned chamber in darkness then joining him abed. When undertaking such a course, it is critical to refrain from reliance upon the continuation of darkness for the entire encounter: arrange your hair and choose a garment in a hue that flatters. The gentleman may light a lamp or candle when first disturbed, and a lady keen for results should plan accordingly in terms of her appearance. Many gentlemen prefer to look upon their partner while taking their pleasure: a little rouge on lips, cheeks and even nipples can improve the view. If the encounter is to take place in your own chamber, you might further set the mood, with a low burning fire, flattering candlelight, and even a strategically placed mirror.

Rouge upon the nipples. Eliza blinked at that advice. And a mirror. Whatever for?

Plan for either a slow seduction or a quick romp, depending upon the tone or your relationship with the gentleman in question. For a seduction, you might enter his chamber in a partial state of undress, that he might assist in the removal of your stockings and stays, for example. If you desire a more immediate result, I suggest nudity beneath your robe: the sudden revelation of a woman's assets often overcomes any hesitation in the most reticent of lovers. If not, you will require a bold touch to gain results.

Eliza devoured the page of counsel, then read it again. She was both scandalized and titillated by the suggestions. Could she ever approach a man during the night, to the point of entering his bedroom uninvited? She could readily imagine that the reward might be worth the risk, and truth be told, she found the notion of a secret liaison quite delicious.

Perhaps she would become *Eliza DeVries: temptress* yet.

She smiled, then her smile faded that such an encounter was unlikely to be with Nicholas.

But there was more.

Upon the merit of forthright touch...

In those instances in which a gentleman insists upon remaining so, a lady may have to be unduly bold to secure her desire of the man in question. If she has exhausted the possibilities of light caresses, welcoming expressions and even glimpses of what might customarily be hidden from view, she may have to become more forthright in her touch to offer encouragement. This is most readily accomplished by many ladies in darkness, and even in secrecy.

Be advised that this counsel will often result in physical union. Once a lady steps upon this path of physical seduction, it may not be possible to halt the delivery of the gentleman's full admiration. If any reader does not wish to proceed so far, then she is advised to stop reading this treatise in this very moment.

Those who continue with this passage are assumed to be seeking more than a caress or a kiss, and will find explicit detail in obtaining their desire.

Now this *was* interesting. Eliza moved closer to the candle, not wanting to miss a single word.

A man's greatest sensitivity is in his member but that is not the only part of his anatomy that will respond to touch. A man's nipples, for example, are often more sensitive even than those of a lady, and there is also the element of surprise in caressing them. Kiss his nipples, gently at first and then with greater vigor. Do not be afraid to use your tongue, or even to graze them with your teeth. Pinch them between finger and thumb. Roll them. Drag your fingernail across them. Each man, like each woman, has a specific menu of items he finds palatable and arousing—I can only encourage the merit of experimentation and observation.

Consider the following illustration to learn best where to touch him and when...

In that moment, a carriage halted in the street below. Haynesdale House could not possibly be the occupant's destination, as they were expecting no one, but the horses stamped and Eliza set aside her reading to go to the window and look. She didn't recognize the carriage and couldn't see those within it. It had stopped on the opposite side of the street, alongside the park, and the footman opened the door on the far side of the carriage. She had a glimpse of a young lady embarking, which was curious. The girl held her cloak closed and had her hood up. She began to walk in the opposite direction that the carriage was facing, and Eliza assumed she visited a neighbor.

How curious that the driver had not stopped on this side of the street. The carriage moved on, the footman leaping off the back to offer a small satchel to the young woman. He passed it to her and raced after the carriage, leaping onto the back so quickly that Eliza thought she might have imagined the exchange. When she looked for the young lady, there was no sign of her.

She must have crossed the street to a neighboring house. She might have continued into the shadowed park in the midst of Grosvenor Square, though that was unlikely at this hour.

Eliza did not know her brother's neighbors in town, though she had passed them once or twice. Their affairs were certainly not her concern.

And Mrs. Oliver's advice was irresistible. Eliza returned to her reading, the young woman's arrival utterly forgotten as she learned more specifics of male anatomy.

NICHOLAS RETURNED to his aunt's home in fine temper after his excellent dinner. All came together for his future with admirable ease and he found himself filled with newfound optimism. No less than six gentlemen had expressed interest in horses from his stables and this before he had even put Sterling to stud there. Even his aunt's summons from the parlor could not influence his good cheer.

He joined her, as requested, casting his hat and gloves onto a chair, then bowed to her. "Good evening, Aunt Fanny."

"You are in fine fettle tonight for a man who has abandoned his sister."

Nicholas glanced up in surprise. "I beg your pardon?"

"You are to be at the theater with Helena and Mrs. North, ensuring that Helena has the opportunity to converse with the Duke of Haynesdale. I had understood that you had some influence over him."

Nicholas straightened. "But Mrs. North abandoned their excursion to the theater."

"When?"

"Yesterday, after I challenged Mr. Melbourne. She thought it unsuitable."

"I thought it unsuitable, but Helena has gone to the theater all the same."

"Alone?"

"Of course not! She attended with you and the duke and his sister..." Aunt Fanny's voice faded to silence and she stared at Nicholas in horror. "Perhaps she did not know," she said, but rose to look out the window in alarm.

"She knew," Nicholas said flatly. "Did Mrs. North collect her all the same?"

"No." Aunt Fanny was pale. "Helena insisted that she would go to Haynesdale House herself, the better to suggest that the duke joined the party."

"But Haynesdale was not there. I was dining with him at White's."

"Good gracious," Aunt Fanny whispered and sank into a chair. She was shaking a little. "This cannot be. There must be some mistake."

"When was this?" Nicholas demanded.

"Three hours ago," his aunt whispered in obvious

horror. "Pettigrew accompanied her there. How could she have so deceived me?"

Nicholas summoned the butler, his heart sinking when he learned that Pettigrew had not actually seen Helena enter Haynesdale House. He charged down to the kitchens, only to notice one of the kitchen maids looking fearful. He reasoned immediately that she knew more, and Kitty admitted not only to delivering a note to Miss Emerson but to contriving that she took a satchel with her.

"Why?" Nicholas demanded so vehemently that the girl broke into tears.

"She was meeting him, sir, to go to Gretna Green, sir. It was so romantic, sir."

Nicholas swore. "Mr. Melbourne?" he asked and the girl nodded tearfully as the remaining staff looked on.

"He sent a letter at noon, sir. She was so pleased."

Nicholas did not share his sister's view. He could scarce believe Helena's folly, but he returned to his aunt to share what he had learned.

"I am going to Haynesdale House to seek assistance," he concluded.

"And the duke will aid you?"

"Haynesdale intended to depart for Dover tonight. He may already be gone."

His aunt dropped her forehead to her hands in defeat, looking more broken than Nicholas had ever seen her.

"Rest assured, Aunt Fanny. I will ride after her." He was surprised when his aunt shook her head.

"It is too late, Nicholas," she said heavily. "It is all too late. It is *night*."

"I will find her. I promise it to you."

The older woman's expression grim. "Even if you do, there will be rumors and there is no more time."

Struck by her emphasis on the last word, Nicholas

paused in the act of leaving and looked back. "Time for what, Aunt?"

She frowned and rose to her feet, pacing a few steps before turning to him again. She gestured and he closed the door, returning to her side. She spoke softly but urgently. "I did not wish to burden you, but there is no escaping it now. My only hope was for Helena to wed well and quickly. I had thought I might manage to keep the house for this season, but it appears that was overly optimistic."

Her words made no sense to him. "What is this?"

"I am at the end of my credit, Nicholas. I knew the house would have to be sold this year, but even that was too much to hope." His aunt took a breath and squared her shoulders, looking him in the eye. "I have a purchase offer from a Sir Murphy Purvis, a newly knighted man of considerable fortune seeking a London home for his family. His four daughters will begin to come out next season and he is most anxious to become established in town." She sniffed. "I believe he was knighted for positioning a cornerstone, of all things. The matter of import, though, is his fortune, which comes from his trade in silk and laces." She sighed. "Alas, he has no son."

Nicholas was astonished. "But your income from investments..."

"The capital is spent at least once over."

"But the silver..."

"All sold and replaced with plate, my boy, and years ago. My situation has been precarious for some time now." She sat down heavily. "In a way, it is a relief to welcome the end."

"But where will you go?"

"I do not know. If Helena *is* married, perhaps there will be a place for me in her new home." His aunt, always proud and often overbearing, appeared much diminished to Nicholas. She sighed. "She was my sole hope," she concluded forlornly.

There was silence between them, a silence broken only by the ticking of the clock upon the mantle. Nicholas realized belatedly that it was the only remaining time piece in the house, and certainly had never been the most expensive one. He calculated, unable to see how he could afford to support both his aunt and his sister, while establishing his stables—even with Haynesdale's generous price for Southpoint. "You do not ask me to return to the gambling tables," he said warily.

His aunt met his gaze with a slow smile. "I would never ask that of you, Nicholas. It was your father's doom, that reckless need for more, and I would not lose you to such a frenzy." She sighed again. "Ride safely. There is rain in the wind."

Nicholas hesitated for a moment, wishing he could console her but knowing there was nothing he could say to offer reassurance. "I wish you had told me," he said finally.

"You have given so much, Nicholas. You think no one knows of your nightmares? And melancholy is your reward after years of service in that war?" She frowned and shook her head. "It is already unjust! I could not have laid another woe at your feet, not for any price."

Nicholas was touched by her unexpected concern. "Did you tell Helena?"

Again, his aunt shook her head. "At her age, one should believe that all will end well. I fear she has learned otherwise or will soon do so." She averted her gaze, her throat working. "I failed her in this, though I endeavored to do my best. I fear that she will be the one to pay the greater price."

"I will find her," he vowed again and left when his

aunt did not reply.

Nicholas took the stairs three at a time, knowing he might never enter this house again. He could not tell what was missing in Helena's chamber, but he went to his own room to retrieve his few possessions of import. He knew he should not have been surprised that the bank notes he had hidden beneath the floor in his own chamber were gone. Too late he recalled the feminine scent he had detected earlier in the day and knew his sister had been the source. He took his father's letters, knowing there was little else he needed, then leapt down the stairs, seizing his hat and gloves from the parlor.

Nicholas strode toward Haynesdale House and, more importantly, the stables where Sterling was kept. Melbourne had three hours' lead upon him and he only hoped he could make up the difference.

It was a long ride to Gretna Green, but the first night the happy pair spent at an inn would damage Helena's reputation beyond repair. He hoped they rode through this night, and he had a day to catch up with them.

In fact, he might have only hours to save his sister from her own folly.

Nicholas broke into a run.

Eliza heard her brother return at half past ten from his club, which was early for him. He paused to speak to their mother and Eliza arrived at her mother's room in time to encounter him there.

He smiled and bowed to her, looking purposeful. "I bid you both farewell, for I ride to Dover tonight."

"Dover!"

"I have business in Paris and will sail with the first

tide. Thomson will drive me there and return with the carriage. I will write when my return is imminent."

"What business?" Eliza asked, but her brother only smiled.

"None of concern to you," he said, maintaining his mysterious manner.

"But how long will you be gone?"

"It is impossible to say. As mentioned, I will write." He kissed their mother's cheek, while she frowned at her plan for the gardens. "Please do not commence upon this endeavor before my return, *Maman*."

Lady Haynesdale gave him an intent look. "Then you had best return quickly. The roses can only be moved before they bloom and if their season is compromised by your whimsy, I will be most displeased, Damien."

"Then I suggest you brace yourself, *Maman*. I doubt I will return before May."

"May!"

"It gives you another year to perfect your plan, to be sure." He bowed then and left, as was his custom, before any more protest could be made. Evidently, he had given instructions as to his packing before leaving for dinner, for he descended the stairs immediately and strode to the stables. Eliza heard the horses stamping and Thomson's voice. A clatter of hooves soon followed and the house seemed suddenly to yawn with emptiness in Damien's absence.

"It is a woman," Lady Haynesdale muttered, moving a placard an increment to the west. "Mark my words, there will be a duchess in this house soon, and the change cannot occur quickly enough to my view."

"No?"

Eliza won a piercing glance for that. "He grows no younger, Eliza." She sat down hard and pursed her lips. "Perhaps the reflecting pond should be square."

Eliza might have helped her mother to draft the new shape, but she heard more ruckus from the hall below. Thinking that Damien had returned for some item, she hastened downstairs, to find Higgins in an uncharacteristic fluster.

"What is it, Higgins?"

"I fear it would be indelicate for me to specify, my lady. Suffice it to say that Captain Emerson has arrived to collect his horse on a mission of some urgency."

Eliza hurried to the stables to learn the truth herself. Nicholas was saddling his horse, his expression grim, and the stablehands looked alarmed. Even Tupper, the stablemaster, had appeared to look askance on proceedings from the end of the stables.

"What is this?" Eliza demanded of Nicholas. "Do you join Damien?"

"No." Nicholas looked beyond her, then stepped closer, lowering his voice. "I tell you in confidence that Helena has fled for Gretna Green with Mr. Melbourne."

Eliza was shocked. "But how? And when?"

"She deceived my aunt with some tale of meeting you here to attend the theater."

"But I cancelled our engagement."

"And she created opportunity from that," he said through his teeth. "They are some three hours ahead of me." He returned to the harness, working quickly. "I cannot fathom why she left with him at all," he continued in frustration. "Melbourne told you that he had an inheritance of six thousand pounds a year. Why would he not simply speak to my aunt?"

Eliza's eyes widened when she realized she knew more than Nicholas. "I had no opportunity to tell you." He turned to look at her, his eyes vehemently blue. "Lady Wentworth confided that could not be true. Mr. Melbourne's father is yet alive, and worse, in no situation to grant such an inheritance to any of his sons, certainly not the youngest."

Nicholas swore so thoroughly that Eliza blinked, then apologized.

"Your vexation is thoroughly understandable, Captain Emerson, but I fear a measure of the fault is mine."

"Nonsense!"

"I should have sent word to your aunt of the change of plans," Eliza said.

"You could not have guessed that Helena would trick her."

"But it was my obligation. I was her chaperone, and charged with her welfare."

"It is done, Mrs. North. I will see it resolved now."

"No," Eliza argued, her tone so sharp that Nicholas looked up. "I must take responsibility for my part in this, and endeavor to set matters to rights."

"I will retrieve my sister, Mrs. North."

"You are not thinking clearly," she chided and Nicholas flicked a hot look her way, never pausing in his labor. "Sterling cannot run to Scotland and you know it well."

"I will change horses as necessary."

"*You* cannot ride all that way without relief."

"Watch me," he vowed grimly. "My sister's reputation is at stake."

"No, it is not a sensible course and you must realize as much," Eliza said. "We will use Damien's resources. He would never protest against it, seeing as I had an unwitting part in the situation." She turned to Tupper without waiting for Nicholas' inevitable protest. The stablemaster, an imposing man of some fifty summers who taught Eliza herself to ride, waited a suitable distance away. Undoubtedly he had guessed that there would be labor this night. "Tupper, we ride for Haynesdale without delay."

"Yes, my lady." He bowed, directing stablehands and grooms with gestures even as he replied to her. "His Grace has taken the smaller carriage to Dover. Will the larger coach suit?"

"Perfectly, Tupper. We may be three on our return and the space may be welcome."

"Very good, my lady." Tupper pivoted. "Oy! The bays! Make haste!" Stablehands hastened to follow his command and even the horses stamped with his urgency.

"Haynesdale?" Nicholas protested. "They make for Gretna Green."

"And Haynesdale lies a third the distance to Scotland," Eliza said. She met his gaze. "If we do not find her before they pause for a night, there will be considerably less cause for haste." She watched his lips tighten and he turned away, but did not dispute this truth.

"Haynesdale is over a hundred miles distant, my lady," Tupper contributed gruffly when she turned back to him. "If you intend to ride in haste, you will need to change horses at least twice, perhaps thrice."

"Precisely, Tupper. Please send grooms with us that they might tend the duke's team where we first change, until they can be collected on our return to London. His Grace will have no patience with the surrender of his horses."

"Indeed he will not, my lady." Tupper snapped his fingers and two young men straightened, a flick of his hand sending them to gather their belongings. "I will drive you myself, my lady, the better that you not be disadvantaged when you do stop. I know the road well."

"Excellent, Tupper." It was a relief to know that his experience would aid in their journey. "And I will send word to Haynesdale that they might be prepared for us. I should think we might arrive there tomorrow for dinner." Eliza invited the stablemaster's opinion of that.

Tupper frowned, undoubtedly calculating, before he spoke. "Likely later than that, my lady, depending upon the road. Rain is promised, after all, and the roads will suffer from it. I would endeavor to reach there by midnight but even that may be ambitious."

"And by then the die will be cast," Nicholas said. He came to stand beside Eliza. "We will have to stop at every coaching inn to enquire after her."

Tupper's brows rose but he did not speak.

"You might as well know the truth of it," Nicholas said to him. "My sister endeavors to elope to Gretna Green and I would stop her, if possible."

Tupper nodded with purpose, no hint of surprise in his expression. "Has the man in question a coach?"

"I think not, though he may have access to one."

"'Twould be a fine friend indeed to lend him a coach and four for such a ride," Tupper noted. "He would be out his team for close to a fortnight."

"The gentleman in question has a curricle," Eliza supplied.

"He will not be riding so far in that," Tupper said with confidence. "It will be the stagecoach for them, then, and they will be on the Great North Road." He pivoted and shouted. "Hawkins! Ride to The Angel and enquire whether the lady and her escort have been seen there."

Nicholas stepped toward Hawkins to give that stablehand a description. "Take Sterling as he is saddled." The younger man rode out of the stable moments later, and Eliza heard Sterling's hoof beats as he trotted down the alley.

"We will see you there, Hawkins, as soon as might be," Tupper called after him, then nodded to Eliza. "We will do our best to find her, my lady. In ten minutes, we will be ready to depart. Be warned that it may be a cold ride. Winter is not out of the wind yet."

"I will ask for a warming brick and fetch a heavy cloak. I thank you, Tupper." Eliza turned to find Nicholas watching her, his expression inscrutable.

"You should not embark on this endeavor, Mrs. North," he said softly. "It is too much for you to undertake such inconvenience and I would not see your own welfare at risk."

"Yet I join it willingly to repair my own error. It is not only gentlemen who have their honor to defend."

"His Grace would not approve," Nicholas said with a frown.

"On the contrary, Captain Emerson, my brother would understand perfectly. Were he here, I would cede to him taking my place in the party, but alas, he is gone. It is my fault. I should have sent word to your aunt myself instead of trusting Miss Emerson to tell her of the change. I knew your sister was inclined to mischief."

Nicholas' expression remained grim and he did not argue this last. "But surely you see the impropriety of our sharing a carriage for so many hours."

He did not even wish to be alone with her. Eliza straightened. It was one matter that he loved another woman, but she had thought they might be friends. "I see us as allies in a common goal, Captain Emerson," she said coolly and his gaze clung to hers in a way she might have mistaken had she not known the truth. "That objective being the good fortune of your sister."

"Yet I will not see your reputation tainted as reward for your kindness." He was resolute. "I will ride with Tupper, Mrs. North, if you refuse to remain here."

And with that, Nicholas turned away.

Eliza raised her voice slightly, and he halted as soon as she spoke. "I remind you, Captain Emerson, that you owe me a secret."

Nicholas pivoted crisply and Eliza met his gaze in challenge.

"I would not withdraw my brother's resources from this quest, but I would think your honor markedly diminished if you did not keep your part of the wager. This journey will provide the opportunity for you to do as much." Before he could reply, Eliza turned away, hastening to gather her belongings and inform her mother. She was a fool and then some to hunger after mere moments in Nicholas' company. He would deny her even this and she would love him until the end of her days all the same.

How she envied the woman who had claimed his heart!

~

HELENA EMERSON WAS COLD.

Her dress had not been intended for traveling and her slippers had certainly not been designed for the muck at coaching inns. Their silk was stained beyond repair, plus they were soaked through. Her aunt always said there was no greater misery than wet feet and Helena found herself in reluctant agreement.

Eloping was rather less romantic than she had hoped. After some hours in a mail coach that was far from luxuriously appointed, Helena was convinced that she was black and blue. She also knew that her new dress was soiled and suspected that her person might be...fragrant.

Worst of all, Ethan seemed to have lost interest in her person. His charming manner was diminished, and when he spoke to her, he seemed to be distracted or even impatient. Was this what the prospect of matrimony did to a man? She sorely regretted ever agreeing to his proposal, for she could not tolerate an entire lifetime of such indifference.

She was wedged in the corner, trapped between the

coach and the considerable bulk of a sturdy woman who had claimed the forward-facing seat with remarkable agility at The Angel. A young girl sat on the other side of this woman and was evidently traveling with the lady in question. Ethan sat opposite them, staring fixedly out the window and making no effort at conversation at all. Helena had a healthy urge to kick him —or worse. The rain had started when they left London and now drummed on the roof of the coach with steady vigor. The girl fell asleep and the woman put her arm around her, a comforting gesture that made Helena feel all the more alone.

And it was her own fault.

She shivered, stifling a sneeze.

"That cape of yours is fine enough but it wouldn't keep a flea warm in summer," the woman said, her tone confidential. "Did I catch a coach to a masquerade ball in error?" She laughed at her own jest. "If so, I am woefully underdressed, to be sure."

Helena smiled thinly. "I daresay not, madame."

"Madame," the woman echoed and offered a meaty hand. "Agnes Dawlish, it is, Mrs. D. they call me, wife of the solicitor in Carting Corners, near Colsterworth." Her grip was resolute, like that of a man, but the glint in her eyes was kindly. "This here is my daughter, Flora." The girl stirred, nestling against her mother more comfortably. Mrs. D. smiled down at her with an affection that made Helena ache.

"I am pleased to make your acquaintance, Mrs. D."

"I suppose you've not got a name," Mrs. D. said cheerfully. "On your way to Gretna Green?"

Helena nodded, only to have Ethan glare at her.

She glared back.

Mrs. D. watched the exchange then eyed Ethan. "A *gentleman* might see to his lady's comfort by surrendering his cloak."

"It is cold!" he protested, drawing that garment more closely around himself. "I will not fall ill on this journey."

Mrs. D. was clearly unsurprised. "That is a fine Romeo you have there, my dear," she advised Helena in an undertone. "Not even wed and he is indifferent to your comfort. I will not be telling you a secret if I confide that situation is scarce likely to improve."

Nor was Mrs. D. telling Helena anything that she did not already suspect.

The older woman rose partly to her feet, rocking with the motion of the coach in a most alarming way, then pounded a mighty fist on the roof. "Hoy there! Stop the coach!"

"What madness is this?" Ethan demanded. "We have need of haste!"

Mrs. D. ignored him.

Helena found the policy a sound one and did the same.

Flora stirred, blinking sleepily at her mother, then offered Helena a tentative smile.

"I'm needing my bag," Mrs. D. said to the man who opened the door. She pointed at the roof. "The dark one, just there."

The man eyed the small space upon the floor of the coach, his intimation clear, but the formidable lady glowered at him. He fetched the bag and dropped it into the carriage so that it landed heavily. It was wet and splashed a bit on impact, then he slammed the door and the coach rolled onward.

"Not so fine as your other frippery, but Flora will not mind lending it," Mrs. D. said, rummaging in the bag.

"I do not mind," Flora said softly, then yawned.

Mrs. D. produced a cape of heavy wool and gave it a shake, then offered it to Helena. "You'll not fall ill when

I am in the vicinity, to be sure. Go on. Wrap up. It won't be biting you, to be sure."

The garment smelled of smoke but it was thick and so warm that Helena was well beyond any criticism. "Thank you, Mrs. Dawlish," she said when she was enfolded in it. "I greatly appreciate your kindness."

"And there is a true smile as a result." They rode in silence, jostling together for some time. Mrs. D. leaned closer and lowered her voice. "Have you a brother, my dear?"

Helena nodded.

"And is he grown to manhood?"

"He is many years my senior and recently returned from the war on the Continent."

"Good." Mrs. D. fixed Melbourne with a disapproving eye, her expectation clear that Nicholas would follow to defend his sister's honor.

"And he shot me," Ethan said hotly.

"Did he then?" Mrs. D. was delighted. "Some sense in the family, then, to be sure. I had always hoped my girls would have a brother, but we were not so fortunate as that."

"He shot me in the arm," Ethan said, indicating the spot.

Mrs. D. feigned alarm. "He missed then, I wager."

Flora laughed.

Ethan's outraged glare made the older lady laugh in her turn.

"And did you smite him down then, sir, and leave him bleeding on the field?" It was clear that Mrs. D. thought this scenario unlikely. Even the jest of it, though, gave Helena a terrible feeling in her belly. What if Nicholas had been injured by Ethan? It would have been her fault.

Ethan straightened. "I could hardly do the man injury, then ask his permission to wed his sister."

"Fair enough, but if you're for Gretna Green, either you didn't ask his permission or he declined your kind offer," Mrs. D. replied with confidence. "Which was it?"

Ethan looked so affronted that the older lady chuckled heartily.

"Fear not, my girl," she said to Helena, giving her a nudge with her elbow. "Your brother will not miss the second time."

"Madame! You presume too much!" Ethan protested, which only made Mrs. D. chortle with glee. The more she laughed, the more annoyed Ethan became, which only made her laugh harder.

But Helena could not laugh, despite her companion's confidence that Nicholas would see all set to rights. She had stolen his money, after all. Her heart sank to her chilly toes. Mindful of her aunt's frequent warnings about cutpurses and thieves, Helena had secreted the banknotes in a small pouch, secured to her undergarments. She clutched it now through her dress, her hand hidden beneath the heavy wool cloak. She also had wound her own stole high around her neck to hide her precious pearls.

Would Nicholas pursue her at all? She certainly did not deserve his gallantry.

She had a terrible feeling that Mrs. D. was right about Melbourne, and that he would be even more careless of her feelings after they were married.

Had Mrs. North been right about hasty weddings in Cumbria, as well?

What if Helena no longer wished to wed Ethan at all?

Was it too late to change her mind and the course of her future?

CHAPTER 10

A secret.

Nicholas had only two and he did not wish to share either with Eliza. Of the two, the secret less humiliating to confess would be that of the battle that haunted him. He could never admit to his secret affection for her, not when he could not provide what she desired most.

But that night in Badajoz...

How could he speak of it to another?

How could he tell a lady of such bloodshed and violence? It was unthinkable to do as much.

And yet, a part of him desired to share the tale, if only in the hope that so doing might loosen its hold upon him. He imagined that Eliza of all women would understand why that night fed his nightmares. It was tempting to confide in her, though he doubted much good could come of it. She might be appalled. She might think him ungentlemanly, even though his confession would be in response to her demand.

Even by the time they reached The Angel, his thoughts were tangled around the conundrum.

Hawkins awaited them there with the tidings he had gathered. To Nicholas' relief, there was some suggestion there that a raven-haired girl and a fashionably at-tired young man had taken the stagecoach north. Reports varied from each other but there was sufficient for Nicholas to be encouraged.

He was glad of Tupper's presence for that man seemed to anticipate every potential obstacle. They spent mere moments at the coaching inn before car-rying on. Hawkins returned to Haynesdale House with Sterling, while they left the city in hot pursuit of the stagecoach.

"Pistols are here, sir," Tupper informed him grimly, knocking his heel against the box that formed the coachman's seat. "I must say as I am glad to have a man of your experience on this journey. It can be perilous to ride at night."

Nicholas nodded agreement. "And I am glad of your foresight, Tupper."

"There are tales of highwaymen near Alconbury," the older man confided softly. "I would not say as much before Lady Eliza, but I wish she had not come along."

Nicholas winced. "I do not think we could have left her behind." He also did not think he could evade the sharing of his tale, not without losing her friendship entirely.

The stablemaster smiled. "No, I reckon you are right in that, but it was good of you to try to change her view. I could not have dared."

They exchanged a glance of understanding.

The rain began in earnest then, a cold onslaught that would have soaked Nicholas through if he had not brought his heavy cloak. When Tupper enquired after his comfort, Nicholas recounted a humorous tale of a wretched night of camping in Spain, much elaborated, that made both of them feel fortunate in their cir-cumstance.

They changed horses at Biggleswade, Nicholas

asking questions of all and sundry while Tupper made his agreements. It was in the darkest hours of the night, the stillness before the dawn, and there was no sound from within the coach. Topkins remained with the team at Biggleswade, waving them on from the yard.

Nicholas hoped Eliza slept.

The sun was riding high as they approached Alconbury and the rain had stopped. The road was riddled with ruts, mud and puddles, a poor sign for their future progress. Eliza left the coach to relieve herself and in her absence, Nicholas took the brick, now cold, to have it heated at the inn. The request gave him an opportunity to speak with the innkeeper. Here, he had a more definite report, though that man believed the young woman traveled with an older female relation. There had been a young gentleman, too, but the innkeeper fancied he had been on his own.

Nicholas reported the details to Eliza as he replaced the hot brick in the carriage. She looked as puzzled and concerned as he felt. "Do you think we gain upon them?"

"They are hours ahead," he said, despondent. "Unless they halt at a coaching inn, it is unlikely that we shall reach Helena in time."

"And if they do, we will be too late to save her reputation," Eliza whispered with frustration. She did not wait for a reply, but granted him a look. "You must be chilled," she said and moved from the middle of the seat to make room, her expectation clear.

His sister was ruined. His aunt was impoverished. That he alone seemed to have experienced Fortune's smile made Nicholas fear that all was about to change and for the worse.

Why not share the tale of Badajoz? It seemed he had little left to lose.

Nicholas stepped back to speak to Tupper, already

in his seat with the reins in hand. "I will ride with Mrs. North for a while," he said. "And endeavor to see her entertained."

"As you wish, Captain."

Nicholas could not help but be charmed by Eliza's triumphant smile when he took the place opposite her and the coach began to move. "You will have your secret, Mrs. North, though you may not be as satisfied with it as you anticipate."

"I suspect you may be wrong in that, Captain Emerson." She beamed at him then, and he could only hope that his confession did not disappoint.

~

HELENA WAS hungry and she had need of a chamberpot. When they halted at Colsterworth to change horses in the late afternoon, she insisted upon leaving the carriage after Mrs. D and her daughter.

"But you will be seen!" Ethan protested.

"I assure you, Mr. Melbourne, I know no one in this proximity."

Helena did not wait for his assistance, but simply leapt out of the carriage. The ground was muddy and the inn was humble, to be sure.

Still, it felt like heaven to stand up.

Mrs. D. had already claimed her bag and was marching toward a waiting cart with a single horse. Flora ran ahead of her and the driver, obviously awaiting them, bowed to her. He stepped forward to claim Mrs. D.'s bag and heft it into the cart.

Helena hurried after her, starting to remove the heavy cloak. "Mrs. Dawlish! I still have Flora's cloak."

The older woman smiled at her. "You keep it, miss. It will not get any warmer."

"But I could not take it from you or Flora."

"Then you can return it to me at your convenience."

Helena smiled. "Mrs. Dawlish, wife of the solicitor at Carting Corners."

"The very one." Mrs. D.'s glance flicked to Ethan, who was evidently following Helena, her sober expression clearly revealing her thoughts. "I wish you luck, my dear. I fear you will need it."

Helena spun to face Ethan, who caught her hand and leaned closer. He smiled for her, the smile that previously made her heart flutter, but in this instance, it had no effect at all. "Let us not loiter here. We must hurry onward to Scotland! I cannot bear any delay in making you my wife."

"I am hungry," Helena repeated.

"I have an apple," he offered, producing a sad specimen from the pocket of his jacket.

Helena eyed the offering, thinking it required no comment. "I want something hot, a bowl of soup or a cup of tea. I am chilled to my very marrow."

And he did not care. Helena saw the truth of it and the sight hardened her heart.

"But any delay will slow our journey," he appealed, then looked over his shoulder. He feared that they would be pursued.

Why did he want to wed her so badly? It could not for her own merit, or he would have been more concerned about her comfort. He had not seen the pearls and could not know about the money she had stolen—and even if he had, it was a paltry sum to fund a lifetime.

Was Nicholas' money sufficient to see her returned to London? It had to be, but she dared not travel alone.

"I also need a chamberpot," she said, knowing there was little argument he could make to that. Helena then turned to walk toward the inn.

There was a silence behind her, a hint that she had surprised her companion.

Ethan caught up to her, seizing her elbow just before she reached the inn. A servant opened the door and Helena inhaled the scent of beef stew, tallow candles and a roaring fire. She continued into the tavern, her stomach growling, and smiled as those gathered there turned to look. The keeper wiped a table, gesturing to it, and Helena sat down with anticipation.

She met Ethan's surprised gaze. "You feel no need for haste, which can only mean that you think we will not be followed," he guessed, then perched on the chair opposite. "Whyever not?"

Helena removed her gloves, finger by finger, choosing not to tell him about the hidden bank notes. "Why would Aunt Fanny want to stop me from marrying a man with six thousand pounds a year?" she asked instead.

Ethan coughed. He sat down hard. He evaded her gaze and Helena sensed that his next confession would not be one she welcomed. "That isn't quite the situation," he acknowledged.

"You told me that was your inheritance." Helena put her gloves down forcefully and glared at him. "Did you lie to me?"

"That is a harsh word," he said, so flustered that Helena's heart sank. "I may have been slightly more optimistic than is warranted."

"How much do you owe?" she demanded in a whisper. The entire inn seemed to have fallen silent to listen.

Ethan fidgeted.

Then he spoke with quiet urgency. "My father yet breathes, as soon you will learn."

"You *did* deceive me!"

"There will be no problem," he insisted hurriedly.

"Once we are wed and my creditors know that the heiress of Hexham is my bride, I will be able to extend my loans until your aunt's passing." He smiled. "You have no cause for concern." He reached for her hand, but Helena pulled it back to her lap.

She frowned in confusion, unable to make sense of his claim. "But there is no heiress of Hexham," she said, before considering the wisdom of this confession. The current viscount, she knew very well, had only two sons.

Ethan's eyes flashed. "Of course, there is! *You* are the heiress of Hexham."

"However did you contrive such nonsense?" Helena thought to make a jest but his expression revealed that he had believed it.

"Your aunt told me so," he hissed, rising to his feet in fury. "Why else would I marry you?"

There was a collective gasp in the tavern. Helena felt the heat rise in her cheeks.

Still, she was no reticent maiden. She rose to her feet to glare back at him. "You vowed you loved me," she said, aware that the women in the tavern found this compelling while the men did not.

"He lied, love," an older lady said with a shake of her head.

"You said you had a legacy, not an accumulation of debts."

"You might speak more quietly, my love."

"You lied about your own father's demise!" Helena watched Ethan's mouth opening and closing as color rose on the back of his neck. She had no doubt that she had finally found the truth. "Did you care nothing for me?" she demanded. "Was this all about some funds that I do not possess?"

"It is not so callous as that," he confessed then

leaned closer to whisper. "But I simply must have an heiress! Surely you understand?"

"You have not found one," Helena said, hoping he would say something more kindly but fearing he would not.

Ethan shook his head, then turned and left the tavern. Helena was outraged. He was abandoning her miles from those she knew and trusted.

What gentleman made such a choice?

"Wretch!" Helena whispered and sat down hard, her thoughts spinning. She had no acquaintances who might come to her aid. Her aunt would likely, as Mrs. North warned, have little assistance to offer her. Nicholas had undoubtedly chosen not to pursue her, thanks to her theft. What would she do when his money was spent? She did not even know what choices she had, but one thing was certain: she was not going to pursue Mr. Ethan Melbourne.

How had he so deceived her?

All the years she had lived with Aunt Fanny and been compelled to abide that woman's obsession with wealth, and she had never thought to check the veracity of Ethan's claim.

There was an error Helena would never make again.

She should have kept her gaze fixed upon the Duke of Haynesdale, regardless of his infirmity.

"If I may say as much, you are well rid of him, Miss Emerson."

This last was uttered in more gentlemanly tones. Helena looked up at the sound of her name to find Mr. Galveston bowing before her.

"If I may be of service," he said, his color rising slightly. "I could not fail to overhear your conversation with Mr. Melbourne. I believe I was so fortunate as to secure the last available room for tonight, but you are welcome to it, Miss Emerson. I will find a place in the stables instead. I would be honored to do you this service."

Helena's heart flooded with relief to find a kindly face. "Mr. Galveston! But how did you come to be here?"

"Pure happenstance, I assure you, Miss Emerson. I left London, having realized that my quest was unlikely to meet with success, and was returning home. This is one of my customary places to spend a night."

"I do not know where you live, sir."

"Outside a small village in Cumbria. Mrs. North was married to the pastor in a nearby parish, thus we were acquainted." He stood and waited. "Will you take the room, Miss Emerson? I think you will find it simple but comfortable."

Helena had learned something in the past day and was cautious to accept. "I would not put myself in your debt, sir."

"I would not consider it a debt but an honor for me." He smiled.

"You are wise not to jump from the fat to the fire," Mrs. D. said, appearing suddenly behind Mr. Galveston. She nodded at Helena. "I am glad that you have learned something on this day. Do you know this gentleman?" Mr. Galveston looked to be intimidated by the solicitor's wife.

"I have been introduced to him in London, yes." She introduced the two of them.

Mrs. D. harrumphed. "Your offer is kindly meant, sir, but I will sit with Miss Emerson until her brother arrives." She nodded as he inclined his head politely. "Miss Emerson had a small bag on the coach from Alconbury. I'm sure she would be most appreciative if you fetched it, Mr. Galveston."

Her manner was so imperious that there was evidently no question of Mr. Galveston failing to comply.

He immediately scurried away to do her bidding and that lady sank into the opposite chair with a smile. "Fear not, my dear. I will wait with you. Your brother will come and all will end well. You will see."

Helena nodded, so suddenly overcome with gratitude that she could scarcely speak. There was a detail, though, that her newfound friend had to know. "Thank you, Mrs. D, but my brother will not come."

"What is this? Is he no better than the other?"

"He is honorable, a true gentleman, and kind to me, but I tricked him. I fear I lost his support in so doing."

Mrs. D. studied her. "I see."

Mr. Galveston reappeared then, a little breathless from retrieving Helena's bag, and set it down beside her with a triumphant smile. She thanked him, then Mrs. D. turned to him. "I wager you know Miss Emerson's family?"

"I know her chaperone, Mrs. North, and have met her brother, Captain Emerson..."

Mrs. D. interrupted this tale, standing abruptly. She was nigh as tall as Mr. Galveston and certainly more imposing. "Then you will write to them, if you please, and advise them that Miss Emerson is a guest of Mrs. Agnes Dawlish, wife of the solicitor in Carting Corners. It is not five miles from here, to the east."

Mr. Galveston looked between Helena and her would-be hostess.

Mrs. D. lowered her voice. "You must see that she cannot stay at a coaching inn, either alone or under the protection of a gentleman." She fixed Mr. Galveston with a hard look. "If you would be of service to the lady, this is the best way."

"Of course!" he said, clearly flustered. "Of course. It is just as you say, Mrs. Dawlish. I will stop at her chaperone's family home in Haynesdale and endeavor to contact Miss Emerson's family there. Captain Emerson is very close friends with the duke, I understand."

"Then I shall rely upon you to do so," Mrs. D. said with resolve. She claimed Helena's bag. "Come along, my dear. I believe you were wanting a chamberpot."

"Yes, indeed."

"And thence for home. You will find comfort at Dawlish Cottage. Flora will undoubtedly be glad of your company. She is so curious about events in town."

"Thank you, Mrs. D."

"Three daughters I have, though none so pretty as you. I should like to think that someone would be of aid to them if they made a foolish choice." She turned to give Helena a hard look.

"I would, if I could," Helena vowed. "If ever I see a young lady in dire circumstance, I will help if I can. You have shown me the merit of that."

"Then all is not lost. Do not give up on your brother just yet, Miss Emerson. He sounds a most principled fellow. I have hopes of him."

~

ELIZA WAITED as they rode in silence, content to let Nicholas choose his moment. The coach was warmer just with his presence opposite her and she took the opportunity to study him. He was looking out the window, frowning slightly, and she saw tumult in his gaze.

His secret was not a happy one.

That made her regret asking for it, in a way, yet she was honored that he chose to trust her with it.

"You asked once why I did not wish to dream," he said finally. He turned to meet her gaze, his own expression inscrutable—save for his eyes, which were that deep blue she associated with strong emotions in him. His jaw was tight and his posture rigid, as if he faced a foe in simply the telling of this tale. "It is because I have been haunted by a single dream these five years, a memory of a battle that I will never forget."

It was precisely as Damien had suggested to her. Eliza only nodded, not wanting to interrupt his tale now that he had begun.

"I should not tell you of that night. I should not give a lady any inkling of what we endured and what few of us survived."

"I ask you as a friend," she said softly.

"Perhaps you know of Badajoz from Haynesdale."

"He says he recalls little of it, save the pain, and that you were responsible for his survival."

Nicholas did not dispute that. He looked out the window again, but Eliza guessed he saw another place entirely. "When I do not drink, I dream of it, again and again." He shook his head, then gestured with one hand, drawing a map in the space between them.

His tone turned brisk and she saw his military experience in his ability to summarize a situation clearly. "Badajoz is sited on a natural peak, one fortified with heavy walls encircling both a town and a fortress. To the north, flowing from west to east, is the Guadiana River, a wide slow river and a formidable obstacle in itself. A tributary called the Revillas breaks from it to flow down the eastern side of the city, descending into fen and swamp to the south and east. On this side, the rock rises in a sheer cliff to the summit of the fortifications. Most previous approaches had been made from the southwest, where the road rose to the gates.

"You must understand that this city was fortified beyond measure, yet Wellington was determined to take it. The curtain walls were over twenty feet high, the eight bastion towers over thirty. Little happened in the vicinity of that town that was not seen from within its walls. The fortress itself occupied the northeast corner of the mount. On this night, it was resolved that we would approach in darkness from two directions at once: from the east, scaling that sheer cliff, and from the west, scaling a less-sheer cliff. In a way, it was madness. In another, no one would have anticipated such a scheme of attack so surprise was on our side."

Nicholas fell silent then, his throat working, and she knew he saw it again. Eliza wanted to touch him, to console him, but she feared to interrupt his tale.

"I was with Haynesdale, of course, and beneath his command. He was calm, I remember, utterly confident of our triumph. Men would follow him blindly, simply due to that confidence. I felt only dread, for I had examined the rock face and knew that many would fall in the attempt to scale it. I feared that we would be assaulted from above, an easy feat for the defenders of the town and one that might spell the doom of many. Haynesdale and I argued over the scheme, but in hindsight, I know it was not his and being ordered to execute it, he had no choice but to follow the command. There were known breaches in the walls above, if we could but reach them, and it was believed that victory would be readily won."

Again he paused, his gaze flicking unseeingly over the map he had drawn in the air between them. "We gathered in the southeast under cover of darkness. The Fourth and Light Divisions were to storm those breaches. The Third Division was to scale the wall, while the Fifth Division was to attack the bastion on the northwest corner of the walls, to divide the defenders. The plan was as sound as it could be. We waited for the hour to grow ever later, in silence and trepidation." He cast her a wan smile. "I remember the croaking of the frogs."

Eliza could envision the scene, men crowded together in darkness, the shadow of the fortress overhead, the sound of the frogs—and she imagined the tang of fear.

"At ten, we placed the ladders against the cliffs and the wall, all the while dreading discovery. There was only a single musket shot from above in response. It made no sense to me but Haynesdale was encouraged." Nicholas swallowed. "I remember his confident wink, then saw him proceed to the ladder. He intended to lead us to victory." He shook his head. "He never hung back in safety to watch. He always led the way, which was why men would follow him anywhere."

Eliza gripped her hands together in her lap, riveted by the tale.

"That wink was the last hint of normalcy, for immediately afterward, there were explosions on all side. The darkness of the night was rent by the flash of fire, the roar of muskets and the shouts of men who were struck." He rolled his fingers and thumb together. "Grapeshot is fine, fired in clusters and a source of much damage. The air was filled with it. It rained upon us like hail stones, tearing into flesh with dreadful power. The very ground shook with the force of their defense and men fell on all sides." He swallowed. "Haynesdale fell. I will never forget the sight of him, the dismay in his expression, the blood as he stumbled. Of course, he tried to rise but was struck again. I knew that he would die there, unless I intervened."

He shook his head and raised his hands. "There was a kind of trench on that side, and it not only filled with the fallen but did so with astonishing speed. I had to get Haynesdale away from there before he was buried alive amidst corpses."

Eliza gasped. "They were not all dead?"

Nicholas met her gaze and shook his head steadily. "Not yet." He inhaled and looked down at the floor, as if he saw that ground again. "Some endeavored to seize me as I retrieved Haynesdale. They clutched at any hope of survival. I remember one man holding my ankle and how hard I had to shake my boot for him to relinquish his grip. By the time I carried Haynesdale to safety and bound his leg to slow the blood, I returned to find that man dead of his injuries. It was chaos. It was carnage. It was horrific." This last he said softly.

"Were you injured, as well?"

Nicholas touched his shoulder fleetingly, disinterested in his own wound. "It healed well enough, but the memory of that night will never leave me." He braced his elbows on his knees and held her gaze grimly. "That is my secret, Mrs. North. That is the dream I fear to have, the dream that haunts me, the dream that will never relinquish its grip upon me. I recall that soldier and his desire to live. I recall the sound of my boots sinking into the mire of bodies as I carried Haynesdale away. I think about the darkness and the fire, the smell of blood and roasting flesh, and I find myself once more in the fen alongside the Revillas, sick with what we had done."

"How many men?" Eliza asked in a whisper. She had heard rumors, but she wanted the truth.

"Over five thousand were lost that night. We took Badajoz, but I could not share in the triumph. The celebration lasted a day and a night within the walls, a glut of whoring and thieving that was as revolting as the price of gaining the town. Haynesdale cannot remember much of it. He was struggling to survive, battling the prospect of infection and a much more lingering death."

"He survived because of you. He told me that he owes you his life."

Nicholas nodded. "He is my friend and he was my commander. There was nothing else to be done." He lifted his gaze to hers. "But when I awaken from that dream, a part of me wishes that I had not survived that carnage, for then I would not be haunted by its memory." He tilted his head and smiled just a little but his expression was not merry. "Perhaps that is a second secret for you, Mrs. North, that such service can adversely affect a man's desire to live."

"Is that why you choose not to wed, or is it a broken heart?"

"Does it matter?"

"Can you not wish for a wife and family?"

Nicholas shook his head with resolve. "Some paths are no longer possible to take, Mrs. North. I will be content with Haynesdale's friendship and success with my horses."

"But will you be content?" she asked quietly. "Or will you yearn for more?"

"It is folly to yearn for what one cannot possess," he said solemnly. "I shall have to learn to be content."

So, it seemed, would Eliza.

He straightened then, seemingly shaking off his mood. "If I am not mistaken, this is Colsterworth," he said, his tone light. "Perhaps we will learn more of Helena here."

Eliza could only hope as much.

PERHAPS THE TELLING of his tale had been an omen. It seemed that all trace of his sister vanished after Colsterworth. There was some suggestion of a young woman of her description pausing at the inn, then no reports of her departure. There was not a whisper of her presence at Grantham and much discussion ensued. Even Nicholas had to admit that there was no point in pushing on to Doncaster when there was no news of his sister.

Had she and Melbourne left the coach for an inn? Had they left the Great North Road and taken a room in some smaller village, away from the road and possible detection?

They charged onward to Haynesdale in darkness and despair welled within Nicholas.

He had failed his sister.

Even at night, he recognized the shape of the land as they entered the duchy of Haynesdale. Each curve in the road, each ancient tree, each cottage and hill was painfully familiar. He had never thought to return here but now, thanks to Haynesdale's generosity, he would live on this property that had claimed a corner of his heart. They passed Southpoint in haste, but not so quickly that he failed to see all the windows dark. The house looked empty, lonely even, and he suddenly recalled his step-mother's conviction that a light should always shine into the darkness to welcome a lonely traveler.

He would do that, when he moved into the house. It would not be his own, but he would treasure the opportunity to reside there again.

"Damien said he had offered it to you," Eliza said softly when Southpoint was behind him. "And that you refused it."

"I did. Your father bought it. It is now Haynesdale's." Nicholas knew he sounded curt, but he did not wish to discuss the matter with her.

"And you saved his life by his accounting. It is only reasonable that he would perceive there to be a debt between you, one he would prefer to resolve."

"It is not about a debt, Mrs. North," Nicholas said. "Your brother owes me nothing, not even his friendship, though I am honored to have that."

"You would not have your valor rewarded?"

"I was not valiant. Any man would have done the same."

"But you did save him, and you were made Captain as a result. Clearly, others believed you had acted nobly on the field."

"It does not matter, not now," Nicholas said, then forced himself to take a more cheerful expression. "You should know that he has rented Southpoint to me, for a ridiculous price, and I was sufficiently grateful to accept."

"Truly?" She was clearly pleased, though he could not fathom why.

He dared not guess.

"Truly. I will raise horses there. Sterling already has been put to stud, but I would have more control over the lineage." He took a breath. "It has been a hope of mine, and Haynesdale helped me to find a way to pursue it."

"But not by returning Southpoint to you?"

"No, by encouraging me to gamble at Brooks's."

She was visibly displeased. "I thought you had no intention of following your father upon that course."

"I do not, but I ceded the merit of one night at the tables. I won, as Haynesdale guessed I might, and while it was not a fortune, the gains were sufficient to see me embark upon my purpose. To aid in that, he insisted upon renting Southpoint to me, declaring that he had need of a reliable tenant. He is a most accommodating friend, to be sure." He sobered at the realization. "And now I owe him again, for this journey will have been costly one, as well as futile."

To his surprise, Eliza touched his hand. "Do not despair as yet, Captain Emerson."

"Odds are long for a happy ending, Mrs. North."

"And yet, I will hope for one until we are certain. I ask only that you do the same."

He met her steady gaze and his heart swelled at her conviction. She did not foolishly insist that all would come aright but hoped for the best. He admired her practicality and good sense, as ever he had. "You must not blame yourself," he said softly, turning his hand to give hers a gentle squeeze.

"Perhaps not, but I will, just as you will blame yourself for a battle gone awry." She smiled as the carriage halted. "No doubt the view will improve by the morning."

Nicholas could only hope as much. He stepped out of the carriage and offered his hand to her, nodding to Tupper. Eliza paused, her hand yet resting on his, to scan Haynesdale Manor with satisfaction and Nicholas watched her. She was at ease with this house in a way that he never could be and he saw that she felt she had arrived home.

Simply standing before it made him keenly aware that he was just the boy from Southpoint, the one the duke permitted to play with his youngest son for there were no other boys of an age. Nicholas did not doubt that Damien being the third and youngest son, and thus considered unlikely to ever inherit, had been part of that choice.

He watched as Eliza strode to the door with purpose and the butler bowed before her.

"Welcome back, Mrs. North."

"It is lovely to be at Haynesdale Manor, Farrell, even in such trying circumstance. I trust you received my note?"

"Of course, my lady, and all the preparations have been made. A cold supper has been laid for you in the dining room, though Mrs. Farley says there is a hot soup if you would like it. She was uncertain of your appetite at such an hour."

"A hot soup would be fortifying and welcome, Farrell. Please thank Mrs. Farley for the suggestion."

"And your usual room has been prepared for you, my lady."

"Excellent, Farrell. You are always so thorough." She smiled at the butler who beamed with pleasure. "I will visit my room before dinner," she said, removing her gloves as she climbed the steps to the house. The staff were lined up to greet her and either curtseyed or bowed as she passed. "I assume you have readied a room for Captain Emerson, as well?"

"The blue guest room, my lady."

"A perfect choice, Farrell. The Captain has no valet and I, no maid."

"Arrangements have been made, my lady." The butler gestured and a young woman stepped forward, as did a young man.

"As organized as ever. It is lovely to come home, Farrell." Eliza turned to survey Nicholas, her expression inscrutable. "Captain? Does that meet with your approval?"

"How can it not?" he said with a smile for the butler and the boy who would act as his valet. "All is always admirably arranged at Haynesdale Manor." He glanced back at Tupper but the older man spoke before he could ask.

"I will send a pair of stablehands on to Doncaster this very night, Captain Emerson, in the hope that there might be tidings there."

Nicholas bowed. "Thank you, Tupper. There truly is no place like Haynesdale."

❧

ELIZA HEARD a bellow just before the dawn, one so loud that it awakened her from a deep sleep. She sat up, heart racing, only to hear it again.

Nicholas!

She flung herself out of bed and seized a robe, not even troubling with a light in her haste to reach him. She knew every inch of this house, even in darkness. She waved away a disheveled Farrell at the summit of the stairs and hesitated only an instant outside the door to the blue bedroom. Nicholas groaned from within, his anguish so acute that she dismissed formalities and opened the door.

He had his nightmare again.

She had to console him, somehow.

Eliza had followed convention for years, but on this night, she would dare to defy it—and she would do as much for Nicholas.

Heart in her throat, she stepped inside. The drapes were open and moonlight streamed through the window panes to illuminate the room.

Nicholas thrashed in the great pillared bed

"No," he whispered, his voice shaking. His fists were clenching the linens and his every muscle was taut. He was sleeping, though, his eyes tightly closed and his lips pulled back in a grimace that bared his teeth. "No, no, *no*."

He was also beautiful. He was almost nude, which granted Eliza a view of the lean power of his body. The moonlight favored him, touching his skin with silver and burnishing his hair, as if he was a divine being who had set foot upon the earth. She approached the bed from the side in shadow, her gaze locked upon his face, her heart twisting that he should suffer so.

It was a poor reward for his valor, never mind his service to Damien. The scar on his shoulder showed that he had paid more than sufficient price for his service.

She should have ordered a brandy for him this night, for surely he had endured enough for one day with Helena's flight—but she had not thought of it.

Had he not requested one out of deference to her view?

"Nicholas," she whispered and touched his shoulder. She felt him shudder, the ripple passing through his body to his very toes, then he seized her hand.

"No," he whispered, but the anguish in his tone was lessened. He clung to her, as if she offered a lifeline, and Eliza perched on the side of the bed.

She clasped his hand in both of hers and whispered to him. "You are safe," she said, hoping her tone was soothing and reassuring. "You are in England again," she said, guessing that he relived a battle. "You are *safe*, Nicholas."

He caught his breath and his eyes flew open suddenly, perhaps because she had used his Christian name. He exhaled shakily, his grip firm upon her hand. She watched him scan the chamber, his unfamiliarity with it as painfully clear as his terror, then his gaze landed upon her and she fairly jumped at the intensity of his stare.

"Eliza," he whispered without comprehension, as if her presence made no sense at all. He frowned and shook his head.

"I am here, Nicholas," she said, bending to touch her lips to his knuckles. "You are safe at Haynesdale Manor." He stared at his hand where her lips had touched him, then studied her face.

He shook his head, then his eyes darkened, a shudder of horror passing through him again. "You should leave," he whispered, torment in his very words. "You should not witness this."

Whether he meant himself or believed her to be sharing his nightmare, Eliza had no intention of leaving. She cast aside her robe and eased into the bed beside him, wrapping her arms around him. Her sole thought was to comfort him, and aid him to endure the dream. He shivered and gasped, then turned his back to her, lost in the torment of his memories.

Eliza chose not to be deterred. She moved beneath the covers, pressing herself against his back and holding him close. One hand slid over his shoulder and beneath his head, while the other wrapped around his waist, landing on the solid warmth of his chest. She could feel the thunder of his heart. Emboldened by Mrs. Oliver's advice, she flattened her hands across his warm skin, closing her eyes at the rush of pleasure that coursed through her. She thought he might pull away, but after a moment's hesitation, he capitulated and surrendered to her embrace. His left hand closed over hers, holding it captive against his chest, and she felt his tears on her other arm.

"You are safe," she whispered again, kissing the back of his shoulder.

"Badajoz," he replied, shaking his head with vigor.

"Haynesdale," she corrected, pressing herself against him. "I will not leave you," she vowed and felt his hand close more tightly over hers.

They remained thus for what seemed an eternity, then she felt his breathing change, slowing just as his heartbeat did the same. The tension eased from his body as he slipped into sleep again, but Eliza did not leave him. It was comforting to lie with Nicholas, to feel his strength and his heat, to press herself against him. It was a forbidden pleasure but one that no one need know about.

She would stay with him, then slip away at dawn.

She smiled at the realization that she would have another secret then.

Eliza did not want to sleep, but to savor each passing moment, to feel his each and every breath. She treasured the pulse of his heart beneath her hand and the weight of his hand over hers. What would it be like to be wed to such a man? What would it be like to lie with Nicholas every night of her life? Eliza could imagine little better, and she knew this night would feed her own dreams in future.

The moon moved slowly across the sky, the angle of its light changing as Nicholas slept in her embrace. Finally, when clouds were flitting across the moon, Eliza dozed, spooned behind the man she loved, content that she had kept his demons at bay.

At least for one night.

CHAPTER 11

Nicholas awakened to pearly grey skies beyond the generous windows alongside the bed. He didn't immediately recognize the room, then recalled that he was at Haynesdale.

With a woman pressed against his back.

That was a surprise.

But there was no mistaking the truth of it. He could feel the softness of her breasts against his skin and smell her skin. Her breathing was slow and deep, evidence that she still slumbered, and her one hand was held captive in his own. When Nicholas glanced over his own shoulder, he was shocked to discover that his bed partner was Eliza North.

If ever there had been a moment that he had been glad of his inability to make love to a woman, this had to be it. He had no ability to soil her, and that was good.

All the same, he could not resist the opportunity to look upon her. Her hair was loose, unbound and falling in dark blonde waves over her shoulders and across the pillow. Her lips were soft and slightly parted in sleep, her dark lashes splayed across her cheeks. Her nightgown gaped open at the bodice and one perfect breast was exposed to his view.

And he had suggested that she was no temptress.

In that moment, Nicholas realized he had been utterly sober the night before. He could not have forgotten himself sufficiently to make such an error as joining Eliza abed…and then he recalled the nightmare, the tang of it on his tongue, the smell of the burning flesh and the overwhelming sense of powerlessness that always accompanied it.

He studied Eliza, recalling his conviction that an angel of mercy had come to him, interrupting his nightmare, gathering him into her embrace and granting him solace. It only made sense that he envisioned such a being as Eliza, as perfect a woman as ever there had been. He smiled and lifted her hand from his skin, pressing a kiss to her palm.

Perhaps Eliza *was* an angel of mercy. Why had she come to him? If pity had brought her to his bed, why had she stayed with him? He could only imagine it had been out of compassion, and that she had fallen asleep herself instead of retreating to her own chamber.

He might have put distance between them, rising to wash and leaving her to slumber, but that rosy nipple tempted him to take just one taste. This opportunity, surely, would never come to him again. Nicholas bent and captured it in a sweet kiss, the sleepy scent of Eliza surrounding and inundating him. There could be no finer scent in all the world. He felt the nipple bead to a taut peak and flicked his tongue across it, liking how she arched her back in capitulation.

He had often guessed that Eliza might be a warm and willing partner abed, but the confirmation of his suspicions only made him yearn for more.

She caught her breath and he glanced up to see her lashes flutter. Nicholas froze, feeling caught and doubting she would be glad to find him where he was.

Eliza's eyes opened and wonder of wonders, she

smiled at him. Her eyes lit, her gaze so clear that there could be no mistake in her thinking. Indeed, she pushed a hand through his hair with a possessive ease. When she smiled sleepily, Nicholas thought his heart might burst. Her fingertips landed on his shoulder and she caressed the breadth of his shoulder slowly, watching her own hand's progress. She traced his scar with a fingertip and her eyes darkened with concern, her touch so gentle that he did not draw away.

Then she met his gaze and smiled at him.

Nicholas had never seen a more beautiful sight and he was beguiled.

"I read a book of late," she whispered, which made no sense at all. Then she reached for him, winding her arms around his neck to draw him closer. Nicholas had a hundred questions, but he dared not utter a sound lest he break the spell. He could not have borne to see her turn away. He knew he should put distance between them, but those soft lips tempted him to take one taste.

He could not take pleasure but he would give it.

Eliza's hair was tousled as he had never seen it, and Nicholas thought it suited her well to be disheveled. She might have been Aphrodite in a Renaissance painting, stepping down upon the earth to claim the affections of a mortal man—or to seize him in thrall. Nicholas had no objections to being her prize. She kissed the pulse at his throat, her tongue touching his flesh in a most electrifying way. He closed his eyes against the delightful torment of her hair against his face, in his hands over his skin. She inhaled deeply after she kissed him, then whispered so that her breath fanned his skin. Nicholas felt a frisson of pleasure right to his toes.

"It spoke of the merit of encouragement," she murmured. That made so little sense that Nicholas wondered if she dreamed in this moment. He had no desire to awaken her, to be sure, though someone would arrive soon to stir the fire, no doubt. Eliza glanced up at him through her lashes, her eyes dancing in a most enticing way. "And I have found the argument very persuasive."

Nicholas said nothing, confused by her words, but Eliza did not seem to care. She stretched up to kiss him full on the mouth. The scent of her made him close his eyes with yearning and his grip tightened upon her—even before the tip of her tongue flicked. A jolt of raw desire shot through his veins.

And then his body stirred, as it had not stirred since Badajoz.

Nicholas blinked in wonder even as a jubilation soared through his veins. That only prompted a more emphatic reaction, one that would lead to an inevitable result after five years of chastity. As glorious as the sensation was, Eliza had to leave his bed before Nicholas committed a deed both of them could only regret.

Sadly, he could think of only one way to encourage her rapid departure.

He would grant her one gift first, though.

～

ELIZA's first initiation of intimacy had less than an encouraging start. To awaken in Nicholas' bed with him studying her so intently had seemed a sign of pending success and a moment that should not be lost. It could not be wrong to make her desire clear, and it was not wrong according to Mrs. Oliver's book of advice.

No sooner had her lips touched his than Eliza feared the worst. Nicholas straightened, like a soldier coming to attention—or perhaps a man realizing who was in his bed. She was certain he would cast her aside, or fling her from his chamber.

Then Nicholas uttered a low growl of such hunger that her heart leapt. He locked his arms around her with thrilling urgency and rolled her to her back. He deepened his kiss, claiming her mouth with a possessive power that made her heart thunder, and proved that she was not alone in her wayward thoughts of this morning.

His kiss was a marvel, both demanding and tender, an embrace that made Eliza glad that she had offered encouragement. It had so little in common with the kisses she and Frederick had shared, that it seemed criminal to describe both with the same word. It even was well beyond the kisses Nicholas and she had shared, which she had believed to be remarkable. Those two embraces had nothing upon this one.

And the meeting of their mouths was not all. Nicholas touched her as Frederick had never done, and Eliza felt such satisfaction in his caress that she knew this was as matters between man and woman should be.

His one hand swept down the length of her in a rough caress, then returned to cup her breast with a reverence that brought tears to her eyes. His thumb eased across her nipple in a movement of such exquisite torment that she feared she might not survive it. Then he did it again, and again, and again, so that she wanted to moan aloud.

At the same time, he held her nape in his hand and kissed her thoroughly, the strength of his fingers in her hair and his bare chest crushing her into the mattress. She was breathless and tingling, aroused beyond measure and desperate for more of whatever he might give.

A heat rose within Eliza, one she had never felt with Frederick, and she dared to give more encouragement with such reward. She locked her fingers into his hair and held him closer, kissing him with a hunger that echoed his own. She wanted more of him, indeed she wanted all of him, and immediately.

She was filled with urgency, a delicious and seductive new sensation. She wanted both to linger over this new experience and to devour it quickly to learn its full extent. She wanted to run her hands over Nicholas' body and explore every inch of it, but she also wanted to lie back and savor his touch, to be worshipped. Her need for more was undeniable—when Nicholas closed his mouth over her nipple again and suckled her with persuasive ease, she thought she would surrender all coherent thought. His hand abandoned her breast and eased over her belly, his fingers sliding between her thighs so seductively that she did moan aloud.

And she was not ashamed.

When she thought she could bear no more, he moved lower, his lips tracing a trail of kisses toward that most intimate part of her. Eliza could only watch him with wonder. Her toes curled when his hands locked around her waist with possessive ease, then he parted her thighs and bent to kiss her sweetly. His touch sent a shock through her, one that changed to a gasp as his mouth closed over her.

He commenced upon a sweet torment beyond anything she had ever experienced before and Eliza parted her thighs, silently beseeching him for more. She writhed beneath his caress, lost to the realms of pleasure, feeling a torrid heat build within her at wondrous speed. She was hot, she was shivering, she was aching for more of whatever he might grant, then all too soon, her desire flamed to a crescendo. She seized his shoulders and cried out as the tumult was loosed within her, then left her trembling in its wake.

"Nicholas," she whispered in wonder, knowing that

Mrs. Oliver needed to add at least one more chapter to her book.

Nicholas moved higher, still pressing kisses to her hip, her belly, her ribs, his movements as powerful as those of a predator. Eliza smiled, knowing she would be glad to be his captive. He laved her nipple, making it taut again, then grazed it with his teeth. "Yvette," he growled with satisfaction and Eliza recoiled in shock.

Yvette?

Yvette?

She braced her hands on his shoulders and pushed him away. He looked sleepy and dazed, his slow smile making her heart leap despite his utterance. He studied her breasts with obvious approval, then reached to cup one with his hand, his intention more than clear.

"Who is Yvette?" Eliza demanded fiercely and Nicholas blinked, lifting his gaze to hers. He frowned, as if puzzled. A horror then dawned in his expression, that change more than sufficient to send Eliza stumbling from the bed.

She knew in that moment that Yvette was the woman whose company had convinced him to linger abroad for so long, the one who had captured his heart and left him despondent, the one so fool as to cast such a man as this aside.

Eliza had no desire to even be confused with such a witless creature.

"I am not *Yvette,*" she whispered with heat, then seized her robe and raced to the door. She was well aware of the weight of Nicholas' gaze upon her, just as she was of the fire in her cheeks. Once again, she was conflicted, both mortified by her own reaction and savoring the tide of pleasure he had loosed within her.

Mercifully, there were no servants as yet in the corridor. She retreated to her own chamber and to the bed, pulling up the covers as if she had been there all night, alone.

Her heart was racing, though, and there remained a slick heat between her thighs. More than that, she felt a languid satisfaction that was all new. She thought of Nicholas touching her with such surety and her breath caught.

But *Yvette*. Eliza rolled over and thumped her pillow hard, even as a chambermaid slipped into the room to light the fire. She feigned sleep, fuming all the while.

How *could* he?

~

NICHOLAS COULD NOT RESTRAIN his good temper.

He doubted Eliza shared his mood and he knew he owed her an apology. But it would be no reward to Haynesdale's hospitality to seduce that man's sister in his own home.

The simple truth was that he was so encouraged by the return of an ability he had once considered to be innate that he could not keep from whistling.

Nicholas Emerson's confidence in the world and the future had been restored by one erection, his first in many years, and the elation of that change in circumstance could not be denied.

There were implications from the return of his abilities, too, ones that could not be overlooked. For if Eliza truly had feelings for him, and he had the ability to father the children she desired, then his future might be rosy indeed. Nicholas could only hope of the opportunity to explain himself and regain her admiration.

She was a marvel, an angel of mercy, a goddess and one who had healed him. He could think of no better reward than to serve her with all of his ability for the rest of their lives.

And so, he whistled.

He had no doubt that victory was not yet complete. He suspected there would be times when all did not respond as expected and he knew his nightmare was not yet banished. But Nicholas was encouraged as he had not been in years, and that was sufficient indeed.

The lady in question entered the breakfast room just as he was finishing an excellent meal. In point of fact, he would have found any meal excellent on this particular morning, but this had been a very good breakfast, particularly one served at so late an hour.

"Whistle again and I will strike you," Eliza warned through her teeth and Nicholas could only smile. She granted him a dark look. "That, sir, is almost as grievous a reaction."

"I do apologize, Mrs. North," he said, bowing low to her. She eyed him skeptically but tightened her lips and served her breakfast. Farrell bustled about, ensuring that she had all she desired, then cleared away Nicholas' plate. Eliza sat down at the opposite end of the table and cast Nicholas a poisonous glance before pouring her tea.

"Who is Yvette?" she demanded once Farrell had closed the door behind himself. Her gaze was steely and Nicholas could only admire that she was so forthright.

He might be engaged before noon.

"There is no Yvette," he admitted easily.

Eliza frowned. "But..."

He moved to the chair alongside her and dropped his voice low. "You had to leave before you were discovered in my bed, lest much be made of your presence there. Assumptions would be made, Mrs. North."

She arched a brow. "Assumptions that were not made as a result of your utterance."

He could not help but smile. "I confess that I did not expect your...annoyance."

She inhaled and her eyes narrowed. "Is it customary for women of your acquaintance to welcome you addressing them with the name of another?"

"I have never done as much before. I strove to protect you, Mrs. North."

"Protect me?"

"I knew you would be insulted but I believed you would leave quietly."

"Quietly," she repeated as if he spoke in tongues.

"I did not know that such passion was in your nature. Perhaps I failed to appreciate your affinity for temptresses."

She considered him for a long moment and he held her gaze, letting her look. "And still your eyes sparkle. Did you enjoy my reaction so much as that?"

"I enjoyed *my* reaction as much as that," he confessed, unable to keep himself from smiling.

"I am mystified, sir."

"You have cured me of a longstanding affliction, Mrs. North, and I am grateful beyond belief."

"How curious that I have no awareness of what I have done that resulted in such a marvel."

"May I speak bluntly?"

"Please do."

He leaned toward her and dropped his voice to a whisper. "You aroused me."

Eliza lifted a brow, her gaze locking with his. Her confusion was clear.

"You came into my bed, you kissed and caressed me, and I," Nicholas took a satisfied breath, feeling powerful and vital all over again. "I *responded*." His smile could not be contained.

"And this is unusual?"

"It was not, until Badajoz."

Her expression became one of concern. "That was five years ago, Captain Emerson."

"And I assure you they have been a very long five years."

"But." She frowned and glanced out the window. "But Damien said you had traveled the Continent, sampling the favors of ladies."

"A tale I knew he would find credible. In truth, I took solace in brandy."

Her lips pursed and she averted her gaze, then studied him anew. "And you do not believe that had a part to play in your...condition."

"The brandy was second. The condition was first."

"Badajoz was first," she corrected and he had to cede that point. "The battle was only part of your secret."

"You are as astute as ever, Mrs. North."

"And you are more accommodating than I know you to be, Captain Emerson."

"I am utterly at your service, Mrs. North."

She caught her breath and eyed him, a reassuring sparkle taking up residence in her eyes. "And what service do you propose to offer to me, sir?"

"I thought to court you, since I believe you once held me in affection."

Her gaze flew to his, and color touched her cheeks. "But you love another," she whispered.

Nicholas shook his head with resolve. "Never. There has never been another queen of my heart save you, Mrs. North."

"But you *left*," she said with urgency.

"Because I had no hope of offering for the daughter of a duke." He held her gaze. "And you wed, purportedly for love, proving my conviction that I loved alone to be correct."

She dismissed this with a gesture, setting aside her knife and fork with welcome purpose. "Because you left," she repeated. "I told you I never loved Frederick in that way."

Nicholas smiled at her. "But I was informed at the time that you wed for love, taking a man of an income of only two thousand pounds. I might be able to match that sum, in a few years."

"Nicholas!" she said with an indignation that warmed him to his toes. "I do not care about fortune! I only ever desired you."

"And I, you, Eliza," he murmured, watching her smile of delight dawn as he said her name. "But I could not pursue you, not when I might be the cause of your unhappiness." She began to protest but he lifted a hand. "You desired children, and I did not believe I could offer you any."

Her lips rounded in a perfect 'o'.

"Until this morning," she whispered.

"You have healed me, and so there is only one deed to be done." Nicholas dropped to one knee beside her and she turned to face him, letting him take both of her hands in his. Her eyes were alight, her happiness so tangible that he could not believe he had ever doubted her regard. "Marry me, Eliza, and build a home with me at Southpoint. I vow I will do my utmost to see you happy and to fill our lives with children."

"You cannot accomplish that feat alone, sir."

"No, only with the lady I love, the woman who will always hold my heart captive." He bent to kiss her hand. "Wed me, Eliza," he whispered. "Please."

"I will, Nicholas," she vowed, then caught his face in her hands and kissed him with a passion he could not doubt.

He was barely aware of the slight click of the door opening, but he definitely heard Farrell clear his throat portentously.

"There is a gentleman to see you, my lady," the butler said. "A Mr. Galveston."

Nicholas straightened.

Eliza looked to be equally startled. "Here?" she said. "Now?"

"Indeed, my lady. I have placed him in the front parlor and hope this is acceptable."

"Of course," Eliza said and rose to her feet. Nicholas followed, rather liking the idea of Galveston being placed in a specific location like a piece of furniture. He would have placed the man in question at somewhat of a greater distance however.

That all changed when Mr. Galveston revealed the reason for his visit.

Helena was not ruined, after all!

~

LADY DALHOUSIE WAS NEVER FOND of obligations but this particular one was overly bitter. She owed a visit to her rival, Lady Haynesdale, as well as an expression of gratitude for that lady's daughter retrieving Helena. The chit had sent her a letter from Haynesdale, confessing all of the tale and revealing that she was in the company of Nicholas and Mrs. North. The relief had been nigh overwhelming, even though it necessitated this mission.

She was obliged to enter Haynesdale House to perform this office, the abode that she had long ago believed would be her own home. It was a burden that she should not have been required to endure, especially in the moment of her own greatest defeat. Her own townhouse was sold. She had no destination. All was in ruins, and she could only believe that Lady Haynesdale would gloat.

Had their places been reversed, Lady Dalhousie would most assuredly have gloated.

She was not late. She was not early. She was not over-dressed. She was not under-dressed. All was precisely as it should be, save the sense of injustice that simmered in her heart.

Constance looked well. Not as young as once she had been and not quite as slender as in their youth, but still attractive. It was on Fanny's tongue to comment how well widowhood suited her former rival but she refrained from saying as much.

She was glad of that choice when Constance spoke.

"And so our families are to be joined in matrimony," that woman said, prompting Fanny to clatter her teacup in the saucer.

Had Helena captured the duke's eye?

She could not imagine a finer ending to this tale.

"I beg your pardon?" she asked, managing to keep the quiver of anticipation from her voice.

"Captain Emerson and my daughter, Mrs. North, are to wed," Constance said smoothly. "I had a letter from Haynesdale this morning. Has your nephew not shared the happy news?"

Fanny felt at disadvantage and knew her old rival noticed. "I had a letter from him this morning but have not read it as yet." She glanced toward her bag where the letter reposed, still sealed. She had been a little fearful of its contents.

Constance smiled and shook her head. "I am requested to seek a special license. They mean to be wed before Easter." She scanned the parlor. "I suppose we will have the wedding luncheon here, if that suits."

"Surely the bride has a preference of more import than mine."

"Eliza asked if it might be thus, but wished for me to confirm as much with you."

Fanny had no objections with someone else hosting the celebration—and assuming its cost—to be sure. "I have no objections, of course." She cleared her throat. "Did she confide where they are to live?"

"Captain Emerson has rented Southpoint from my son. Perhaps you did not know. It was arranged just before Damien departed for Paris. I understand that Captain Emerson intends to breed horses."

"He always had such a gift with them."

Constance picked up a letter from the table. "And Eliza suggests that she might continue to seek a match for Helena, if a removal from town to the country is deemed suitable by you." She frowned at the letter. "It sounds as if she has a particular gentleman in mind."

"I have no objections," Fanny said. "Of course, Helena has no memory of Southpoint, but it was always a lovely property. I think that being from town might be of benefit to her."

If nothing else, it would be more challenging for Helena to find trouble.

"I always think a young girl should experience London, but it is in the country where she best finds her footing, to my view."

"She did always love Hexham when we visited."

"Precisely." The two women smiled at each other politely, though Fanny was keenly aware that she was the only one lacking plans. "I understand you have sold your house in town," Constance invited.

Fanny laughed lightly. "The country does beckon us all."

Constance smiled at her, her expression unexpectedly kind. "I think you should read your letter," she said. "I can leave you for a few moments to enquire after the menus for the week."

She was possessed of an alarming confidence, one that fed Fanny's curiosity. Once she was alone, she set her tea aside and studied the letter from Nicholas for a long moment, before taking a breath and opening it. She scanned its contents, reassured by his steady hand and fairly hearing his voice.

Then she gasped aloud when she reached the detail of import.

I am hoping, Aunt, that you will avail yourself of a service I am able to do for you. There is a small cottage at Southpoint, perhaps one that you recall, with a garden in need of some attention. It is a sufficient walk from the main house to allow for privacy, nestled into a dale with a fine hedge surrounding it. Do you remember Bramble Cottage? It is part of the holding that I have leased from the Duke of Haynesdale and currently sits empty. I would be most obliged if you would take the garden in hand and make a home there. Of course, I could not ask you for rent after your years of caring for Helena, but would simply like to see the property occupied...

Fanny blinked back tears, crumpling the letter in her hand, then smoothing it across her lap again. Her heart swelled with gratitude and relief so that it took a moment to compose herself.

Her sister's boy had become a fine man, to be sure.

"Will you accept?" Constance asked softly when she returned. A maid followed her with a fresh pot of tea.

"Mrs. North told you."

"She mentioned that it was Captain Emerson's intent."

"And we will be so close."

Their gazes met and Constance smiled. "I would seek your advice about the *Apothecary Roses*. They have such an inclination to mildew that I despair of them ever flourishing."

"There is not sufficient sun for them, then," Fanny said with authority. They discussed roses with such gusto that the hours flew by until Higgins declared that dinner would be served. Fanny was shocked to note the hour, but Constance appealed to her.

"Do stay and dine with me," she said. "I would greatly enjoy your company."

And Fanny, who knew how dismal it could be to eat alone, realized that she and Constance had more in common than their admiration of the late duke. It was time to put that old feud behind them, to be sure.

She smiled. "I should be delighted, Lady Haynesdale," she said with an enthusiasm she herself would never have anticipated just hours before.

IT WAS WRETCHEDLY FAR from Haynesdale to London. Helena thought they would never reach town again. On the other hand, she was not anxious to encounter Mr. Melbourne again, or even to face her aunt's inevitable chastising. Her short visit to the Dawlish home had given her a new appreciation of her own situation—and her experience with Mr. Melbourne had secured her resolve to wed a rich man.

The Duke of Haynesdale would suit her well. For the sake of comfort, she would turn a blind eye to his infirmity and his advanced years.

She was glad that Nicholas and Mrs. North would wed, as the prospect seemed to give them both joy. She supposed that two persons so aged must be glad to have someone with whom to share their dotage. Their union also would give her the opportunity to frequently encounter the duke.

Helena did not intend to let opportunity be lost.

Their return to London was at a more stately pace than their departure and Tupper seemed to expend a tremendous amount of concern on horses that were not even the duke's own. He talked long with the ostlers at each inn, and Nicholas often joined the discussion. They stayed at The Bell, the inn at Stilton, for one night before continuing to London. That evening, in the room she shared with Mrs. North, Helena noticed that her brother's intended read late into the night. It seemed that she had a treatise that fascinated her, though she declined to tell Helena anything about it.

That only ensured that Helena was resolved to read it before they reached London.

On that last day, Nicholas rode with Tupper atop the coach and Mrs. North dozed off in the coach during the afternoon.

Helena supposed that the lady's great age could only lead to such fatigue, especially when she had read long into the night.

She opened Mrs. North's satchel slowly and steadily, watching for any change in that lady's posture or breathing. There was none. She recognized the document immediately, for it was a sheaf of loose pages, covered with elegant handwriting. Helena secured the top one and retreated to the far side of the coach to read it.

Upon the merit of a forthright touch...

Helena felt her lips part in amazement as she read the page, then she sat up to avidly read the entire page while she had the opportunity. Once she had read it all, and considered the illustration, she viewed Mrs. North with newfound appreciation.

Her chaperone, it seemed, had a far larger knowledge than Helena had ever guessed. She eyed the satchel and wondered how many more pages she could read before Mrs. North awakened.

There was only one way to find out.

IN THE END, it was Eliza North who wed before Easter Sunday, not Helena Emerson. The Saturday in question dawned a glorious spring day, with a clear blue sky overhead and an abundance of sunshine.

Eliza was awake early, still unable to believe her good fortune. Nicholas had been to Haynesdale again to ensure that all would be in readiness for their arrival at Southpoint and that of his aunt at the cottage, which had need for some repairs. Upon his return, they had agreed upon the date, despite Damien's continued absence, rather than delay their nuptials any longer. The duke had sent his good wishes and arranged for the special license.

Eliza left the house for the church with her mother, waving to those neighbors who appeared to wish her well. All the staff had gathered to wish her well, and her mother was hosting a luncheon afterward. She wore a new dress of silk so fine that it might have been gossamer, with golden embroidery of such lavishness upon the hems that she felt like a queen. Roses not yet being in bloom, she carried a nosegay of blue hyacinths and their sweet fragrance had already filled her chamber. The larger coach waited before the house, the team of four bays tossing their heads with impatience, and Tupper beamed at her like a benevolent uncle.

In the carriage, her mother conjured a letter and presented it to her.

"What is this?" Eliza asked.

"A gift for the happy couple." Her mother's smile was mysterious.

"*Maman*! You have already planned a luncheon..."

"It is not from me," her mother said, interrupting her protest. "Read it now so I may see your reaction."

In that moment, Eliza recognized that the letter was addressed to her, and the script was in Damien's bold hand. She opened it, thinking he sent her good wishes for the day or perhaps sent word of his return. Instead she gave a gasp of delight and looked then to her mother.

"He always planned to settle a sum upon you when you wed again," her mother confided. "But this, I believe, will be more welcome."

It was, for Damien declared that he was returning Southpoint to Nicholas outright, as a wedding gift to both of them. He had written to his estate manager as well, who would finalize the details when next they arrived at Haynesdale.

"Did you contrive this, *Maman?*"

Her mother shook her head. "Damien insisted upon it. He asked my approval, for he said Nicholas had declined the gift before and he did not wish to give offence."

"I am certain there can be none, *Maman.*"

"So am I, my dear. So am I." They embraced in the carriage and Eliza watched her mother wipe away a joyous tear. "To have you so happily wed and so close, as well." She pressed Eliza's hand. "It is a gift beyond expectation." Then she smiled impishly. "Though there could be one more to make matters complete."

Eliza had to tease her. "Indeed? You were the one to tell me that children were not required for happiness."

Her mother laughed. "I said nothing of grandchildren, Eliza."

They laughed together, then Eliza was startled to realize they had arrived.

The church interior seemed dark after the sunlight and there were only a few good friends and relations gathered to witness the ceremony. Eliza recognized Lady Dalhousie, Helena smiling beside her, then her heart leapt with familiar vigor when she saw Nicholas waiting for her at the altar. He smiled, his eyes fairly glowing with satisfaction.

He had abandoned his regimentals in recent weeks, insisting that he enter private life again with the move to Southpoint. To the satisfaction of Jenkins, his valet, he had visited Damien's excellent tailor. His navy jacket was crisply tailored and his silk vest of gold with threads of blue matched her own dress. Her heart fluttered, as she knew it always would in his presence, when she halted beside him to make her vows.

"Last chance to escape me," he murmured, a merry twinkle lighting his eyes.

"Never," she said, vehement even in an undertone and was gratified by his smile. Then the service began and she listened solemnly, repeating her vows and savoring the conviction in Nicholas' tone when he swore his own.

Then his ring was on her finger, her hand captured fast within his own, and they were leaving the church to the merry pealing of bells and the congratulations of all around them. To Eliza's astonishment, there was an unexpected figure on the steps of the chapel. The old woman wore shawls and cloaks aplenty, and truly was so draped in fabric that she could barely be discerned beneath her hat.

She offered a flower to Eliza. "A posy for the bride," she crowed and Eliza halted to speak to the crooked older woman.

"I thank you for this kindness, my lady."

"It is a conviction of mine that a new bride should be wished well by all of her acquaintances," the woman said. Eliza could discern the gleam of her eyes behind the veils but could not see her clearly.

"Are we acquainted, madame?"

The woman cackled. "I am known as Mrs. Oliver," she confessed and Eliza was startled.

This woman was the one granting her such intimate advice? She was astounded.

"Cannot believe as much, can you, my lady?" Mrs. Oliver continued, clearly deriving great satisfaction from the surprise she had given. She smacked her lips audibly. "Three husbands I have buried and I have savored each and every one of them, as I believe you may know."

"My lady?" Nicholas asked from beside Eliza, clearly puzzled.

She introduced him quickly to her newfound companion then smiled. "Though we have not wed previously, I have relied upon the advice of Mrs. Oliver these past weeks," she informed him. "In matters unknown to me without her counsel."

His eyes widened in surprise as he clearly understood her meaning. "So, that was how you knew," he said beneath his breath. He bowed before the older lady. "And do I owe you a debt, Mrs. Oliver, for ensuring my bride and I have been so happily joined?"

"You will owe me one for ensuring that you remain happily wed, to be sure."

Eliza almost laughed at Nicholas' surprise.

Mrs. Oliver meanwhile rummaged beneath her copious cloak and produced a leather satchel that had become most familiar.

"Dare I hope there is more of your book to be reviewed?" Eliza asked.

"I found your comments most illuminating on earlier passages, Mrs. Emerson, and should be delighted if you had the opportunity to review these additions." She leaned closer to whisper. "You might indulge in a look before night falls, if you mark my meaning."

Eliza smiled. "I am honored by your trust, Mrs. Oliver. I will see them returned to you before we depart for Haynesdale this coming week."

"Haynesdale, is it then? I should be obliged if you might leave your address for me."

"At Carruthers & Carruthers," Eliza agreed with a nod. "I will indeed."

The older lady then swept a curtsey of remarkable depth and wished them well. Eliza was smiling as they continued to the carriage.

"You look most mysterious, my Eliza," Nicholas murmured. "What is in that satchel?"

"I will show you, tonight," she promised and he kissed her hand, vowing to hold her to that.

And then he kissed her lips, and Eliza forgot all about Mrs. Oliver and her book.

"THIS IS QUITE OUTRAGEOUS," Nicholas said that evening after all the guests had left and Lady Haynesdale had retreated to her room and her garden plans. He was standing in his nightshirt in Eliza's chamber, examining the pages given to her earlier that day by Mrs. Oliver. Eliza had taken the liberty of reading them before he joined her. Her mother had assigned Nicholas the chamber next to her own, one that Frederick had occupied on those few occasions when they visited London while married.

Eliza was glad to have so few memories of Frederick here or at Haynesdale Manor, for she wished to think only of Nicholas. Indeed, her first marriage seemed a distant dream, and certainly not one that stirred her as much as her current situation. Just having Nicholas in her chamber, his shirt open, his hair tousled, was sufficient to give her palpitations.

He flicked her a glance, his eyes very blue. "Scandalous even," he added in a low rumble that made her toes curl.

"What is outrageous is that I had to resort to such tactics," Eliza said, moving to his side. "Intimate advice from strangers. That *is* scandalous. Particularly when you could have simply proposed to me yourself." She turned her back to him. "Will you unfasten this necklace for me, please?

"Was your maid remiss in her duties?"

Eliza chuckled. "Simply unable to complete them because I dismissed her."

His fingertips landed on the back of her neck, then slid across her skin in a slow caress. "Whyever would you do such an impulsive thing, Mrs. Emerson?" he murmured, then replaced his fingertips with his lips.

Eliza closed her eyes and tilted her head back in satisfaction. "So, I could be better prepared for your arrival, of course."

"By reading this? My lady, you have no need of such counsel."

"Why not?"

The necklace was removed and dropped to the table, then his arms closed around her waist. He leaned against her, his lips on her ear, his breath making her shiver. "Because you are utterly seductive already. No one need advise you on the merit of a forthright touch."

She turned in his embrace, sliding her arms around his neck. "But when we met again in the breakfast room just weeks ago, I had no notion you were susceptible to my presence, Captain Emerson."

He grinned. "Be assured that I am utterly and completely so." He drew Eliza closer. "You truly have my undivided attention, now and forever." He lowered his head and captured her lips beneath his own, giving her a kiss so slow and thorough that she nearly forgot her own name. When he lifted his head, satisfaction lighting his eyes, she nigh did forget the topic of their conversation.

"What of your nightmares?"

He shrugged. "They are less frequent and less vigorous, thanks to you. I will retreat to the other chamber later to ensure that I do not disturb your sleep."

"You will do no such thing," she said fiercely, holding him fast.

Nicholas' smile was slow and lit his eyes. Eliza was pleased to see that the shadows were vastly diminished. "Perhaps you liked the result of awakening abed with me."

"Perhaps I did, sir, and that had nothing to do with the book." They smiled at each other for a long warm moment.

"That drawing," he said, nodding toward the discarded pages from Mrs. Oliver.

"What of it?"

He coughed lightly. "It shows a male member."

Eliza smiled, then pulled back slightly to look down between them. "Rather smaller than the actual one before me," she said playfully, then reached down to caress him. She felt uncommonly bold, but he rose to her touch in a most encouraging way, just as foretold. "Your recovery appears to be complete, Captain Emerson."

"I believe we should check thoroughly to be certain," he growled, gripping her waist and pulled her against him. He kissed her more urgently this time, his hunger feeding her own. He swept her into his arms to carry her to the bed without breaking his kiss, then stepped back to look upon her. Recalling the merit of a bold invitation, Eliza pulled her chemise over her head and discarded it, shaking out her hair so it fell over her shoulders.

"It appears I have wed a temptress," Nicholas said, his admiration more than clear.

"Oh, I hope so. It has been my dream to become one."

"You?" He feigned astonishment. "Such an upstanding and respectable lady?"

"Me!" she replied playfully. "You are over-dressed for seduction, sir."

He removed his own nightshirt and watched as she surveyed him, then moved onto the bed. His anticipation was palpable, but she liked that he moved slowly, drawing out the moment. He kissed her hand and then her elbow, flicking a glance up at her as he trailed kisses to her shoulder. "Is it possible, Mrs. Emerson, that your choice of reading material has led you astray?"

She shook her head, smiling. "It has led me to precisely the place I most wish to be."

"Then I must ensure that you find satisfaction in your situation," Nicholas declared, pausing to kiss her nipple and coaxing it to pert attention.

"I believe we should consult the new pages," she said, guessing his reaction. "To verify that all is correct."

"You will not be reading on this particular night, my lady."

Eliza laughed. "Not if I have successfully tempted you."

"Consider it done," he vowed and lowered his weight atop her, kissing her sweetly as he pinned her against the bed. Eliza ran her hands over him, happy beyond her wildest imagining, and gasped when he lifted his head to look down upon her.

"I believe *I* should give that book a recommendation," he whispered. "For I am well content with the results of your consulting it."

"Wait until I check the advice offered in these new pages," she threatened and he laughed.

"Wait until I show you that there is no need of a book on this night," he vowed and kissed her to silence.

"I love you, Nicholas," she whispered when she could.

He ran a hand up her arm to her cheek and cupping

her face in his hand. "And I love you, my Eliza," he murmured, bending to kiss her soundly again.

Eliza let her hand slide down the length of him, her fingertips dancing over his flesh until she reached the area featured in the illustration. She heard him catch his breath as she wrapped her fingers around him, and felt him go still when she touched the spot at the base recommended for the cultivation of arousal. The way he whispered her name against her throat was most assuredly a testimonial to that counsel being correct.

Eliza had time to smile, then Nicholas caught her close. His fingers slid between her thighs with welcome surety, and she doubted she would sleep much at all that night.

Or perhaps not even the following morning. The nights of a temptress might prove exhausting but Eliza saw no cause to complain about that.

*R*oses, roses, and more roses.

Would that such flowers had never come into existence.

By the time the entire party left London for Haynesdale, it was not only a veritable entourage, but Helena was certain she had heard sufficient conversation about roses to last her until she became even more elderly than Aunt Fanny and Lady Haynesdale. Their communion over the flowers had progressed from mutual admiration through at least three intervals of heated disagreement—the first about the finest of all roses, the veritable queen; the second about the merit of the newest cultivars from the Continent; and the third, the most contentious yet, about the shape of the planned reflecting pond to be constructed at Haynesdale Manor. Helena was resolved to die before she reached such dotage that would require her to be fascinated with gardens.

The only mercy was that she was traveling in the smaller of the duke's coaches, along with Aunt Fanny, while Lady Haynesdale occupied the larger coach, along with her daughter, now Mrs. Emerson. Nicholas had cruelly abandoned Helena on the journey, choosing to either ride Sterling alongside the party or join the other party in the larger coach. It was perfectly horrid of him to prefer his new wife's company to that of his sister, but he only laughed at Helena when she commented as much.

Worse, the duke was yet away from England and no one knew when he intended to return.

What so occupied his attention? Helena wished to know.

How could she charm him when he was so persistently absent?

How could she utilize what she had learned from the treatise surreptitiously borrowed from the former Mrs. North? Those passages had been most illuminating and only made Helena more curious about intimate matters.

The duke would be captivated by her, if only he deigned to return.

As days and weeks passed, though, Helena began to be convinced that he would not.

Aunt Fanny talked endlessly as they rode north, first about the triumph of Nicholas' wedding, then about their happy return to Southpoint, then about her vexation with Lady Haynesdale for refusing to share all of her views. She endeavored to solicit Helena's interest in the cottage, which might as well have been a tomb at the end of the world, and failed.

Helena kept her face close to the window for miles as they departed, drinking in every detail of the city they were leaving behind. She would die an old maid, with blisters on her hands from tending roses, forgotten by every man of interest, a veritable orphan in the wilds of Nottingham. The duke would never return and even abiding in his own duchy would offer no opportunities to steal his heart.

As fates went, Helena's was an undeservedly cruel one.

"You will like it well enough, once you meet some new friends," Aunt Fanny declared, as if it was of no import to leave London behind. She was very content these days, and more inclined to treat herself to a sweet at tea than had recently been the case. "There might be any number of eligible young men in the area."

Helena sighed. Doubtless she would be obliged to tend chickens or milk cows. Her silk slippers would be ruined.

But then, there was no cause for dancing in the duke's absence.

She frowned at the passing view, such as it was.

"Consider it a new adventure," her aunt advised. "You have had a season in town, now you will become acquainted with country living. I imagine there are many reputable families in the area. You have only to recall your new acquaintances, Mrs. Dawlish and her daughters, to be reassured."

Helena did like Mrs. D. and she was obliged to her, to be sure. And Flora had been nice enough, once she had overcome her shyness and talked a little.

But still, Helena was convinced that all country suitors would be like Mr. Galveston, and she could not abide the thought of marrying such a man.

Nor could she abide the thought of living forever with Aunt Fanny.

Doubtless some hideous match would be arranged and she would be obliged to wed a man she despised.

"Perhaps we shall get a little dog," Aunt Fanny said brightly.

Helena sighed again. She had no desire for a dog.

"And look!" The carriage lurched as it took a turn, and evidently the road they continued upon was both narrower and rougher. "We take the turn into Haynesdale! Doubtless these are the woods said to thickly cover this estate. It is rumored, you know, that Robin Hood plied these very forests."

Helena sat up with new interest. She could be abducted by a dashing outlaw, compelled to ride by his side, stealing from the rich to give to the poor.

He would have to be a local man, in disguise; a nobleman, to be sure, but one cheated of his inheritance, determined to benefit the people as much as his wicked relation had abused them.

She peered into the forest on either side of the road with curiosity. The shadows were dark, sunlight filtering through the trees to illuminate spots in the distance, a clearing or a flashing stream. She shivered in delight, imagining that a dangerous rogue watched their progress, planning his scheme to steal her away.

"There! Your mood is evidently improved. We *will* get a little dog," her aunt continued. "Soon enough, you will have your first glimpse of Haynesdale Manor, but better yet, we will linger at Southpoint for a night before continuing on to the Bramble Cottage." Aunt Fanny gave a rapturous sigh. "Even the name is satisfying," she murmured with a contentment Helena did not share.

Doubtless there would be blackberries and Helena would be obliged to pick them, then make jam herself.

Her aunt blithely continued. "I would carry on without delay, but Nicholas would ensure first that all has been repaired and made ready. I cannot wait to see it, Helena!"

She continued upon the same subject for the next hour as Helena sought a glimpse of her captor and salvation, but without success.

When they finally stopped, it was late in the afternoon and the sun was lowering toward the trees. Southpoint was a tidy house, perhaps a little larger than her aunt's London townhouse, but there was something comfortable and reassuring about the sight of it. Helena did not remember it, but she felt as if she had come home.

The house was symmetrical, a pair of doors of deep green in the middle of the façade, with large windows paired on either side. Above were five windows of goodly size, the whole of the structure made of cut stone. To the left was a gate leading to what appeared to be a garden and to the right was one that led to the stables, barely visible behind. An older man and a woman in an apron stood on the steps, obviously to greet Nicholas, with two young girls beside them.

Nicholas led Sterling toward the right gate, where an ostler met him to take the horse. Nicholas then handed Eliza out of the larger carriage, leading her to the door. Helena watched him smile and knew he made a jest, for the older man waiting there smiled and nodded approval.

Nicholas then came to open the carriage door for Aunt Fanny and Helena. No sooner were they standing before the house, than Lady Haynesdale called from the big coach. "I spoke to Eliza already, Lady Dalhousie, but I do hope that you will join me for tea tomorrow before departing for your cottage. I should so like to have your opinion upon the gardens once you have seen them."

"We should be delighted," Aunt Fanny said, clearly unable to resist the temptation of seeing the roses.

"And Miss Emerson, you need not fear that you will be obliged to endure too much discussion of gardens." Lady Haynesdale had the look of a person with a secret, though Helena could not imagine what it might be. "Eliza has made a most wonderful suggestion and I intend to act upon it."

Helena looked to find Eliza smiling at her, and wondered what jest these two had planned. Her aunt nudged her. "I cannot wait to learn of it, Lady Haynesdale," she said politely.

"You need not wait, my dear," that woman confided. "We are going to host a ball at Haynesdale Manor in a fortnight, and you had best bring your dancing slippers. The young men in these parts like nothing better than to dance and I wager you will be popular indeed."

Oh!

"That sounds a marvel, Lady Haynesdale."

"It will be, Miss Emerson."

"Will the duke return in time to enjoy it?"

"Who can say, my dear." Lady Haynesdale smiled. "It is years since I planned such a party, but I have not forgotten all I know. It will be the talk of the shire!" She waved to her driver, then waved farewell to all of them as the team of four horses trotted away.

"A ball!" Aunt Fanny said with satisfaction. "You might be wed this season, after all, my dear."

Helena had no objections to a wedding, so long as the right man stood by her side. She fiercely wished that either the duke would return by the date of the ball, or a dangerous stanger would make his attentions known to her.

Either would be more interesting than the incessant talk of gardens.

WEST OF PARIS, the Duke of Haynesdale was driven down a rutted lane in his rented coach. He felt as if he was at war again, confronted by obstacles and half-truths at every turn. The sole detail of promise that he possessed was this address. He had failed to confront Jacques Desjardins, though he had come close enough to see that man's back as he fled into the darkened streets of Paris. If nothing else, he had frightened the man.

It was little consolation when he wanted so much more.

This foray into the countryside was the last clue he held in the mystery of Desjardins' hold over Miss Ballantyne.

A convent seemed a most unlikely destination in this matter. An almost-forgotten one, hidden in the forests of Brittany and far from any thoroughfare or town, seemed even less likely. The dialect in these parts was so thick as to be another language altogether and he did not relish the inevitable interview with the Mother Superior. He had written in advance but had no notion whether his missive would have arrived before himself.

The mail in France could stand improvement, to be sure.

At least Eliza was happily wed and he had been able to contribute to her future with Nicholas. He had no doubt they would be happy but wanted them to be comfortable as well.

Sometimes, it was not all bad to be duke, though he did miss his older brothers.

The wind had been relentless, the last town far behind them and the warming brick at his feet cold by the time the coach slowed. The sky was dark and he could see clouds rolling above the treetops, a winter sky if ever he had seen one. Doubtless there would be a storm soon. He would be obliged to drive on after his visit, despite the hour and the weather. Damien was chilled to the bone but would be more than glad of the opportunity to walk. His leg ached with a vengeance and he leaned heavily upon his cane as he approached the entrance.

The building was ancient, covered with vines, so

much moss on the stones that it might have been part of the forest itself. It looked to be built around a cloister, like a medieval abbey, and the church tower rose high at the right. Clearly, the foundation was of some age and he marveled that it had not been damaged in the unrest of forty years before.

Perhaps in this corner of France, the tumult had been less.

There was a welcome light at the portal and a stout porter who clearly anticipated his arrival, though Damien did not know why. He had not written to advise of his visit, preferring an element of surprise. He was ushered into a room of welcome warmth, where a small fire burned on the hearth and a lantern cast a welcome glow. The windows were small and the furnishings spare, leaving no doubt that people came to this place for simplicity and reflection.

"Good afternoon, sir," a woman said softly in Parisian French.

Damien was startled that he was no longer alone and spun to look. A slender older woman had entered the room silently from behind him, and he realized there was another door to the room. She was dressed simply, in a dark dress of severe lines that fell to the floor, her hair and neck hidden beneath a wimple that spread over her shoulders. Her face was devoid of paint, her expression stern but serene, her eyes a deep brown. She stood utterly still and might have been a statue, save that she blinked on occasion.

Again, he had the sense that he had journeyed back in time to this place, or perhaps that time had no place in this part of the forest. He bowed deeply to her as he greeted her.

"Good afternoon. I have come..." he began, but she lifted one pale hand for silence.

"We do not utter names here, sir. Indeed, we speak

as little as can be contrived." She reached out, indicating his signet ring with one slender finger, then his cane. "I believe you are from England."

Damien inclined his head in agreement.

"Is she well?"

He hesitated, uncertain of his reply.

"A mutual acquaintance wrote to me recently," the woman said, her gaze locked upon his. He sensed that she would recognize a lie before he even uttered it aloud, if he had been inclined to deceive her. "She advised me that you could be trusted."

Doris? Miss Ballantyne? He could not be certain.

"Is our friend well?"

He could only guess that she meant Miss Esmeralda Ballantyne.

"She is well, but I wish her circumstance was better."

The woman was unsurprised. She nodded, as if a decision had been made, though Damien expected it had been made long before. "That can be the only reason for your presence," she said, then turned, raising a hand in invitation. A young girl entered the room from that same shadowed doorway, her head bowed, and the older woman touched her shoulder gently. "Be brave, *petite*," she said quietly when the girl's steps faltered. "All will be well."

The girl stepped forward and lifted her chin, her eyes such a clear hue of green that Damien caught his breath in recognition. Even in such youth, she was a beauty, a younger version of Miss Ballantyne, her hair as black and her skin as fair. There was an innocence in her gaze instead of Miss Ballantyne's knowing glint. He immediately felt an emphatic need to defend her at any price.

"Your sister summons you, just as always she vowed she would," the nun advised. "Remember all we have taught you, and think kindly of us."

This was the mysterious Sylvie, who Miss Ballantyne defended from Jacques Desjardins.

Her sister. Damien had no ability to assess the age of young woman but he guessed this one to be perhaps twelve years of age. She would have been an infant, then, at the beginning of the war, too young perhaps for the journey to England or any uncertainty in Miss Ballantyne's future.

So she had entrusted the babe to the care of these sisters.

The older woman kissed the girl's cheeks, then stepped back, her steady gaze expectant. *"Bon voyage, monsieur."*

THE GIRL'S THROAT WORKED, her tears welling, but she stepped toward Damien with a surety and trust that humbled him. She straightened then offered her hand. He heard the tremor in her voice. "If you know my sister, I am glad to accompany you to her side."

"It will be my honor to escort you there. I give you my solemn vow and my word of honor that you will come to no harm in my company," he said to her in French. "I will do all in my power to reunite you safely with Miss—"

The nun caught her breath. "We do not say that name, monsieur!" she chided.

"Forgive me. With your sister," he concluded and the girl nodded. "You do realize that I ride for England?"

The nun nodded once as did the girl. She gripped a very small bag, her chin lifted proudly, and if this was the sum of her possessions, she had lived a simple life indeed. Damien opened his purse and offered a donation to the nun. She hesitated only a moment before accepting it, then he gestured to the girl and headed for the door.

They would cross at LeHavre. The crossing would

be longer, but the port was closer, and he felt an imperative to reach England's shores as soon as possible.

The Duke of Haynesdale's concern was justified, for unbeknownst to him, he had been followed from Paris by the very man he had sought there. As they left the convent, Damien and his companion were watched from the shadow of the forest, and another coach followed shortly afterward.

~

IN DISTANT VENICE, the rain was falling in sheets. It glistened on the stone walls and rippled the surface of the canal, turning all the world to shimmering grey. It gathered in puddles in the square outside the accommodation rented by Lady Beckham, ensuring that the dampness could not be readily dispelled.

Arthur Beckham, blessed with a headache after his revels of the night before, paced through the lavish rooms, impatient with his situation. It was early in the morning, and it seemed only he and the resident cats were awake—the pair followed him down a hallway hung with silk brocade to the reception room his mother favored. It was empty, though he could hear his younger sister at her lessons. She was conjugating verbs in French aloud, periodically being corrected by her tutor.

Arthur yawned and rummaged through the books borrowed and bought from Carruthers & Carruthers. He wished for London, a hot cup of cocoa, familiar friends, and an entertaining read.

Childe Harold. There was a poem Arthur had been advised to read many a time. A curious choice on his mother's part. Perhaps she was trying to improve him.

Arthur smiled at the very notion, for he was already excelled in all pursuits of import, to his own thinking.

Like any competent rakehell, he was a master at racing, gambling and womanizing, plus it was said he could charm the very birds from the trees. What other skills remained?

His mother, however, had never been a lady quick to admit defeat.

He flung himself into a chair near the window, ignored the view of all that rain, and chuckled as the cats followed him. One—a long-haired silver beast, with knowing eyes of green—settled on the window sill to watch him with what Arthur had realized was characteristic suspicion. The other—the short-haired black one with yellow eyes and one white paw—curled in his lap. Arthur stroked the creature absently, enjoying the low thrum of its contented purr, and opened the book.

He was so startled by its contents that he nearly dislodged the cat.

Harris's List of Covent Garden Ladies. What was this?

He had heard of the volume, but never had the opportunity to read a copy. He seized the moment and did just that, reading it avidly from one cover to the other. Arthur only wondered how this volume had come to be in his mother's possessions after he was done.

He thought of the young lady who often worked at Carruthers & Carruthers, the one he liked to tease. Had there ever been a woman who blushed as crimson as Carruther's daughter? Arthur did not think so.

The youngest sister, Miss Carruthers, always packed his mother's orders. He eyed the book again. She had two older sisters, as well, the oldest recently married to Rhys Bettencourt, Baron Trevelaine. He had always thought all three to be a most serious young women.

This book, however, hinted at a mischievous disposition, if not a daring one.

Arthur, it must be noted, had a fascination with audacious young women—thus his interest in the volume he held now.

If this unexpected revelation was not sufficient to make him yearn for their return to London and an encounter with the lady in question, he could not imagine what was.

~

AUTHOR'S NOTE

Harris's List of Covent Garden Ladies was a real publication, printed in London from 1757 through 1795, being updated most years. It was a guide to prostitutes and courtesans, complete with their names—perhaps with one letter missing—and addresses, as well as notes upon appearance, specialities and prices. The excerpts that Catherine and Eurydice read in the prologue are from editions of the guide.

The volume was originally compiled by Samuel Derrick, a linen draper from Dublin who came to London to pursue his dream of becoming an actor, dramatist and famed poet. In London, Derrick frequented The Shakespear's Head, a coffeehouse in Covent Garden, whose chief waiter, one John Harrison, called himself the Pimp-General of All England. Inspired by this procurer's own notes on the local ladies, Derrick created and published his own volume when in desperate need of money. There was likely an agreement with Jack Harris for the use of his name—although he subsequently published a competing title, which was not a success — although Derrick used his own observations. Derrick's contribution remained anonymous for decades. It was a very popular little volume and it was believed to have sold 8000 copies per year in the 1760s. After Derrick's death in 1769, the book continued to be updated by others, until its publication was ceased in 1795.

Hallie Rubenhold has written about this book—*Harris's List of Covent Garden Ladies: Sex in the City in Georgian Britain*—as well as 18th century courtesans like Charlotte Hayes in *The Covent Garden Ladies*.

~

ABOUT THE AUTHOR

Deborah Cooke sold her first book in 1992, a medieval romance called **Romance of the Rose** published under her pseudonym Claire Delacroix. Since then, she has published over ninety novels in a wide variety of sub-genres, including historical romance, contemporary romance, paranormal romance, fantasy romance, time-travel romance, women's fiction, paranormal young adult and fantasy with romantic elements. She has published under the names Claire Delacroix, Claire Cross and Deborah Cooke. **The Beauty**, part of her successful Bride Quest series of historical romances, was her first title to land on the *New York Times* List of Bestselling Books. Her books routinely appear on other bestseller lists and have won numerous awards. In 2009, she was the writer-in-residence at the Toronto Public Library, the first time the library has hosted a residency focused on the romance genre. In 2012, she was honored to receive the Romance Writers of America's Mentor of the Year Award.

Currently, she writes paranormal romances featuring dragon shape shifter heroes under the name Deborah Cooke. She also writes medieval romances as Claire Delacroix. Deborah lives in Canada with her husband and family, as well as far too many unfinished knitting projects.

Visit Deborah's websites to learn more about her books:

DeborahCooke.com

Delacroix.net

THE CRUSADER'S HANDFAST

The Rogues of Ravensmuir
THE ROGUE
THE SCOUNDREL
THE WARRIOR

The Jewels of Kinfairlie
THE BEAUTY BRIDE
THE ROSE RED BRIDE
THE SNOW WHITE BRIDE
The Ballad of Rosamunde

The True Love Brides
THE RENEGADE'S HEART
THE HIGHLANDER'S CURSE
THE FROST MAIDEN'S KISS
THE WARRIOR'S PRIZE

The Brides of Inverfyre
THE MERCENARY'S BRIDE
THE RUNAWAY BRIDE

The Bride Quest
THE PRINCESS
THE DAMSEL
THE HEIRESS
THE COUNTESS
THE BEAUTY
THE TEMPTRESS

Harlequin Historicals

UNICORN BRIDE

PEARL BEYOND PRICE

Time Travel Romance

ONCE UPON A KISS

THE LAST HIGHLANDER

THE MOONSTONE

LOVE POTION #9

Short Stories and Novellas

BEGUILED

An Elegy for Melusine

To learn more about Deborah's contemporary and paranormal
romances,

please visit

DeborahCooke.com